MISCHIEVOUSLY MINE

LEIGH W. STUART

CITY OWL
PRESS

MISCHIEVOUSLY MINE
Sycamore Cove Games, Book 2

CITY OWL PRESS
www.cityowlpress.com

Cover Design by Mibl Art. All stock photos licensed appropriately.

Edited by Mary Cain.

For information on subsidiary rights, please contact the publisher at info@cityowlpress.com.

Print Edition ISBN: 978-1-949090-34-5

Digital Edition ISBN: 978-1-949090-33-8

Printed in the United States of America

need a pick me up or just a cute read for the holidays then I recommend this book it will lighten your heart!"
- WICKEDLY TWISTED BOOK REVIEWS

"loved the dares! They were hot and sexy to read! I really enjoyed the secondary character too. I want more of Cooper! Overall this was a fun quick read!"
- ONCE UPON A ROMANCE BLOG

For my husband -
Here's to another twenty years of love and laughter.

SYCAMORE COVE PEACE TREATY

The Terms:

Both parties agree as of today, February 12, 2009, to end any, and all, of the following activities:

* Pranks, big or small, expensive or cheap
* Tricks, see the 1ˢᵗ point
* Boasting of pranks (past, present or future pranks**). Including, but not limited to:

   - incidents with spiders, real or fake
   - reminiscing about Cooper's tighty-whities

*Posting or exhibiting photographic evidence of pranks

The Conditions:

Both parties agree to respect each other's private property, including but not limited to:

- *cars, vehicles*
- *homes*
- *clothes*
- *toiletries*
- *school or office supplies*
- *anything else imaginable*

This peace treaty stands for the duration of both parties' lives.

Any action that breaks the cease-fire will be grounds for swift retribution in the form of posting pictures, being pranked in return or forced to listen to jokes of dubious humor.

Territory includes but is not limited to—all land, water, and air surrounding or affixed to planet earth, undiscovered worlds in all known and unknown universes, whether parallel, inverse, or two-dimensional.

We, the undersigned, agree to generally act like the adults we are now and not like the teenagers we used to be, upon pain of extreme embarrassment, of our fears and phobias being exploited, or our personal property decorated in ways that are difficult to clean up.

Sandra Mercy Kelly

Cooper Dwain Hall

**Treaty addendum: In fact, these pranks should never be spoken of again. Ever.

CHAPTER 1

Cooper Hall reclined on a white lawn chair in a beam of sunshine that lit up his head like a saint's halo. It knocked her breathless. It burned her up. Sandra crossed her arms and fumed over being in the same place as him.

The Sycamore Cove Central Park buzzed with excitement as fifty people gathered to hear the mayor's much anticipated announcement. Rumors were that the mayor's office wanted to host the first ever Townsperson of the Year contest, awarded by cash prizes for the winner and runners up. Whether or not it was true, Sandra hadn't seen this much energy in the town since the fire station needed renovations and the firefighters held a wet t-shirt contest to raise funds. She had been there to interview them after they dumped buckets of water on one another. A smile twitched at the corner of her lips.

One of the perks of being a reporter in a small town.

From Sandra's standing position behind the assembled chairs in the park, she had a good view of the back of the audience, but no matter how often she turned her attention elsewhere, Cooper inexorably drew her gaze.

Her chest tightened a little harder each time. It wasn't supposed to do that. There was nothing between them. She could live the rest of her life perfectly content to never see him again in fact. Telling herself to relax and do her job, she leaned against the sprawling sycamore behind her.

A warm breeze brought the scent of freshly mown grass, and the pink peonies surrounding the wooden gazebo bobbed. A couple of dogs, belonging to joggers, barked as they crossed on the walking paths under the trees. It was a perfect May afternoon. Or it would be if she didn't have to share the park with Cooper.

Lauren, Cooper's sister, walked up the gazebo steps and tapped on the microphone.

Her whole body radiated energy, and she smiled at the crowd. "Hello."

Since being hired as an assistant in Parks and Recreation, Lauren had bloomed in confidence. "Thank you so much for joining us today as I, along with the mayor's team, announce the very first Townsperson of the Year contest in Sycamore Cove."

And the rumors were confirmed. Sandra shifted her pen and paper to one hand in order to shoot off a message to her boss as Lauren continued to explain the details of the contest.

A few seconds later, Sandra was writing again, pen rolling across the paper.

"While we might encounter some bumps and snags during our first go, we are excited to make this an annual contest," Lauren said. "This will allow us to put a spotlight on the spirit of our town and reward the best among us, the people who are out there working every day to make a real difference. We will offer cash prizes to the winner and free advertising for businesses or organizations. Everyone is welcome to sign up on the online submission form, but the initial contestant list will be curated by our judges, who are looking at things like local business entrepreneurs, volunteer work, participation in town events, overall positive community impact."

A gust of wind blew a twig on Sandra's notebook and she paused to brush it off. She missed a sentence, but the words *popular vote* echoed in her ears. Popular vote?

"Candidates can and should encourage everyone they know to vote, one vote per person, per day, and remember to keep it fair and honest," Lauren continued.

All right. Popular vote it is.

"The last Friday and Saturday will be a blind vote, so we won't know who is on top, and then the grand finale will be on Sunday, two weeks from this weekend, with the winner and second and third places to be announced." Lauren scanned the crowd, a huge smile on her face. "Keep it fair, keep it friendly, and most of all, keep it fun in order to prove to us that you best represent this wonderful town."

This wonderful town. Sandra's heart swelled. This town had saved her a long time ago. She belonged to it and it to her.

She tapped her notepad with her pencil, then underlined *popular vote*. She didn't usually approve of popularity contests, but it was true that the person who represented the town should inspire followers. That was what leaders did—forged a path.

From the corner of her eye, she watched her coworker, John, walk around, getting snippets of video of unsuspecting audience members. The cameraman from the Warrosquoake County Channel 12 News had a peculiar fondness for sneaking up on people.

Sandra's gaze shifted from him and wandered over the audience.

Cooper ran his fingers through his chestnut hair, and she frowned. No, actually, she glared. Her cheeks drew inward as she narrowed her eyes. His hair was too long, too messy with those loose curls. But she knew it to be oh, so silky to the touch. The kind of hair a woman could really fist during a kiss.

The thought grated her nerves and sent longing to her core at the same time. Why was he here? It must be to support his sister. He certainly couldn't hope to compete to become the Townsperson of the Year.

And that heavenly light had no business landing on him. It was false advertising in the extreme. There was nothing angelic about him, aside from his soulful steel-blue eyes. But a saint?

She snorted. Hardly.

He was the bane of her high school existence. The itch she couldn't scratch. The lemon juice in her paper cut. The sun-drenched, sexed-up Loki who never ceased getting under her skin. Pushing all her buttons. In all the wrong ways.

And he was up and walking in her direction.

Her spine stiffened.

Several people nodded or waved as he strolled to the back of the assembly. Everyone loved Cooper. Everyone except her, of course. Although, she couldn't deny he had eye-candy appeal, especially since he sported a beard in addition to that silky hair.

His eyes met hers, and he pressed his lips together, then continued a slow and steady path directly toward her.

She ignored him, turning her attention to the speaker, the director of Parks and Recreation.

He leaned a shoulder next to hers against the tree trunk. "Sandra. Nice to see you."

"As always, Cooper, it's a pleasure." Her nerves prickled with his nearness. She checked her nails, wrote a few more notes on her pad of paper, and tried to train her senses towards anything but him.

Cooper cleared his throat. "You'll be covering the contest, I assume?"

"Of course. I might even do more than cover it," she said, voice deliberately sharp. Surely, he would take the hint and go.

"It is tempting, I agree. You know, since it's based on popular vote, I'd get loads of love based on my charming personality alone."

"I wouldn't call your personality charming," she said. "Besides, have you forgotten the competition? There are some impressive people in this town who will certainly sign up."

He shrugged, as if dismissing potential candidates. "Any ideas what the finale will entail?"

"Probably the usual—interview, presentation."

"Swimsuit competition?"

"Because you'd like to see that? Cooper, Cooper." She tsked. "Always *that* guy, hoping to see women in bikinis."

"Please, Sandra, I don't need to watch a beauty competition to see women in bikinis. In fact, I avoid watching that sort of thing. No, it's because if there is swimsuit competition, I'll kill it. It's been ages since I've had to shave my legs to put on my Speedos, but I'll do it if I have to."

"Wait. Are you seriously considering submitting your candidature? This should be entertaining." She flipped to a clean page and wrote *Competitors* at the top. Shaking her head slowly, she wrote his name, followed by a huge question mark.

"I am seriously considering it, yes. A sweet amount of free publicity, some prize money—everything a growing business needs. The judges will love me. I've been attending charity events, fundraisers, and community service projects for years."

"If the judges love you, it's because they don't know you like I know you. Your sister has been twisting your arm since she got back from college to give her a hand with her projects. We both know the truth. Your contributions to this town are quite lacking. I could even say *unsatisfying*." She bit her tongue the second after the words came out of her mouth. She should know better than to try and rattle Cooper.

He shifted to face her, his back to the gazebo and the speaker. But she wasn't listening to the presentation anymore. His face was too close to hers.

"If anyone in the town complains about being unsatisfied, I am happy to make amends. I pride myself on fulfilling every expectation."

She beckoned him to follow her around the tree. There were a few truths that needed to be said and she intended to say them.

"Listen, Cooper…" The wide tree screened them from the audience and mayor's people on the gazebo. "I know you think you are the answer to every woman's prayer in this town, but allow me to be blunt and say I will never make the mistake of getting into your bed again. And for me to like you, you'd have to get a brain transplant, as in an entirely new and palatable personality, because what you are now is insufferable."

He scratched his chin, a wry, half-grin on his face. "What, you think I should get a lobotomy? Sounds about right. No one's opinions are worth more than yours, are they? No matter what, you are always right."

"Out of curiosity, did you hope to start impressing the judges just by showing up today? Is that your secret, superpower? The ability to look like a decent human being when you are actually deceiving people?"

"My superpower is the ability to keep a smile on my face, despite the people around me. And you?" he asked.

"Oh, honey, I have come out alive and on top of every encounter I've ever had with you. No small feat, considering your penchant for playing dirty." She jabbed a finger at his chest, but he didn't even blink.

"And yet, you came running to me last Christmas."

"To my eternal shame. Then again, I went running the other direction when I realized you were still *you* after all these years." She forced herself to keep eye contact. This close she could make out the golden flecks in his eyes, individual strands of hair, and the fine laugh lines in his cheeks.

He smirked, shaking his head. "You were hoping I'd been lobotomized?"

"I was hoping you had matured since graduating from high school. I was also hoping for a good time. But you left me terribly disappointed."

"You expected me to come at your beck and call like a cocker spaniel. And, as I recall, you were starting to have a pretty good time. You wanted a rebound fling. I was there to give you a rebound fling. You wanted..." His voice trailed off, his eyes glancing downwards. They stayed there, zeroed in on her breasts.

Apparently, Cooper thought she was here today for his viewing pleasure.

Anger flash flooded her body. She took a deep breath, ready to flay him alive when he took her chin in his hand.

"Don't look down right now," he said. "Sandra, look at me and nowhere else."

She froze at the warning in his tone. Something was wrong. Her anger dissipated, leaving her cold. No matter what a pain in the ass he could be, he would also throw himself in front of moving car to save another person. Even her. "Why?"

"Don't look down, no matter what. Do you understand?"

"Don't look down? What the hell? Is it a—" She squeezed her eyes shut. Her muscles clenched, her chest tightened. Heart lodged in her throat, she tried to breathe, but could only get a sliver of air. "Cooper, tell me it isn't a spider."

Fibbing wasn't one of Cooper's strengths. He considered himself to be a straight shooter, although he could maneuver his way out of uncomfortable situations with partial truths.

But with Sandra gasping and trembling in his arms, it wasn't the time for mind games.

"Eyes on me." He swallowed. "As for what's wrong, you should know by now I'd never lie to you. Hold very still."

"It *is* a spider. Get it off me," she said, voice squeaking. "Just hit it off!"

"The spider happens to be on your left breast. I'm not going to hit it off." It had to be the biggest wolf spider he'd ever seen. Not deadly, but any bites would swell and hurt, and it was in between the ruffles of her shirt. Flicking wouldn't be wise.

He cupped his free hand, descending slowly.

She made a keening whimper through her clenched jaw. Sweat glistened on her forehead and her chest heaved for air, which didn't make his task any easier. He'd never witnessed her arachnophobia up close. His movements were also hampered by the death grip she had on his biceps, confined to the small space between their bodies. His muscles bunched hard in response to her nails.

"Try not to tear my arms off," Cooper said through clenched teeth.

She peeked out from narrowed eyelids. "This isn't a prank, is it?"

"Sandra, the treaty still stands. Call Holy Hot Tamales for a truce, or simply look down if you need to."

There was a beat of silence and she shook her head. "No, I believe you. Is it a big one? Is it hairy?"

"It's tiny. The size of a pencil eraser. And no hair. Ignore what my hand is doing and try to think about your next vacation on the beach."

Electric tingles flickered to life in his fingertips at the silk of her shirt when his fingers began to curl. He was only touching her shirt but could have been on her bare skin for the way the muscles in his abdomen clenched. He had to keep calm. Somehow.

Her nipple hardened under his palm. And he hardened in response. His mind knew this was not the time, but his body had other ideas. Every single part of her that was touching him—thighs brushing his, the edge of her hip, her hands on his arms, and the nub of her nipple—lit up his nerves and sent his blood racing. In the wrong direction.

Focus, Cooper.

The change in Sandra was rougher than whiplash. When he had seen her at the back of the audience, he wanted to reach out and see if she had softened since the fiasco of their almost-fling. The answer had been a swift, hard no, and he'd regretted speaking to her. Then the spider had crawled out from nowhere, and she was falling apart in his arms.

He held his breath, his hand on her breast. And he wanted to do so much more than save her from a spider.

CHAPTER 2

The two-and-half inch arachnid clung to the thin silk shirt with spindly legs, the stripes on its back a warning. Cooper steadied his resolve, concentrating on the spider and not the swell of Sandra's breast under his hand.

"Cooper." She gasped, head up. "Faster!"

"If you say harder, I'll die."

"Will it get the spider off my chest faster?"

"These things take time," he whispered. "You can't force Mother Nature, only draw her out gently with sweet promises until she sits in the palm…of…your…hand."

His hand closed, accidentally rubbing her nipple, but he had the spider. The creature stirred and scrambled to escape his grip.

Chances were good Sandra hadn't noticed him touching her nipple, or the uncomfortable hard-on forming in his jeans, what with her panic attack barely kept in check. He exhaled slowly.

"You can remove your nails from my arms, not that I didn't enjoy it just a little." In an awkward maneuver, he threw the spider onto the lawn and wiped his hand on his jeans, the whole time prisoner to her iron grip.

"I can't move my fingers." She didn't seem to be joking. "I think there are more. I feel like there are hundreds crawling under my shirt."

"That's most likely your imagination."

"What if the wind blew an egg pouch on me? There could be hatchlings in my hair. Or under my clothes! Check my back."

He glanced over her shoulder. Long, sensual curves and a hint of brown skin at the top of her collar. No spiders on her white blouse or dark skirt. "You're clear."

She began breathing again as he pried her hands loose. "Are you sure? Check again."

If he was any judge of character, it was taking all her self-control not to scream and jump up and down while stripping to her skivvies.

Of course, if she wanted him to check again...

He leaned over her and lifted her hair. With his other hand, he ran his fingers under the silky collar of her shirt, directly on her bronze skin.

Her shoulders quivered at his touch. "See anything?"

"Indeed, I do."

Oh, the things he saw. The long planes of her back interrupted only by the pale lace straps of her bra and the arch of her spine as it drew his gaze downward. These were the kind of things he could spend hours contemplating.

"What?" she asked, hands clasping the sides of his shirt and drawing him nearer.

"If you are worried about spiders, your back is fine," he whispered, bringing his lips as close as he could to her ear without kissing it. "However, I haven't checked everywhere."

There was a sensitive zone on her nape, right at her hairline behind her ear. He had discovered it last Christmas accidentally.

He skimmed his fingertips on the velvet skin there now, making her quiver again.

She whimpered so softly, he would have missed it if he hadn't been listening. But it wasn't in fear of arachnids.

He ran his fingers upwards to the vulnerable hollow below her earlobe and then into the springy curls of her hair, as if searching. He almost felt guilty for exploiting her weaknesses.

"Anything?" she asked, voice husky and eyes partly closed.

"No. No spiders." He tilted her head to *check* the other side, his pants growing uncomfortably tight. Too many memories crowded the forefront of his mind, flashing by one after the other. He had to stop. It was too much. Lifting his hands, he released her. "You see? I have changed. You needed to be saved, and here I am."

She twisted to face him, dark brown eyes smoldering. "Save me? You can't be serious. You aren't saving me. I have arachnophobia because of you."

He took a measured breath—she was doubting his seriousness again, for the love of... This was exactly why he shouldn't be touching her anymore. "That was a long time ago. No more pranks."

She studied him, arms crossed. "You were feeling up my tit. Confess."

It was on the tip of his tongue to deny everything. But he was classier than that. He squared his shoulders. "Only in-so-far as it was necessary to remove the spider. Which, you will remember, you begged me to do."

"I...begged?"

He immediately regretted bringing up the facts.

"Listen carefully, Cooper Hall, you and I—" Footsteps crunched in the gravel not far from them.

For once, Cooper was glad to see Vic.

"Cooper," Vic said, flashing his wide, phony smile.

"Vic, glad you could make it." He sensed his blood pressure rising as Vic's gaze roamed freely up and down Sandra and seemed to linger on her long legs. Anger tightened his gut.

The dickweed. He had to drool on everything living within a ten-foot reach. The wolf spider should still be near. Cooper hadn't thrown it too far. He should find it and leave it in Vic's car.

Although, that would be cruel for the spider. Biting Vic's ass was too hideous to even contemplate.

"Hello." Vic held out a hand for Sandra. "And you are?"

"Sandra Kelly, for WCC 12 News."

"Vic, partner in Homeward Bound with our buddy here." He clapped Cooper on the shoulder harder than was necessary.

Sandra nodded, face a smooth mask. "Nice to meet you. Thank you for speaking with me, Mr. Hall, but I should get to the other interviews." She strode off, shoulders squared and white heels rasping in the gravel at a smart pace.

Vic tilted his head and watched her go. "Good friend of yours?"

"From high school, yeah," Cooper said, stretching the truth. "Were you here for the contest announcement or did you just show up for the free coffee?"

"I was passing by. You can fill me in with the details later. So, what do you think of this opportunity?" Vic handed him a brochure.

"It's definitely a possibility for the business. This would be great if one of us won. There are a few sweet prizes. We'd have the next two and half weeks to get in the votes and then a couple of days for the judges to wrap things up."

"Votes? Who is voting?"

"Anyone. Everyone. The winner will mostly be determined by the popular vote. This is a small town. We need to get our names on the list and start wooing. You know how it goes."

"No. I didn't grow up in a small town, so I don't know how it goes," Vic said, his voice dropping. "We need to talk."

Cooper frowned, leaning in closer.

"I've been thinking about our business plan. More and more it doesn't make sense to have our headquarters here. Sycamore Cove is the middle of nowhere. It's hard to meet with clients, it's hard to convince people we are serious, and it's boring."

With a scoff, Cooper crossed his arms. "It's also cheap, which, at this time, is the determining factor."

"It's cheap, but it's also costing us business. Listen, we have to move. I'm pulling out if we don't leave for Richmond or an even bigger city."

"We have an agreement. You can't pull out." No way was Cooper leaving.

Homeward Bound was his start-up company and Sycamore Cove was his town. He had built his tech business from scratch before Vic had shown up with much needed investment funds. Cooper would sink without the money. But he couldn't leave his home.

"I could arrange for my freedom, make no mistake." Vic curled his lips in a smirk. "However, this contest has me thinking. The prize money is peanuts, but winning would be good for the business, and the publicity we could get for free might be worth sticking around here for another year. Like you said, it's small town. I won't win because no one here knows me."

Cooper, a knot twisting in his chest, clapped a hand to Vic's shoulder, showing more confidence than he felt. "Don't worry. They know me."

"What about competition? Like that journalist?" He lifted his head toward Sandra, now surrounded by a small group of people. "I've seen her around town talking to people. If she competes, she'd be a shoo-in. I'd vote for her."

"Thanks for your support, Vic. With or without you, though, I can win this thing."

"Good. And if you don't, we'll find new headquarters." He backed away, raising a hand in farewell. "See you Monday at the office."

Cooper waited for him to go. He uncrossed his arms, expelling his breath slowly. So much for enjoying the spring day, or any day, until he could guarantee a win for his business. Getting rid of Vic in the process would be a bonus, although he shouldn't dream too big.

But he could do it. He would have to have one hell of a game plan, but he could do it. His start-up would be saved, he could begin making money, and most importantly, Vic wouldn't dictate whether or not he could stay in Sycamore Cove.

Unless Sandra competed, too.

She wouldn't, though. Covering the competition should exclude her from being in the running, no? It hadn't occurred to him to be worried earlier, but the more he thought about it the worse the situation got.

And if she did compete?

It would be a tough competition, in any case. The list of competitors would be announced in a couple of days when they got all the submissions, and he'd see if Sandra's name was on it or not. He shook off the tension growing in his shoulders. Now was the time to organize and plan. He finally had the details of how the judging would go and he had some ideas of how to garner the town's favor. Time for action.

Someone yelled Sandra's name from the gazebo and waved her up to the group with the mayor. Cooper paused, watching her glide across the lawn and up the stairs. She could star in a detective novel with her legs as long as the day, smooth dark skin, and almond eyes that saw through bullshit faster than a hot knife went through butter. And a whip-smart tongue, too. He had been on the receiving end of her observations—it wasn't something he enjoyed. Much.

There was one simple way to know if she was entering the competition.

Cooper chuckled. He must be a sucker for punishment. The warm sunlight beat on his back and he ran his fingers through his hair to cool his head as he took the path to the gazebo.

Sandra stood at the top, a hip jauntily to the side in the take-no-prisoners stance he was terribly familiar with.

He smiled and approached. But slowly.

"Sandra, nice to see—"

"Wait a minute." Her hand went up to keep him from approaching, and she peered into the dusty, cobweb filled rafters above her head. "As much as it is a pleasure to see you, as always, I'd hate to have to owe you my life twice in one day."

"Chances are slim I would have to de-spider you again. It's fairly unusual. But I'm here for you should you have a sudden need of me."

"Of course, I couldn't let you live if you felt me up a second time. Once can be an accident. Twice, and your ass is mine. But not the way you'd like." She smiled, fluttering her eyelashes at him.

If any other woman did that, he'd be ready to flirt until he charmed her into diving under the covers with him. Sandra's fluttering lashes were like missile alarms blaring on a non-test day.

"Not to change the subject from anatomy," he said, "but I have to know, are you going to submit your name for Townsperson? You know you have nothing to prove to this town."

The glance she gave him could have cut down a swath of oak trees. In one second, she deciphered his true purpose in asking her, and also in buttering her up. Actually, she laid bare his soul for her scrutiny. It was not pleasant.

Way to be subtle, Cooper.

"Cooper Hall, I do believe you are afraid that I'll run, and if I run, I'll beat you. Wouldn't that be awful?"

"I'm planning ahead for all contingencies. Taking stock of the competition. That's all. Besides, do you really want to compete against me?" He couldn't back down now.

"Oh, yes, I would very much enjoy competing against you, and I have every intention of winning."

His gut clenched. She was in. This was the worst-case scenario. Sandra was, to put it mildly, adored by this town. He had to head her off somehow. Convincing Sandra to change her mind because he wanted her to, though? Right. And with a little more wishful thinking maybe he could make it rain beer this weekend. That would be awesome.

Reverse psychology?

Appeal to her practical nature?

Send her a very convincing letter pretending to be a prince in love, but she'd have to take a two-week hiatus from social media to be eligible for his hand in marriage?

All right, no one was that gullible.

There was no right way of doing this.

Which only left the wrong way of doing it.

"Then I suppose it's good that our treaty still stands," he said slowly. "Think of the mess if it wasn't. I doubt we could compete in the contest and wage a prank war at the same time." He tsked, shaking his head.

Sandra licked her lips and sashayed a little bit closer. "Are you under the impression I can't multitask? You have realized I'm a woman, right?"

"The thought occurred to me, in passing, yes." He broke into a sweat. "But I don't believe now would be a good time to start filling each other's cars with ping-pong balls or hiding taxidermied tarantulas in closets."

"Cooper, please. We never did the same pranks twice. At least, I never did."

"My point exactly. I'd hate to put that kind of pressure on you when you need to focus all of your energy on getting more votes than me. People in this town love me. I'd hate for you to not be able to handle it."

"Is that a threat? Do you want to break the treaty?"

Another prank war between them would be a major distraction. She would be in a battle on two fronts. Could she run a secret campaign against him and a public one for herself to win the contest? For that matter, could he?

Screw it. At this point, he didn't have a choice.

Cooper swept his arms wide. "A challenge. I know it won't be a problem for me, but I'm not standing in the eye of the camera every day in front of the whole town."

A smile spread across her lips, but it chilled him. "You think I can't handle *you*? Oh, honey, if you want a prank war, then so be it. Bring it on, Cooper Hall."

Leaning forward, she kissed his cheek, light as a breeze. Her lips hovered near his ear and she whispered, "Bring it on."

CHAPTER 3

A shivery thrill raced through Sandra's body. Finally, a chance to get back at him after everything he had done to her through their high school years and the fiasco last Christmas. A war, which she intended to win, was overdue.

It wouldn't be easy—nothing was easy where Cooper was involved—but she was ready for whatever he had to throw at her.

A worm of doubt wiggled in her chest.

Cooper was a master at pranking. Little, petty stuff, like plastic-wrapping cars or hiding dead tarantulas in her locker were his warm-up exercises while planning finely orchestrated pranks. This time he would strike hard and fast. There was no time to lose between now and the finale in two-and-a-half weeks. Which meant she had to be faster and smarter.

Her gaze zeroed in on Lauren, his sister. If anyone would give her a hand, it would be his little sister. Cooper had made her life miserable by terrorizing all potential boyfriends until very recently. The second Lauren was free, Sandra sidled to her side. A quick glance over her shoulder showed that John was busy setting up the camera. No one else was close by.

"Lauren, hello." She shook her hand. "I have so many questions about the contest, but could I ask you an odd favor first?"

"Sure, no problem," Lauren said, a wide smile sparkling all the way to her eyes.

"You know I'm old friends with your brother. I'd like to borrow his house key so I could drop off a little surprise for him. A harmless, fun-filled surprise."

Lauren side-eyed her, silent for a second. "Harmless?"

"As a kitten. But not a kitten. I know better than to give animals as gifts."

The smile returned to Lauren's face and she nodded. "I see. All right. I guess I can trust you, Sandra. As an old friend of his." She found her ring of keys in her purse and twisted one of them free. "So long as it's harmless."

"He'll love it. I promise."

John revved the news van to life as Sandra jumped in the passenger seat. She rubbed her hands together and gave a muffled squeal.

"Radio?" she asked.

"There's a polka CD under the seat somewhere."

Polka? Where did this man find his taste in music?

"I'll take care of it." Seconds later, she found her favorite radio station and cranked up the sound.

By the time they reached the WCC 12 parking lot, they had no choice but to roll down the windows and idle while blasting JLo's "I Ain't Your Mama" and waving their arms in the air.

John was a horrible singer. Maybe he was a baritone in an alternate universe, but he pitched his voice up to a squeaky falsetto and sang off tune, off rhythm, and with approximate lyrics.

But he could car twerk. All two hundred pounds of him.

Sandra's door popped open in the middle of a refrain. Her boss —her ex—glared at them.

John switched off the music sheepishly.

"I could hear you from inside reception," Brad snapped, still glaring. "Are we professionals here or not?" He glanced over her and sniffed. Disapproval was thick in the air. He was perfect on the outside as usual. Impeccable light grey suit, luxury watch on his wrist, his light brown hair, longer on top and trim on the sides, was brushed carefully back. While she had once found his hazel eyes and strong chin attractive, all she could think of now was that he was shorter and heavier than Cooper—a boy pretending to be a man.

Sandra swung her legs from the interior, pushing him aside to get out and taking her time adjusting her skirt.

"How is the receptionist?" she asked. "Settled in and working hard?" She and Brad might have been able to keep their relationship a secret from their co-workers, but when he dumped her last winter, Sandra immediately noticed the attention the new girl, Sandy, was receiving.

Sandy. What a stupid name.

Brad blinked and shrank visibly. "Can I speak with you in my office?"

John joined them at the side of van to slide the door open. "I can take care of the equipment, Sandra, and get started editing. Join me when you're ready."

She patted him on the shoulder and left him humming the song, two octaves too high and wiggling his backside.

If only all her colleagues had such a great sense of humor.

She fell into step with Brad. The five months since their breakup hadn't eased the tension. He had said she was the one and had hinted at getting a ring. Then he met the brainless wonder recently hired at the front desk.

It wasn't his fault she had reacted so badly, though. Her rebound relationship due to a broken heart was her choice, and she wasn't proud of what she had done.

He walked fast and directly to his office on the second floor of the news channel building. As producer, he carried the huge weight of putting together the stories and shows every day, but he micromanaged. Everything was a haystack and he was constantly sifting through to find needles. Control was everything to him.

As the station's youngest and most recent reporter on board, he especially stuck his nose in her work. He was always looking for something to criticize or a way to undermine her projects. And she was sick of it.

"Tell me everything about this Townsperson contest," he said before they had even sat. He tipped his seat back to watch her.

"It's a great project. The mayor's office supports it as part of Lauren Hall's work to promote the town for tourism and business. I have the list of judges. Candidates can submit their names and dossiers for consideration over the next three days. They filter through the names and make a first selection, then it's a popular vote for two weeks. The last weekend is blind voting leading up to the finale. They are looking for people with community service, a business that promotes the town or brings in jobs, volunteer work, or who participate in some of the other contests and tourism activities."

"We should follow this closely, especially because it's the first time. It would also be good to have one of our own in the running for it. To bring extra exposure to the station. Can you think of anyone?"

"Funny you should mention it, as I had the same thought. In fact —" Cooper's words popped into her head. *You would be better off covering the contest from the sidelines.* Her mouth went dry.

"Yes?"

She silently renewed her vow to send Cooper down in flames. The king of pranks was about to be dethroned in more ways than one. "I will be submitting my candidature."

Brad scoffed. "You're free to do what you want, but I wasn't thinking of one of my journalists. You have too much on your plate as it is, remember? You are behind on that report of the school recycling program. Now brainstorm with me, Sandra. Who would be qualified to represent both this town and the station, but not be too busy? When we find the right person, we can use him to boost our ratings, too. Absolute win."

It was painfully obvious where he wanted to go with this speech. No one was more worthy than him, in his eyes. "I don't know, Brad. Oh, wait. Why don't you run?"

He didn't hear her sarcasm. Fake surprise lit his face and he nodded in approval. He picked up a pencil to twirl.

"I like it. You could be right. Let's keep me in mind for now and I want you to go downstairs, find John and start editing—"

"Stop right there. You do what you want, but I am submitting my name for this contest and what's more, you are going to stop dictating my every move."

"Submit if you want, but I am in charge of stories around here. I will tell you where to go and what to do." He jabbed the pencil end toward her, nostrils flared. "You jump when I tell you to."

"Yeah, about that. I believe the time has come for me to have the freedom to report the stories I choose and that are important to the town. Not the ones you think I should cover. I decide from now on. The reason I'm late on the recycling story is because there isn't a story. I've been junior reporter here since finishing college, and I've proven my worth a dozen times over."

"Where is this speech leading?"

Sandra paused, heart racing. She had rehearsed this conversation a hundred times in her bedroom or car, but hadn't planned on bringing it up today. It was do or die time, though. There was one solution to this situation. She wouldn't leave her town for another news group, unless as a last resort, but she had to get out from under his constant control. Since staying on as a junior reporter was out of the question...

"I'm asking for a promotion and the raise to go with it," she said in a quick rush.

"Promotions are earned, not handed out." His answer came so

fast, he must have been rehearsing in his head, too, while she worked up to asking him.

Of course, he would imply she hadn't already earned it. Most likely, he credited himself with her quality field work and comfortable rapport with the people she interviewed.

"Last year, I won an Outstanding Rising Reporter Award," she said.

"You know what I love most about you? The way you are so passionate about everything you do. It's truly beautiful."

She pressed her hands to his desk so as to not smack him. He was bringing up passion and love now? With his new buxom and blond girlfriend downstairs? Last December, she had been too devastated to strike back and since then, too worried about her reputation to allow hint of any scandal between them. If he didn't want to give her the promotion she deserved, she would force his hand. "And this year, I intend to win the Townsperson contest. I think that would deserve a promotion.

He twiddled a pen, considering her proposal. "You can't use your broadcasts to promote yourself. It would be unethical."

"I know. I wouldn't." Although, he had hinted at using the station to advertise its candidate, aka himself, only two minutes ago. He was despicable. "Deal?"

"Sandra, if you actually win, I'll give you your own office, plus the promotion to go with it. I don't imagine I'm running much a risk, though. In the meantime, you have editing to do with John and not much time get it ready." He shooed her with a wave of his hand.

Without a word, she slammed the door on the way out.

John would have to wait for her help. He was probably snacking on beef jerky and wandering the halls, scrolling through his messages, anyway.

Wending her way through the open office desks, Sandra fumed. What a craptastic day it was turning out to be, thanks to Cooper and her boss. She wished she could smack some sense into her younger self for falling for Brad's superficial charms. Not to mention her fling with Cooper. But Brad was far worse. She hadn't seen it in the beginning. She knew who he was now, though, and she wouldn't let him push her.

She had no choice but to win this contest. It was time to start kicking some ass.

Her freedom at the station depended on it. Putting Cooper in his place depended on it.

CHAPTER 4

Local legend claimed Captain Kearn's Lighthouse was haunted, but the thin heels of Sandra's four-inch pumps clipped confidently on the gravel as she marched onwards to the tower. The afternoon sunlight blazed on the peeling white paint and glowed red on the exposed bricks. Over the ridge of wind-blown grass and sand, the waves crashed steadily on the beach, and the air was salty and fresh.

John and Chad, their newest intern, followed her down the trail, carrying the equipment. They reached the base and the door, choked over with brushy weeds.

The abandoned tower loomed four stories high. She craned her neck to study the balcony circling the very top part. Steel bars and wooden planks. Despite its age, it lacked signs of rust or crumbling bricks. It seemed sturdy enough. She'd find out soon enough.

"Ready to go up?" she asked. "How much time until we're live?"

Chad checked his watch. "Exactly one hour and eight minutes." He hefted the huge bag higher on his shoulder and motioned the way to the lighthouse door.

That morning, Brad had informed Sandra of a slight change in plans for the day's broadcast. Her work would be in two parts. First, they had to do a pre-recorded video at the top of the lighthouse and then get downstairs and outside in order to do a live broadcast during the Saturday evening "Local Gems" segment.

He had her jumping through hoops because she had dared ask for a raise and recognition.

A breeze from the coast set the grasses shivering along the shore. The susurration sounded like ghosts whispering to each other. She smiled. Perfect for a haunted broadcast.

"Then let's not waste time." Sandra grabbed hold of the heavy steel door. It swung open with a nerve-grating squeal.

"Thumbs up for the fire-department unlocking it for us," Chad said, turning sideways to get himself and the bag through the opening. "At least we don't have to climb up the pipes with the camera and lights."

Sandra put her hand to his arm to stop him. "What are you talking about?"

"Climbing the pipes. Didn't you used to do that? Climb up the other side of the wall to the balcony in order to get in?"

"You mean for the parties." She scoffed and shook her head. "I'm afraid I partied elsewhere, thanks to a certain person."

"Who was that?"

Sandra tiptoed inside the dank tower. "No one of importance." It might not have been a genuine, working lighthouse, but it was built that way. No frills. The hollow, circular building had one winding staircase all the way up to the landing. There were four windows for light, which was barely sufficient, as the glass panes were coated with grime.

She stepped onto the first metal stair, and the slick sole of her four-inch high pumps slid on the metal. She eyed the narrow stairs askance. She would be climbing this thing on her tip-toes to keep the heel from hooking on the steps' edges, but that was life. Reporters couldn't allow obstacles to keep them from continuing—not even footwear.

Soon, three pairs of shoes reverberated on the steps, echoing painfully in her ears. At least the noise should scare off the spiders. The place was practically dripping with cobwebs, and Sandra watched the bricks for skittering movement. They finally reached the landing and the fourth window. The floor was divided by a wall and a door, to make a small room on one side. The wood creaked and groaned as Sandra walked to the door.

John climbed the final step and glanced around. "Is this place safe?"

"Probably. As long as you don't have asthma, that is," she said. Clouds of dust billowed in the faint light from the window. She peeked through the open door into a tiny room, about half the size of the tower. There were two small windows and a wooden ladder which led to the very top. That was where the light would be, if there was one. The top floor had full glass windows and a balcony. But she wasn't sure they could get up there with the equipment. "Come on. We'll set up on this floor."

She strode through the opening. And jerked to a stop. Ice formed in her veins. A figure in black floated above the floor. Skeletal hands reached for her. Black tatters brushed the floor instead of feet. An empty face loomed under a dark hood. Fear crawled over her skin as the dead thing kept reaching for her.

She couldn't breathe.

John bumped into her, saw the creature and screamed, high pitched and panicked.

Sandra's chest convulsed for air. She covered her mouth and laughed.

Chad pushed in to see and whistled in appreciation. "Not bad. I wonder who left this here."

"Well, it certainly caught me by surprise," Sandra said. As for who left it there... Who else but Cooper? Although, she wasn't sure how he knew she'd be visiting the lighthouse. The ghost was well done, no doubt. Larger than life, wrapped in gobs of store-bought cobwebs and floating above the floor. It must have been a left over Halloween costume he'd stuffed.

How mundane. The man was losing his touch after all these years. Sandra poked the outstretched arm. Straw, or perhaps paper shreds, crackled. Once upon a time, he had tricked her with fake blood coming out of a water fountain at a sports camp. This ghost behind the door? She was not impressed. "Let's use it for the recording. It will be a nice background prop."

Chad and John set up the lamp next to the wooden ladder and took several minutes adjusting the angle and placement. Sandra brushed debris and a bit of broken glass from the spot on the floor next to the ghost. It was cramped in the room. A few pieces of old furniture were shoved against the wall, the ladder took up space in the middle, and behind the door—where the ghost was—was a pile of crates and broken odds and ends. An old photograph of a young woman hung between two windows. Sandra leaned forward to study the picture.

A sigh whispered nearby. A draft of cold air chilled the room. The hairs on Sandra's neck and arms lifted. Darting a look at the open door, she checked for danger.

No one.

But she couldn't shake the feeling of being watched. Only Chad, John, and herself were in the tight space, but it felt as if something else moved between them. Was in there with them. She tried to shake it off.

A faint, sniffling noise came from far away. She crossed glances with Chad, who was frozen in the act of setting up the lamp.

"Did you hear that?" he asked.

A soft sob sounded. Close by, but not in the room.

"Oh, I'm pretty sure I didn't hear anything," John said, his eyes wide. Beads of sweat appeared on his forehead, and he wiped them with his sleeve.

"Did anyone check the lens room?" Chad pointed upwards.

"Nope. Why don't you stick your head through the trapdoor and take a look for us?" John suggested.

Sandra waved them both aside. "Allow me to handle the situation." Lips pursed in determination, she balanced the tips of her heels on the round, rickety rungs. She climbed slow and steady, and paused when her head reached the level of the trapdoor.

There are no such things as ghosts. That was one childhood fear she had managed to conquer, thanks to Cooper Hall.

Sucking in a breath for courage, she climbed the final steps into the lens room. It was beautiful. Pale blue paint still decorated the wooden floor and window frames. Through the glass, there was a three-hundred-sixty-degree view of the hills, beach, and ocean, Captain Kearn's hundred-year-old house on the cliff. The lens took up most of the middle of the floor, but it had never been used. Just a rich man's hobby. She clucked her tongue. "Don't come up, boys. The carnage, sweet angels above, the carnage."

Chad scrambled up, and then John. He hummed a polka tune in appreciation.

Sandra clapped her hands. "We better get to work."

Back on the landing, Sandra swiped shards of broken bottles to the side with her feet and planted herself next to the ghost. Chad tilted the lamp until the light shone in her eyes.

"Test?" John asked.

"And go," Sandra said. "This is Sandra for your news on all things spooky and weird in Warrosquoake County. We are standing in the haunted lighthouse today with a new friend, so grab your popcorn, and don't freak out if your closet door swings open by itself tonight. I'm sure no one's in there."

"Did you know my closet actually does that?" Chad asked.

"In that case, it was nice knowing you. You'll be dead within three days, I'd say." Sandra tsked in mock pity.

John chuckled and checked the digital replay. "We're good." He pointed at her.

"Hello, and good evening, this is Sandra Kelly for your news on

Local Gems, reporting from inside the tower known as Captain Kearn's Lighthouse." She smiled for the camera. "We've all heard the ghost stories, including St. Elmo-like lights in the hills, the sound of a child or woman crying, or sightings of a young woman in blue pacing along the beach. Our research shows there may be some truth to the stories." A shiver ran from her toes to her scalp. That crying was back. She motioned towards the Halloween prop. "Although the fellow beside me is just some prankster's idea of a good time, the story of the young woman dates back to 1930, shortly after the market crash of '29. In fact, Captain Kearn's daughter died in mysterious circumstances near the lighthouse after her mother reported her missing. The last time she was seen alive, she was dressed in blue and standing on the beach."

The air turned cold in the room. Had they left the door open downstairs? The windows?

Chad's eyes bugged and he drew back.

"On the other hand," Sandra continued, forcing her voice to remain steady, "many people attribute the floating lights to nothing other than party-goers, walking over the dunes with their flashlights in the middle of the night. At least two psychics contradict this practical explanation, though, and have insisted over the years that this very room is haunted by a ghost of a middle-aged man. A man none other than Captain Kearn, the millionaire turned pauper after the crash. They claim he walks from the house to here, carrying his lantern in his search for his daughter, and then climbs the stairs to where he took his own life."

Another cry sounded. Goose bumps and hairs on her arms and neck stood. This one was closer and louder. And it wasn't a person yelling or any animal or bird cry that she could identify. The cry choked and faded.

"Outro," John hissed, reminding her to wrap things up.

No way was she going to panic during a shoot the second things got tough. Or weird. Not a chance, because remaining calm was how people moved up in her line of business. She would absolutely deserve any and every promotion she got.

She swept her hand to include the whole room. "The ambience just keeps getting better and better, folks. Now, let's take a look from outside the lighthouse and see if the Historical Society of Sycamore Cove is right about wanting to renovate this building."

John cut the recording and Chad heaved a sigh of relief.

"Is anyone else freaked out by this lighthouse?" the intern asked, switching off the light. "I came and got drunk here a hundred times at night, but today—" He broke off his sentence and shook his head. "I can't."

"You know what," Sandra said. "Go on down without me. I want to leave a note for the person who decorated the room."

"Are you sure?" Chad asked.

"Honey, nothing is going to come after me and survive. I'll be right down."

"We are live in twenty-two minutes, but you want to stay in the creepy tower," he said, shouldering his bag. "And you think the thing in my closet is going to get me." His muttering died off as John followed him out the small door to the staircase. They began the metal-clanging, spiraling descent to the ground.

Sandra's gaze swept the room. Chest rising and falling too fast, she held herself in place instead of running after her coworkers. The ghost was nice touch. She wanted to leave Cooper a little message to remind him who he was dealing with, though. It took more than old costumes to rattle her.

There was a whisper of a sob. Faint. Far away. She shook off the feeling that something was wrong with the room and dug a pen and pad of paper from her bag.

There was a rustle like dry grass in the corner. The tiny scratch of a rock or piece of glass on wood. She scribbled a few words on the paper and tore it from the pad. The sooner she could join the rest of the crew, the better.

Sandra rolled the paper and tucked it in the ratty robe of the ghost costume.

It shivered, coming alive. A scream caught in her throat as adrenaline flooded her muscles. The creature stumbled forward. It hit the floor with a hollow thump and lunged for her. Clawed hands grasped.

CHAPTER 5

The faceless horror reached for her, cobwebs and torn cloth waving.

Shouting, Sandra jumped back and knocked against the open door. She stumbled to right herself, but the door slammed shut with a crack. There was a man. There was a man coming for her.

With a cry for help, she grabbed the only weapon she had—her blue suede, four-inch pump—and brandished it, spiked heel outward, like a kung fu warrior. Man, ghost, phantom, whatever, she was not going down without a fight. It crouched, bent at the middle and moaning, arms outstretched.

Not knowing whether John or Chad heard her, Sandra jumped for the door.

Pain flared in her foot. Glass. Hissing at the white-hot cut, she threw herself at the handle and turned. The door wouldn't budge. She banged and shouted at it.

The man stood upright and came for her.

"Stop!" She menaced him with her shoe, teetering on one foot. "Stop right there, or I will use this!"

Funny. Her voice sounded so much tougher than she felt. Inside, she was shaking as bad as a fruit salad on a trampoline. Her inner Jackie Chan was shining through like a boss, though.

The man took slow step and leaned forward, closer. Her heart flipped then pounded against her ribs, and cold sweat broke out. She could barely breathe. She opened her mouth to yell for help.

"Wait." He grabbed her hands and pinned her arms to her body.

Self-defense lessons kicked in and her knee came up to connect with his phantom junk. He grunted, doubling over and coughing in pain. He groaned, "Sandra."

That voice.

He hunched over, holding his stomach and crotch. With a trembling hand, she pulled off the hood and exposed a tussle of silky brown hair. How had she not guessed? She pressed her forefingers in the pressure points under his ears, at the top of the jaw bone.

"Cooper." She pressed harder to turn his face towards hers. "Oh, I should have known. It had to be you or some psycho. Get ready to experience the most epic, man-tittie-twister of all times."

She let up on the pressure points, ready to pinch his nipples, but made the mistake of putting weight on her injured foot. The glass dug in deeper. The pain was blinding. Reflexively, she grabbed ahold of the only thing within reach—Cooper. Tangled up and off-balance, she tumbled sideways. He caught her around the waist, but her weight pulled him down, too. Right on top of her.

Her heel burned, shooting sharp flares up her whole leg. Desperate to make the pain stop, she reached around Cooper to press the top half of her foot. But mostly, she just managed to squeeze him tighter to her chest.

"Sandra," he groaned in her ear, "this isn't the time or place."

"Get. Off. Me."

"I'm trying, but you kneed me pretty damn hard."

She wriggled underneath him, getting a noseful of his natural, buttery scent. A scent she hated herself for knowing too well. Christmas. She was putting all the blame on the holidays and too much eggnog.

"Are you hurt?" He rolled limply off and to the floor, starting to uncurl himself like a pill bug that had sensed the danger had passed. How very wrong he was.

"Yes," she said.

His hands were suddenly on her leg, exploring up and down. "Where? What happened?"

"Don't touch me." She batted him away. That thrill that bubbled through her stomach at his fingertips was immediately dismissed as nothing but nervous energy. "It was you, wasn't it? The scary noises, the weirdness? Dammit, you nearly gave me a heart-attack. I could have fallen down the stairs!"

"Never. I was watching the whole time." He sat back on his ankles, the costume settling around his shoulders and legs, crunching.

Sandra plucked at the threadbare cloth and dark bits of paper fluttered to the floor. "Nice. A little padding to make up for what you lack in size."

"All part of the disguise. I would have jumped out earlier, but Chad was too close to the open door and then I didn't want to interrupt the broadcast. But when I saw you leaving me a note, my heart was overwhelmed. Now, tell me where you are hurt."

She lifted her foot to the level of his face. Blood dripped to the floor. Just a drop or two, burgundy on the dusty boards. Her head spun at the sight and she grabbed her heel.

It was his turn to bat her hands away as he held her heel and inspected the wound. "We really need to get this cleaned. Come on, I'll help you down the stairs." He grunted and stood. Acting the part of a gentleman, he took her elbow and helped her stand, but when she put her foot down, she winced in pain.

"Wonderful. I can't move an inch." Her voice was razor sharp, trying to warn him off, but Cooper wasn't impressed.

Nonplussed, he reached for her. "Lean on me."

"No—"

He wasn't listening. Despite her height and athletic build, which intimidated most guys, he wrapped an arm around her waist, supporting her weight. "Good thing for you, I've recovered from your vicious attack."

"Don't worry, I have more where that came from."

"I'm looking forward to it." He paused, lips pressed together. "I'm sorry about your foot. Really."

An apology? From Cooper? She quirked an eyebrow. The apocalypse was coming. She could already hear the horsemen's hooves pounding on the sand.

"I can see you don't believe me, but I am sorry. I never wanted you to get hurt." Cooper moved them both to the door and grabbed the handle. It wouldn't turn. He yanked, trying to force it left and right.

A sigh came up from deep within her chest. "Cooper, the door is jammed. I already tried it."

"Nonsense, it's just—" The handle popped off and he stared at it. "Maybe I can jimmy it."

"With your imaginary crow bar?" She pulled free of his arm to lean against the wall, hands in fists. "I have to be downstairs giving a live transmission in twenty minutes. Which you already know because you were here listening to us. This could get me fired. At the very least, it will make me look bad. And you don't want that, Cooper, because I don't want that."

"You won't be late." He held up a finger for her to wait or be silent, and anger churned in her chest. "I promise, you won't be late."

The noises from the stairwell had died. Chad and John must have reached the ground and would be setting up the camera.

"Hey," she said, poking him. "Try yelling for the guys from the balcony. Maybe they can get it open from the other side."

"I will take care of everything. You won't be late, and we'll get your foot bandaged." He pulled off the costume robe and tossed it in the corner. A second later, he was up the ladder in the lens room. His steps echoed hollow on the wooden floor above her and a window screeched as he opened it. She closed her eyes as he yelled for John and Chad. There was no reply or steps on the stairs as far as she could tell. Her watch said there were only eighteen minutes left.

Brad would take advantage of this screw up—he wouldn't hesitate. Her opinions and planning would be brushed aside for months.

No, not months. She would either win this contest or leave town for a new position. An iron resolution settled on her shoulders. She would win. But first she had to get out of the tower and show everyone at home she could do her job.

"I'll be right back," Cooper called from the trap door. There was a scuffle on the floor and a grunt.

"What are you doing?" She huffed. The man was impossible. Where did he think he could go up there?

The balcony.

Climbing up the walls. The high school guys used to brag about it. They would come out here on weekend nights and climb the pipes and bricks up to the top to get in and party. Cooper must have remembered.

Her heart leapt to her throat and she limped to the ladder. "Cooper! Don't you dare! We'll call the fire-department." Where was her phone? She limped to her bag and flung the contents out. "Wait, I'm calling John to get back up here right now!"

"Give me two minutes, Sandra," Cooper called faintly.

Pulse racing, she tried to follow his path along the balcony based on the sounds from outside. From this height, he would die if he fell. He would die, all for a stupid prank and because he felt guilty for it. She wrapped her arms across her stomach, holding in her fear. If he fell, her life, everything she loved, would be meaningless.

There was a bump from the landing outside the door. She hobbled across the tiny room and pressed her ear to the wood. Another bump. Cooper's voice, probably cursing. A squeal of metal. A louder thump, as loud as her own heart pounding, when he hit the landing.

He was safe.

Her legs went weak as tension fled. She wanted to yell at him, insult him, tell him what she thought of his idiotic heroics, but there was no air in her lungs. The handle on the far side of the door rattled. Stepping back, she waited as the door swung smoothly open, revealing Cooper with a cocky grin and a ripped t-shirt.

That strip of bare skin on his shoulder tempted her like ice cream on a hot summer day. But she wouldn't give him the satisfaction of ever letting him know. "Cooper Hall, you are the most vacuous, dimwitted, cheese nug, and how the hell did you get in exactly?"

The underside of the balcony was visible from the open window next to the stairs. She shook her head, amazed. "Seriously? You used the bottom of the balcony like monkey bars, opened the window one-handed, and then crawled inside? From three stories off the ground? Do I know you?"

He grinned wider and ducked his head in mock modesty. "Remember the discussion we had about my superpower? Now you know. But I'd like to keep it a secret, so hush-hush."

John yelled her name from the bottom of the lighthouse and his footsteps crashed on the metal stairs.

Nothing like your work buddies coming to save you right after the nick of time.

Cooper could have fallen trying to climb off the balcony and to the window. On the other hand, if Cooper had been a psychopath, hiding in the costume, she would be dead by now, and John would have had to explain to the cops he thought she was writing a quick note. For ten whole minutes.

"She's here!" Cooper's deep voice rumbled in the tight space.

The footsteps on the stairs paused.

"Sandra?" Chad called, squeaking. "Is that you?"

"Stay down there, I'm coming." She waved to Cooper to come and help her. This was his fault, and she would make him pay. Now and later.

Sandra gritted her teeth as Cooper supported her at his side and they walked slowly to the stairs. Though it was hard to ignore the rippling muscle holding her up, the memory of him jumping at her steeled her nerves. His hair tickled her face, setting off a brush fire in her veins, and she had to restrain herself from combing her fingers through it

With his deep brown eyes and self-assured smile, he was a mash up of an Italian lover and a moonshine-making, Appalachian mountain man. One crook of his finger and any woman would be tempted to take some time off her feet on his porch, sipping his homemade brew.

Then staying the night in a delirious, steamy mess, to wake up to fresh coffee in the morning.

No—she was done. She was done imagining Cooper was hiding his sweet, sexy, true self behind the cavalier exterior. He had broken the treaty.

But damn, he smelled good.

CHAPTER 6

Anyone could steal undies and tie them to a pole. Cooper should know. He'd spent years perfecting his skills, planning and orchestrating pranks that went well beyond toothpaste on toilet seats and tighty-whities flapping like flags of surrender in the wind.

Cooper's inner caveman warred with his civilized self, wanting to cry out his victory in this latest hard-fought battle. He had come. He had hidden. He had pranked, and now he was carrying off his woman as his prize. A growl rose up through his chest.

Just before it could spring from his throat, his civilized self wrested back the control of his brain (and body). Sandra certainly wasn't his woman or his prize to take home to his lair, and his prank had been far from perfect.

Getting them stuck in the room. Sandra cutting open her heel on glass. No. He could do better, but at least nothing else bad had happened. No real harm done.

He focused on the present. He had to get Sandra down in time for her broadcast. As he half-carried her a couple of steps across the landing, her hair tickled his nose and neck. The younger guy, Chad, thundered up the spiraling staircase and froze at the sight of Cooper.

"Aren't you the Halloween decoration?" he asked.

Sandra blew a curl from her face. "Chad, this is Cooper. Cooper, Chad. And that's enough niceties. Let's move, people, we have a show to do."

"Right!" Chad pivoted on the narrow step and clomped downward, shaking the whole structure.

"I'm sure this thing is in better condition than the door handle," Cooper said, guiding Sandra to the rail.

"If it's not, we'll both die atrocious, painful deaths." She held tight to the rail and Cooper's shoulder, and hopped on her good foot.

Cooper stayed one step ahead, careful to go at her pace. "From this height, we might make it out with only twisted, broken bones and puncture wounds from rusty metal."

"How much do I have to pay you to make you stop talking?"

"Just ask me nicely. You know I'm here to please."

"Nicely?" She scoffed. "Cooper, I know all your tricks and I've seen all of your cards."

"Not all of my tricks. Not yet."

She shook her head, gritting her teeth as she navigated the narrow passage.

When they reached the halfway point, Chad returned, hair sweaty and sticking up. He raked his fingers through it and cleared his throat. "No pressure, and not sure what's going on, but shouldn't you be getting set up for the shot already?"

"What's going on is that my shoe is filling up with blood and I have at least twelve more minutes before we are live, so stop bugging me."

"Right. You're right." He swiveled to go, then completed a full three-hundred sixty degree turn. "Why is your shoe—"

"I'm coming! Tell John to be ready at the base of the tower. Now."

He clamped his mouth shut and hurried down, out of her way.

Cooper smiled and patted the rail. "You'll be fine. No worries. You're doing gr—"

She lifted her pointer finger to silence him. "No motivational platitudes from you, Cooper. Not now. Not later. And to think I was hesitating on whether or not I should break the treaty."

"No platitudes. Got it. Do you want me to carry you down on my back?"

"Just help me hop faster."

They were both out of breath by the time they reached the bottom, but they had made good speed. Sandra checked the time on her phone and sighed in relief.

Outside, the late afternoon sun shone slanted straight into their eyes without a single cloud to break the solid blue sky. John bustled over, ecstatic to see them.

"This is great, let me line this up." John peered into his viewer and adjusted the angle on the camera. "This is gold for Pavel over in social media. He's been after me for more behind the scenes footage. I caught the whole thing. Really fun stuff. Where's the mic?"

"The mic?" Sandra patted herself, as if it could be hiding in her form-hugging suit. "No. I must have left it in the tower. Wait, you want footage for Pavel for what?"

"Magic," said John. "You know, the behind the scenes madness and mayhem."

One eyebrow went way up in a silent what-are-you-rambling-about question that made Cooper glad she wasn't glaring at him.

"Pavel's words, not mine," John protested. "To post on our site, and Facebook, and to tweet. Fun stuff."

"Does this look fun to you?" She reached down for her heel.

Cooper, suspecting she was going to show him the blood-stained inner sole, was quicker.

"Was this the mic you wanted?" He produced the mic from the satchel he used to hide the rest of his costume.

"That's the one. Sandra, do you want to say a word? This is so great." John aimed his camera, and she blinked at him a second.

"I think I'd better prepare for the broadcast," she said. "There were lots of words I could say, but none of them would be appropriate for posting online for our friends at home. If you follow me?"

"Right." Chad popped up next to them. "IFB?" Cooper stepped aside as Chad helped Sandra adjust her earpiece that allowed her to hear her coworkers at the station.

"Test?" John asked.

Someone must have been speaking through the IFB. She smiled and whispered, "No time."

"Ready? Go."

"You've heard the ghost stories and the legends, but what is the truth about this building and should it be preserved as a historical monument?" Sandra asked the viewers at home, smiling broadly.

If Cooper didn't know there was a hole in her heel, he never would have guessed by her poised, calm manner and sparkling smile.

She continued without missing a beat. "Everyone is entitled to their opinion, including the real estate group trying to purchase this land and knock it down, but here are the facts. Built over several years in the late 1920s, this has never been an official working lighthouse, but was expertly modeled to resemble one from the turn of the century, including the light and machinery. It is also an unofficial landmark for many people in Sycamore Cove and has been featured on postcards and in travel brochures. Abandoned and belonging to no one as it is, I believe that we could say it belongs to all of us. I hope you've enjoyed this segment of Local Gems. This is Sandra, and I'll be seeing you again soon."

"And cut," John whispered. "Fabulous."

The second he lowered the camera, Sandra slumped forward with a tired groan. He was done waiting. In two quick steps, he was at her side and he lifted her up to tuck her against his chest. As Cooper eased past her coworkers, he noticed John was recording them.

"What are you doing?" Sandra hissed.

"Carrying you to my car. What is John doing?"

"Following us with his camera. How did you get your car behind the trees?"

He had to duck to navigate a few lower branches, but there was an old path. And there was his car, at the end of the party road. People coming on picnics and to visit the tower usually took the main road and then the short driveway to the base of the tower. Partiers took the back way that was more path than road.

"You really need to get out and have more fun, Sandra. I can help you with that, you know." Cooper set her down at the passenger side of his Jeep. He opened the door for her.

She took a seat, collapsing back and letting her feet dangle at the side while he dug out his emergency first aid kit from the back. He found the kit, a bottle of water, and a towel before kneeling on the dirt and flattened grass in front of her.

"Let's get this cleaned." He lifted her foot, and inspected the bottom of her heel, ignoring the feel of her smooth ankle and calf. Blood was smeared everywhere and beginning to dry. He poured the cold water over it, wiping at the sole of her foot with the towel.

"Bad news is, the glass is really stuck in there."

"How stuck in there? A trip to the doctor's stuck?"

He grinned. "I think I can handle it. It's small, you won't need stitches, but we will have to disinfect. Maybe let some blood flow."

"That sounds perfect. I'd love to make some blood flow."

"I bet you would." He shifted his grip and for a few seconds to lift her foot higher, and his warm hands slid up and down her calf and back to her heel. This had absolutely no effect on him whatsoever. No effect. His fingers grazed her arch on accident. She gasped.

His jaw clenched. Considering his experience on interpreting gasps, he was fairly certain it wasn't a gasp of pain. But he couldn't take advantage of it.

His breathing was faster, but only because he was trying to get a good grip on the glass jammed in her foot with the mini-tweezers supplied by his kit. Not because of any weird fantasies. A line formed between his eyebrows as he concentrated.

"Do you want me to count to three or just yank it out?"

"Is this a trick question? If I say count, you'll just do it after two."

"No counting then?" he asked.

"No counting. Just do—"

He squeezed the tweezers and pulled.

Sandra yelled bloody murder and flexed her muscles to kick. She would probably aim for his face if he didn't hold tight. "You didn't warn me!"

Kneeling in the dirt, holding a pair of the longest, sexiest legs imaginable, he figured there were probably worse ways to go, but he wasn't ready to check out of this life, yet. "I'm sorry. You said not to count." He dodged the uninjured foot that escaped his hands and came straight for his nose.

"Sorry? Not yet, you aren't. She inspected the bottom of her foot, twisting around in the seat and accidently flashing her panties. Red and frilly.

Sweat broke out on his forehead. He wanted those things in his teeth.

"Your bedside manners leave something to be desired. I need a Band-Aid. This is bleeding."

"Your highness," he said and chuckled. She would never see his true bedside manners, but pointing that out might earn another kick to his head. Besides, he had to put the disinfectant on first and it was the stinging kind, so he didn't want to provoke her more than necessary.

Movement caught his eye. John was sneaking up on them with his camera held on his shoulder to film.

"Hey, can we get some privacy? I'm not sure this is news," Cooper said. The news station was always digging for a story. Not many counties were more boring than Warrosquoake, but he didn't think Sandra wanted her red panties on display.

"Technically, everything has the potential to be news, but this is for behind the scenes fun. Sandra, are you all right?" John asked. "Need to go the emergency room? I brought the van around to the trees."

Cooper noticed that he didn't stop recording.

"I'm fine," she said. "This fine gentleman is going to give me a Band-Aid and—"

Cooper poured the disinfectant on the puncture wound and squeezed, which cut off the rest of her sentence. A pained groan escaped her throat.

"For crying out loud, would you warn me first?"

"There's really no way to prepare for it. It's hurts whether I announce it or not. Puncture wounds are dangerous. Blood helps flush out the nasties. There. This looks good now." He wiped her sole clean with a cotton pad and gently applied a square Band-Aid.

John breathed noisily at his shoulder and zeroed in on Sandra's foot with the camera.

Without asking, Cooper stood and reached into the car to pick up Sandra again.

"You can thank me later when you don't get an infection," he whispered, conscious of both John and Chad tagging close behind.

They reached the news van, but for the second time in the space of a few minutes, Cooper found his arms rebelling at the idea of letting Sandra go. Admittedly, he enjoyed holding beautiful women.

"You can put me down now," she said.

He reluctantly obeyed. "Kudos for the report. You did good."

"You're not getting mushy on me, are you?"

His phone buzzed in his pocket. A message. "Not by a long shot. I have too many pranks ready to go on my dash to winning the Townsperson Contest."

"You're so cute. I'll see you later, Cooper." She climbed onto the passenger seat. "Sleep well while you still can."

The other two hustled to store the camera and lamp in the back of the van and as soon as John could get in his seat, they were driving off, not a glance in his direction.

He stayed rooted to the spot while the smell of exhaust and the scent of her perfume—earthy spices and flowers—faded.

His phone buzzed again. He ignored it, strolling slowly to the trees toward his own car. And his phone buzzed again, but this time someone was calling.

He pulled it from his pocket. Lauren was calling him.

Despite his brain telling him to stay calm, a sliver of fear snaked through his chest. She hardly ever called. Something might be wrong.

"Hey, what's up?" he asked.

"Are you insane? Are you trying to get yourself killed?"

Good—she was worried about him. Nothing serious. "Not that I know of. What exactly is the situation?"

"Climbing around the top of that tower as if you were Spiderman? That was not normal or healthy. Do I need to stage an intervention?"

"Wait, Lauren, don't—"

His phone buzzed with an incoming call. He glanced at the screen. Vic. His stomach began a slow, steady descent to his shoes. "Keep cool. I'll call you right back."

He hung up on her and swiped for Vic. "Yes?"

"So this was your ingenious plan to get the town to vote for you to represent them professionally? Nothing says *I'm the best this town has to offer* like swinging from the underside of a balcony four stories from the ground to break in a window."

John had posted footage of his climb to free Sandra. It had taken less than a half an hour for his sister and his business partner to see it—neither of whom were heavy into social media or watched the news much. He was dead.

"My strategy for the Townsperson contest isn't your worry," Cooper said.

"But you represent the business as my partner. So when you do stupid shit, I look like I work with an asshole."

Vic hung up without another word.

Cooper rubbed his face with his palm, gut twisting in knots. Even if he asked John to have Pavel take it down, the damage was done. The contest hadn't started yet and he was out of the running.

CHAPTER 7

The news van rumbled and John's *Greatest Hits of Polka* piped from the speakers, both lulling Sandra into a hazy stupor. A hand-crocheted action figure of Annie Leibovitz, complete with a yarn camera, and made by Sandra herself, danced on the end of a string under the rearview mirror. They pulled off the pothole-filled drive onto the road toward town and she closed her eyes.

Her phone rang.

And that would be Brad, because he simply can't let ten minutes go by without criticizing my work.

His name was on the screen. She muttered a string of curses and turned off the music to answer.

"Hi, Brad, can I help you?" Her voice was sugar and cream.

"Would you care to explain what that was about? Hair and clothes a mess? No prep before going live. And that video John sent in for our behind the scenes stuff? Some random monkey boy, who isn't a part of our team, playing on his makeshift gymnasium was not what I had in mind. *Behind the scenes* are supposed to make us look good, not like slapstick amateurs."

"But tell me how you really feel. I can take it."

"This sarcasm," he said, spitting the word out, "is exactly why you are still Junior Reporter. What the hell was going on at the lighthouse?"

She took a deep breath—she needed her job, she loved her job. This trying time would pass and she would be a tougher badass because of it. "Mr. Hall happened to be in the area and went in to visit the lighthouse before we arrived. As we were leaving, the door got jammed shut when the handle broke. Mr. Hall, being a sportsman and a gentleman, climbed out to the balcony and to a window in order to push the door open and allow me to exit."

"I'm supposed to believe that? Door getting mysteriously jammed? Why was it shut in the first place with the two of you upstairs? Do you realize how this makes the news station look?"

"Like we have amazing citizen heroes in our town?"

"Sarcasm, Sandra. I just warned you about it."

The audio on her phone clicked with an incoming call. Probably her mom. She only waited fifteen minutes after a broadcast to call.

"Listen," Sandra said. "I'm not going to throw John or Pavel under the bus for posting the kind of footage you specifically requested. Things happen in the field. Crazy things, in fact. You don't know half the shit I've had to put up with or deal with on the spot. If you don't like it, then don't ask for it."

"I don't think asking for professionalism is asking too much. I want you in my office first thing Monday morning. This discussion is not over."

Oh, you sweet summer child. Yes, it is. "I'll be at my desk on Monday. Goodbye."

She swiped and tossed the phone in her purse at her feet. Speaking of, her cut throbbed like being hit with a burning red poker. John scratched his rounded jaw and coughed, nervous.

"I got you in trouble, didn't I?"

"Sweetie, just don't play any more polka when I'm in the car with you," she said and patted his shoulder.

Her phone rang. Again? What was his problem? "If you think for one second I will acquiesce to your every demand and allow you to control my every move, you have another thing coming, producer or not, you had better watch out."

"Sandra, that's harsh and I really don't see why you think I'm controlling your every move, but yes, I will be watching my ass closely from now on."

She rolled her eyes up, studying the van's ceiling. "Cooper. Why the hell are you calling me?"

He paused and then stammered out, "I might be calling because there is a slim sort of possibility that I could use your help."

"My help?" She gave a good belly laugh. This was rich. "You are calling me for help? That seems masochistic even for you."

"Yeah, I need your help, but only because your news station posted a video of me when I climbed out of the tower. This could kill my bid for Townsperson of the Year. Now I'm sure you would think it was great if I couldn't even submit my candidature, but fair is fair. You got me in a difficult situation. You are the only person I can think of to help me dig out of this hole."

"Did you forget you got us locked in the tower in the first place?"

"And I got us out. And your colleagues posted it for the whole town to see. By the way, my arms were stunning, if I do say so."

She drummed her fingers on her leg. It might have been his fault, but they were both facing judgment. But she'd have to work with him to pull it off. Any time with Cooper was too much time. Then again, she couldn't let Brad win. "I might have a solution." A devilish plan was forming in her mind.

"I'm in, whatever it is."

If he was willing, she could find the strength to be around him for a few more minutes. But not today. She would need help to pull this off—a flamboyant, take-no-prisoners performer to lend her a hand. If her friend was free tomorrow, she could get an interview with Cooper right after some serenading fun in the middle of the park. Sunshine, love, and community all together—it would be perfect. "First of all, you are not backing out of this contest, Cooper.

It will be so much sweeter when I grind you to dust than if you give up now. Understood?"

"Yes."

"Are you busy tomorrow?" So much for her weekend.

"No," he said.

"Meet me at River Crossing in the afternoon. I'll send you a message for the time."

"Wait. Is this a trap of some kind?"

"Why, Cooper Hall, you know me better than to ask such a question. You want help for your little problem? I can help you, but remember, you broke the treaty, not me. Oh, and you owe me a pair of blue suede Guess pumps. These are ruined."

A grin spread across her face and she hung up on him. However, it faded almost as fast as it had arrived when she called Brad back.

"Brad, this problem has given me an idea for how to handle the Townsperson contest. Except it isn't a problem, it's an opportunity, and this situation ties into it perfectly."

Cooper leaned back on the park bench, arm out as though around an invisible girlfriend and his face to the warm sun. The park overlooked the bluffs and the river, which emptied into ocean nearby, and was filled with people out to enjoy the Sunday afternoon.

He took another sip of his iced, cold-brew coffee and pretended to be relaxing. He had learned long ago not to show anxiety when Sandra could be near. It made her thirstier for blood—his blood, specifically.

The temperatures were warm enough these days to sit in a t-shirt until the sun went down. The last gulp of coffee washed down his throat. He closed his eyes, face to the setting sun and letting the heat warm him. Her text had said to be there at five, ready for an interview. It was nearly five-fifteen. He loosened his button-up shirt collar at his neck. Maybe she simply wasn't coming.

A hand landed on his shoulder and he jumped in his seat. Shielding his eyes, he glanced up. Sandra was behind the park bench, one hand on her hip and a small, portable camera in the other. Her skin and golden-brown curls glowed warm in the sunlight.

"Mr. Hall. I'd like to interview you this lovely afternoon, if you don't mind?"

He stood, ducking his head in acknowledgement. "I would like that very much. Much more so than this being a set up for a prank."

A smile spread on her wide, glossy lips. "Good. I limped all the way across the park just for you. You get one interview to tell the town about why you'd be the perfect Townsperson of the year, same as I'll offer all the candidates. I make amends for your stunt getting posted and my producer is satisfied. Ready?"

"What, right here, right now?"

"Did you have somewhere else in mind?" She didn't wait for his answer but lifted the small camera level with her eyes and made a couple of adjustments.

He ran his fingers through his hair and rolled his shoulders. If she wanted him to talk about himself, he could handle it. Someone tapped his shoulder.

"Excuse me," a man asked.

He turned, then squinted into the sun's rays.

"Are you Cooper Hall?"

A young guy in black pants and a leather jacket stood on the path in front of him, holding a pizza box. A large bag was on the grass next to him. He held the pizza towards him.

"Did you order a large pepperoni and pineapple pizza? You like it salty and sweet, am I right?"

That was the sort of pizza he usually ordered. Weird. Then a cold finger of suspicion brushed his spine. Had she arranged something? He threw a glance over his shoulder to where Sandra stood. She wouldn't do this in the park, would she?

Innocent surprise was all over her face. And she was filming. "Why Mr. Hall, you shouldn't have gone to the trouble."

"I didn't." He shook his head the pizza delivery guy. "It's not mine, but you can leave it with me if you want and I'll eat it later."

"But you are Cooper, right? Phone number 757—"

"I'm Cooper. Listen, I'll pay for the pizza, it's not a problem. How much do I owe you?"

"Don't mind me if you need to take care of this, Mr. Hall. I'll edit it out later. Promise."

She would. A prank in a park. And he had hoped she would actually help him to fix the lighthouse stunt? He was out of his mind. "Thank you, Ms. Kelly, that is kind of you."

"I don't want your money," the man said. "I came for your heart and nothing else will do."

"Oh, isn't this wonderful?" Sandra cooed.

Tossing the pizza box like a Frisbee, the young man ripped off his jacket—really tore it in a way that set off alarm bells in Cooper's head. The kind from old World War II movies, where a boat has been hit and the alarms are blaring, and sailors are racing to shut the valves and the captain is gazing off into the camera with steely eyes and vowing to go down with the ship.

Then the guy pulled off his shirt, too.

Cooper was glad he wasn't a captain. He was not going down with this ship.

"I think I'll be going—"

The now topless dude whose prominent six-pack and hairless chest could give most women a mild heat stroke put his hands in his rainbow-colored gym bag and pulled out an Eighties size boom box.

Legs planted firmly, boom box overhead, and puppy-dog face on, the guy kissed the air.

Cooper knew that stance.

Peter Gabriel's "Your Eyes" poured from the boom box, drifting cotton candy sweet through the park and attracting the attention of every person lazing about. Squeals of excitement reached his ears despite the music, and he could sense the cell phones being whipped out and turned towards him. With Sandra filming, too, it was a major event by Sycamore Cove's standards.

"Thank you," he shouted. "That will do."

Shirtless Lloyd Dobler nodded. But the music kept playing.

He had hated *Say Anything* after the first ten minutes of watching it at Meredith Monroe's house during a Saturday movie-athon his sophomore year. First love, sacrifice, and gushy romance. Not interested.

Now the movie was back to haunt him in the form of Sandra's newest, public prank.

"Mr. Hall," Sandra called. "Would you like to *say anything* to the people of Sycamore Cove about being serenaded in the park?"

"Indeed, I would. This comes as a complete surprise, but obviously, I have an admirer. I respect that." Time for him to turn the situation around and salvage what he could. He motioned to get the guy's attention. "Hey, how about a song with more bounce?"

"You're right, I hate that song, too," boom box boy yelled in reply. He fiddled with something behind the player and "Bad Romance" filled the air. He added a hip swivel and his pecs twitched alternately.

A gaggle of girls and a couple of women had formed a half circle behind Sandra, and one of women winked at him, knowingly. They were enjoying the show, and probably imagining all sort of things.

"Can I get a picture with you?" a teenage girl asked the guy. She held up her phone and made a duckface at it.

"Great show, isn't it?" Cooper asked, facing Sandra and the group. "I love that we can keep the community close through music and fun. Don't forget, voting for the Townsperson of the Year starts—"

"Oh, shit." The music cut off.

Someone grabbed his arm, yanking him.

"My boyfriend is here," the guy said frantically, his nose nearly rubbing Cooper's. "You have to come with me."

"No, I don't think—"

"He will kill you. Look over there."

Cooper craned his neck. A body-builder type with too much testosterone and protein bars in his daily diet parked his motorcycle in the parking lot about fifty yards up the hill. From that distance, it wasn't clear where one bulging muscle ended and another started. He could be part of Sandra's prank. But she frowned at the approaching figure and then shook her head at Cooper.

"Scares small children, makes the ground shake, black leather boots guy?" Cooper asked.

"Yes. I don't think he's seen us, but he must have noticed my car.

Sandra stepped up next to them and leaned in. "Is there a problem?"

"I think he saw me," boom box guy said.

"Who?"

"My jealous boyfriend."

Cooper crossed his arms. "Sandra, did you plan this? The scary hulk?"

"What are you talking about? Did you plan on locking us in the tower the other day? Things happen. Let me distract him for a moment."

Boom box guy took Cooper's arm, eyes on the menace coming straight their way. "Honey, I wish you the best of luck. Now, you, hot stuff, I need you to do exactly what I say."

"Crazy suggestion, but why don't we explain the situation?" Despite that rational part of Cooper's brain telling him it was all part of Sandra's plan, the other part couldn't help but notice the guy was about to panic. She headed off to intercept the leather-studded boyfriend. Cooper didn't know which of the two had more determination in their step, despite Sandra's slight limp.

"Explain that I was serenading you and starting a great performance? That would go over like a ton of horse-shit. He is insanely jealous. It's so hot." He fanned himself. "Except when he tries to kill nice people because he thinks I'm cheating on him."

Cooper looked down. A bright pink feather boa and matching pair of heels had appeared from the bag. Among the other items in the guy's bag, Cooper had time to see a blender, some rhinestone jewelry, and a bottle of edible eggnog body oil.

"Put it on." The guy waved the boa under his nose. "He knows I only go for tough, manly men and never drag queens. Change your shirt, too. I promise. It will protect you."

"Before I go drag with you, what did you say your name was?"

His new friend winked at him and lowered his voice to conspirator levels. "They call me Valentino il Grande."

"Right. Can I call you Val?" No way was he saying that whole name out loud. "As in Val Kilmer?"

Valentino smiled. "Oh, baby, only if you say it like you mean it." He wrapped the boa around Cooper's neck.

Cooper had to try one last time. "Read my lips. Explain. Things. To. Him."

"Baby, please. Put on the feather boa and heels if you want to live."

CHAPTER 8

The scowling six-foot-and-something man stomped through the park in black leather boots, chewing up the distance between Sandra and himself as if she was a trespasser on his private hunting grounds. This was not part of the plan.

Nonplussed, she squared her shoulders and hefted the camera to make sure it was plainly visible. She smiled and strode up the grassy knoll to intercept him. "Good afternoon, may I introduce myself?"

He grunted, squinting at the small group of people who had gathered around Cooper and Valentino for the serenade show.

She sidestepped around him, drawing his gaze in the other direction. Sunlight glinted dangerously on his studded dog collar, and his leather jacket creaked. "Sandra Kelly from WCC 12 News. I'm here interviewing citizens in the park today. Nothing too formal, but we always enjoy featuring people on our local gems show. Could I ask you a few questions? Starting with your name, sir?"

Another grunt. He narrowed his eyes at her and bent closer. The tattoos on his neck and face shifted as his jaw tightened and his veins pulsed. "My name is Clarence Saintmire."

"Well, Mr. Saintmire—"

"No. I'm Clarence." His fist bunched and he pounded it in the other palm.

"Right. Clarence. And what brings you to the park today?"

He twisted his mouth in an ugly grimace. "My man is here. Have you seen him?"

"Do you have a description of this person? Clothes, hairstyle, notable features?"

"Blond. Dreamboat. And I'll crush anyone who tries to touch him." Clarence craned his neck, gazing past her and down the hill. "The hell am I seeing?" He stormed off towards Cooper and Valentino, who by now had lost their crowd.

Cooper stood, leaning precariously, looking slightly confused, a hot pink feather boa around his neck and matching heels on his feet. He hobbled forward. On instinct, Sandra lifted her camera.

And zoom.

A shirtless Valentino was right behind him, swinging a huge bag onto one shoulder. He rushed forward to hold back the towering giant of muscle and fear.

The drama and beauty of the moment was Perfect. With a capital P.

She panned the scene. The park teemed with families and picnicking couples, most of whom had their heads turned to watch the trio, and the park fell noticeably quieter as everyone held their breath.

Cooper edged his way up the hill, obviously nervous, but Valentino was glued to the biker and even stood on tiptoes for a kiss.

Enough filming. Sandra rushed forward to take Cooper's arm. "There you are. I'm so happy you came for an interview. Would you like to talk here at the park or go somewhere to sit indoors?"

"Someone want to explain what happened to his shirt before I get angry?" Clarence demanded.

"Sunbathing is what happened to my shirt. You wouldn't want me to get a farmer's tan, right? This is my friend Cooper," Val said, waving at him. "Remember I said I might be helping out a guy with a costume?"

"No. I don't remember that."

"Was this something fun you planned for the news interview and your upcoming bid for the Townsperson of the Year contest?" Sandra asked, exaggerating her enunciation.

Take a hint, Coop.

He frowned his fuchsia lips for a second, rubbing the feathers on the boa. Then he tossed her a smile. "Exactly. You know me. Reaching out and getting close to people, understanding people, and..."

"You wanted to experience what it means to feel wild and free," Val said, saving him when he floundered. "And also beautiful. I would like to add, that you look beautiful."

Clarence glanced from Val to Cooper. In one quick step, he reached Cooper, his fist in his face. "Are you trying to attract my man?"

Sandra forced a laugh. She grabbed Cooper's hand, pulling him firmly to her side. "Of course, he isn't. He wouldn't. Because..." She paused. To save Cooper she was going to have to say something she would regret. But it was necessary. "I know him better than you could imagine. He and I have this complicated relationship going on. But I don't want to dwell on us. Cooper, let's take this interview to a café. What do you say?"

"What kind of complicated relationship?" Clarence asked. He planted his feet and crossed his arms.

She swallowed. "An on-again, off-again, rebound fling sort of relationship. But let me assure you, he is not only interested in women, but he is currently..."

One of Cooper's eyebrows went up slowly as he turned to face her. "I'm currently?"

"I mean, *I* am currently pursuing Mr. Hall," Sandra said. Embarrassment rushed hot through her chest, neck, and onto her cheeks. "And I believe the feeling is mutual." Clearing her throat, she stepped closer and squeezed his arm.

"Put your arm around me and hold me close," Cooper said. "If you want to, of course."

"I don't think I could handle that level of intimacy with you at this point."

"Take all the time you need. We can go at your pace."

Full credits went to Cooper for acting exactly like the trickster he was. Sandra cleared her throat and yanked on him to start walking. "My pace is strolling to the nearest café." She glanced over her shoulder. "I'd love to do that interview, Clarence. Perhaps another time?"

He sniffed, upper lip curling. "Give me your bag, Val. Let's get out of here."

Next to her, Cooper wobbled and righted himself with a lurch. He leaned closer. "Actually, could you put your arm around me and hold me up? These damn heels are too small, and I have no idea how women can walk in these evil contraptions."

She pressed her lips to keep from smirking and wrapped her arm around his waist. The warm, soap scent of his body took her mind back to winter when she pulled him into a corner at the dance club and kissed his neck when he was looking the other way.

Sparks danced on her nerves at every spot she was pressed against him and an ache throbbed in her chest.

Forget it. Forget him. So he smelled good? That was the best thing he had going for him.

"Is the leather studded biker following us?"

She snapped her head up at the sound of his voice. She had to hope he hadn't noticed she was smelling him. "Yes. Yes, he is."

"How far to the car?" Cooper asked.

"If I can make it with my injury, you can make it in those stilettos. Breathe."

"I'm sorry. I forgot about your heel, but how do you do it?" He looked down at her, brown eyes wide in amazement. "Honestly?

The spikes stick in the ground. My toes are screaming in agony with tiny, high-pitched voices. I can hear them in my head."

"Oh, honey, I don't feel the pain of high heels anymore. I trained for twelve years under Master Hankami of the Blue Mountains to be able to walk with ultimate grace and ease in all forms of shoes."

"That would explain it." He inhaled slowly. They were reaching the top of the hill and the parking lot. "Question. Did you arrange for the boyfriend to show up and act like he was going to kill me, or is this just a bonus for you?"

"Cooper Hall, you have the keen mind of a journalist. Striking straight to the heart of the situation with the right question. But let me ask you this, would I pretend to be interested in you if that jealous boyfriend wasn't an actual threat? Ever?"

"This isn't helping me keep my cool. How is my makeup holding up?"

"It's admirable. Valentino did an excellent job." They hit the pavement of the parking lot and Sandra steered them towards her car.

"So about this interview," called Clarence behind them. "Are you doing it?"

They swiveled, still attached by their hooked arms.

"The interview with Cooper?" Sandra asked. "Yes. I thought we'd go somewhere…"

Clarence narrowed his eyes, teeth flashing white.

Sandra dropped Cooper's arm and lifted the camera at the same time. "So Mr. Hall, thanks for coming to River Crossing Park to talk with me today."

Without a blink, he smiled. "I wouldn't have missed it for the world. I am thrilled to be your guest and I would like to say that I'm looking forward to this competition. This town is one of the best towns in the United States to live in, the schools are good, the streets are safe, and the parks are full of surprises."

"Yes, speaking of which, would you like to tell us why you are wearing a feather boa, lipstick, and a pair of magnificent high heels on this fine spring afternoon in the park?"

Valentino and his boyfriend remained a couple of feet away, listening to the exchange. She panned the camera to take them in.

Valentino blew a kiss. "Hi, Mom!"

"Tell her what you were doing," the boyfriend barked at Cooper, arms crossed.

"An exercise in going drag, something that has fascinated me for...it's hard to say for how long, but I appreciated Val's help. It's harder to walk in heels than I ever imagined. In fact, I need more practice."

The boyfriend grunted. "Let's go." He dropped a possessive hand on Val's shoulder and steered him forward. "And you," he snarled at Sandra, "I've seen you at the Yarnucopia. I'll be waiting for my interview."

"Yarnucopia?" she asked. "Getting...yarn? We'll be in touch as soon as possible."

"It was so nice *practicing* in the park for a change," Val said, breezing by.

"Wasn't it?" Cooper replied. He lifted a foot, barely keeping his balance, and pointed at the shoe. "Could I keep these for a while? Until we meet up next time..." It seemed as though he would add more, but the boyfriend growled at him and Valentino waved goodbye.

"I'll take that as a yes," Cooper said.

Val accompanied his jealous man to the bike, gazing up at him with adoration.

Sandra cleared her throat. "Love can certainly be surprising. Mr. Hall, considering your experience here in the park today with so many people watching, would you have any words of support for the members of our LGBTQ communities who struggle with stigmatization and discrimination, here and across the country?"

He paused thoughtfully, playing with the end of his boa. "We should all spend time walking in shoes that are not our own, if I may paraphrase a cliché."

"Well, said, Mr. Hall. Thank you." She panned the camera from his head to his feet, as he nodded and shifted uncomfortably in the heels. "And cut."

He kicked the shoes off and sank to the sidewalk to sit. "Goddam, that was torture. Those things hurt more than I ever, ever imagined." He pinched the top of his nose and shook his head, laughing silently. Or perhaps he was trying not to cry. Poor baby.

She knelt by his side and rubbed his arm to comfort him. "I know. I know, but you're all right now." Remembering that she no longer needed to pretend to be pursuing him, she patted him to cover the awkwardness of petting him for the last minute and dropped her hand.

Chest constricted and stomach in a flighty turmoil, she cleared her throat and backed away. As she moved to her car, though, Cooper stood and stepped in sync with her.

"Why don't I buy you chicken wings and tequila shots to celebrate still being alive? Then we can talk strategies on fabricating scandals for all the other candidates for Townsperson of the Year."

"I should go. I have to edit this for work…" She had to get a cool drink somewhere alone, was what she needed to do. Even wearing bright pink lipstick and a glittery shirt, he was devastating. The playful crinkles around his eyes clashed with the intense, dark gaze that never left her face.

He flipped the end of his boa. "Sandra, I believe it's time you admitted your feelings. I'm too much man for you."

"Mm-hmm." She focused the camera on his face. All it took was the real Cooper to cure herself of him. "What else can you tell me about yourself?"

CHAPTER 9

The knot in his gut loosened as Cooper returned to familiar territory with Sandra. Her arm in his, her body moving next to him, and the only thing he could imagine was cupping her nape and pulling her in for a kiss. He had been a heartbeat away from wrapping her in his arms to breathe in the perfume of her hair.

"I could tell you all about my wine collection. The cellar is full of bottles. Would you care to come and see it?" he asked.

She rolled her eyes. "Cooper, I swear—"

The low rumble of an engine approached, and the tires crunched on gravel as a car pulled in beside them. Cooper grabbed Sandra's hand, pulling her to the sidewalk and safety.

Inside the car, the driver was fumbling with a coffee thermos, an open map, and a cell phone. She seemed to notice them suddenly and lowered her window.

"This is Sycamore Cove Park, right?" the woman asked. Her gaze traveled to Cooper and she frowned.

"No," Sandra said, picking up her camera to cradle it in her arms. "This is River Crossing. The one you want is in the center of town with a gazebo."

"Thanks! I'm supposed to meet some clients who live in town. I didn't interrupt anything, did I?"

"No," Sandra said, shaking her head emphatically. "Nothing going on."

"Good. I saw the camera and thought maybe you were filming something and I butted my car in the middle of it."

"The camera? Right, the camera. I'm from WCC 12 News and we were doing a quick interview. But we are done now."

"For the Townsperson the Year contest," Cooper said. He might as well campaign. Nothing else was mattered, right? "Voting starts tomorrow. Remind your clients to vote for their favorite candidate. There are prizes for voters, too, I heard."

"That's so nice. I will." She paused and wrinkled her nose, studying Cooper. "Please don't take this the wrong way, but fuchsia is really not your color. Here." She whipped out a card from her dash and extended it to him. "I'm with Avon. Call me. You won't regret it."

Cooper pressed his lips closed and took the card with a nod. "Thank you. Well, I hope you have a lovely afternoon."

"No problem, you too! And..." She pantomimed answering a phone and mouthed *call me*. Cooper waved as she left.

Laughing softly, Sandra brushed by him as she circled her car. She popped the trunk and set the camera in its case, and slammed it closed. Her expression tightened, growing cold. "Voting starts tomorrow. To be fair to the other candidates, I need to figure out who is in the running and book interviews as soon as possible."

Admittedly, he preferred when she laughed. But he had a contest to win. "We aren't really done with the interview, are we?"

"We are even now, Cooper Hall. You saved me, I saved you, and since your interview will be the first one posted, it should make up for the bad publicity of the lighthouse." She brushed her hands as if done with the matter.

He gestured to his sparkly shirt. "How does this make me look better than I did before? The pink boa isn't even my color."

"Worried? You should know I'm an ace at edits. You'll be great. But I promised this to Brad first thing in the morning, and I twisted John's arm to help me get it ready this evening. The prank won't show on the broadcast. Oh, and you still owe me a pair of shoes."

"If you wear ten and a halves I can hook you up with a killer pair of hot pink stilettos right this minute."

"I wear nines. And I chipped two nails climbing down the stairs yesterday."

"Shoes and nails. It's noted. If you could give me Val's number, he has my shoes." Cooper tilted his head, studying her as she fidgeted with her fingers and pursed her lips. "Are you all right?"

"I've got a lot to do this evening."

"I see. You know, even with the contest, I'm here if you need to talk. You could come over. I'll fix you dinner. I actually know how to make some tasty chicken and zucchini pasta. Except I don't have the ingredients. Grilled steaks?"

"I'd have to be out of my mind to go to your place. We can't be together for more than two minutes without disaster striking, or hadn't you noticed? Besides the fact that we are competing. And we are competing. You will register for the contest tonight and in three weeks, I will trounce you at the finale."

She waggled her fingers in a goodbye and dropped into her seat. Cooper scooped up the heels Val had loaned him as she pulled from the parking lot. He rubbed his face.

"Come over and talk? I'll fix you dinner?" Shaking his head, he walked to his car. "I might as well throw rose petals in the air and confess I still fantasize about what almost happened last Christmas."

If he was going to win and save his place in Sycamore Cove, he had to focus. And he had to hope that her edits would be miraculous, because only divine intervention would help him look like a serious candidate for the contest at that point.

※

The third time Cooper called her Monday morning, Sandra accidently laughed out loud during a meeting.

He must have been truly terrified about the interview airing. She coughed to cover up the mistake and signaled to the ten colleagues frowning at her.

"Excuse me for a moment, please." She stood and walked quickly from the room and then steered straight to the kitchenette on the second floor where the coffee pot was.

The news channel coffee usually tasted like Mississippi River water filtered through a coffee-stained sock. This morning was no different, but she hadn't taken the time to stop for real coffee, and she needed the caffeine.

She took a steaming sip and stared at the black screen of her phone. A smile tilted her lips upwards. Yeah, she would call him back. After three tries, he deserved a little something for his efforts.

"Hi, did you want to talk to me or is your phone rubbing your butt?" she asked as soon as he answered.

"Interesting. I call and you immediately think of my butt."

"You wanted to see how fast I can hang up, is that it?"

"Nope, not at all. Sandra, I'm not going to beat around any proverbial bushes here. When do you show the interview and is it too late to ask for a second try?"

She leaned back against the counter, grinning at his obvious discomfort. "Are you nervous? What for? This town loves you, or at least everyone who goes to Murphey's on weekends loves you." A scritch-scritch noise came through the earpiece. She closed her eyes and pictured him scratching his out-of-control beard.

What she wouldn't give for a secluded cabin and lazy summer afternoons alone with a man like him.

As long as it wasn't Cooper.

"Incidentally, it's pulled pork taco Monday at Murphey's. If you had answered my calls earlier, I would have reserved you a spot at my table," he said.

"And why on earth should I answer your calls?" She took another sip from her mug.

"Because you're secretly in love with me?"

Steaming hot coffee scorched a path up and out her nose. Snorting coffee out her nose hurt worse than she could have imagined. She reached blindly for a towel to wipe her face.

"Hardly! I'm not at your beck and call, no pun intended." She finished wiping at her nose and under her eyes, trying not to smear her makeup. "I have to get back to a meeting."

"Seriously, though. Voting doesn't start until noon and the list isn't posted yet, and the interview hasn't gone on. Why do I have over a dozen messages in my box from women who want to meet up with me?"

"What?" She took a deep breath. He didn't seem to be boasting, just genuinely confused. "Cooper, I can't for the life of me imagine why anyone—especially a woman—would want to see you. Unless..."

The clips John filmed during the broadcast were on social media and had gone practically viral. People loved watching Cooper climb through the fourth story window and then afterwards, carry her to his car. Everyone wanted to know more. What had happened in the lighthouse? Why had this man appeared out of nowhere to help her? And was he related to the ghost somehow? That one killed her.

People were frantic to pin this on fate.

Even Brad had asked her about Cooper. She reminded him again that same morning he was a candidate for the Townsperson contest and she had the park interview to air. They would remind viewers about the two-week contest and voting, then go straight to the first candidate on her list. It should boost ratings for them and give more exposure to the contest. Win-win, no question about it.

And if Cooper thought he could continue to pull pranks and get away with it, he was in for a surprise. Everything was more difficult when you were in the public's eye.

"You left me dangling here, Sandra," he said, breaking into her thoughts. "Unless what?"

"They found your email address after seeing you in our clip."

"You mean I've got a dozen potential dates because you guys posted a video of me? Sandra, really, you shouldn't have."

She scoffed. "Don't get too excited. I can show you my inbox and all the dating offers I receive. If it's too much for you to handle, I'd back out of the contest now. All right, I have to go. Don't forget about my shoes you ruined." She gulped her last mouthful and hurried back to the meeting room.

Apparently, not much had happened and Brad had launched into another spiel about how to correctly cover high school sports. Two seconds later her phone vibrated. Hiding the phone under the table, she swiped.

Cooper: I bought you new ones
Sandra: No thanks. I don't trust your taste in heels
Cooper: I found the blue suede Guess pumps, 4" online. They are
    coming in a week

Sandra's thumbs froze above the cell phone. He had replaced her $200 heels and they were being delivered to his house? The man had an ulterior motive. This was a trick or another prank.

Sandra: Accepted. But what about my new nails. I broke 2
Cooper: send me the bills

Another message popped into view.

Cooper: how much does nail polish cost?

It was too precious. The man had no clue.

*Sandra: do u think I buy a bottle of polish and invite my girlfriends
over on Friday nights for a pajama party?*

She breathed deeply. That should make him understand.

Cooper: Sweet Jesus

Pause.

Cooper: would you invite me the next time if you do?

Indeed. She cleared her throat and tried not to laugh at the
image of Cooper in pink pajamas getting his nails done.

Cooper: how much are you asking?

Brad must have posed a general question she hadn't heard.
Nonchalant, she frowned as if in deep thought.
Sandra's phone buzzed as Phoebe snapped an answer.

Cooper: how much?

Actually, she hadn't intended to make him pay for her trip to the
nail salon—she needed to go anyway. But if he insisted....

Sandra: $50
*Cooper: I'll pay it. What time does the party start? Should I bring
drinks? I have vodka and crème de menthe*
Sandra: $50 for the nail salon. There is no party.
Cooper: you're killing me
*Sandra: I know. There is a party, but you can't come. The lingerie
will be too sexy*
Cooper: you're killing me

She smothered a smile by clearing her throat. This was great.

Sandra: and we touch each other's feet all evening

Long pause.

Sandra: until we get the whipped cream out
Cooper: please invite me
Sandra: It could kill you and I don't want that on my conscience.

No reply. She could just picture him—he must be in agony. The Cooper she knew was a serial dater, refusing to commit or be tied down.

Although, she didn't know that for sure. Maybe he liked to be tied down in a literal sense. Could she prank him with that somehow? And not want to take advantage of him? Heat rushed to her head and a tingling set up in her stomach.

That was enough unhealthy interaction with Cooper for one day.

It was also, thankfully, the end of the meeting. The time was eleven o'clock. She gathered her notebook and pen, and returned slowly to her desk. One hour to kill until the voting began. Two hours until Cooper's interview and the afternoon in the park segment would roll, along with the information on the contest. Her heart lurched and then began racing. She knew her whole family would be glued to their screens in order to vote the second the site opened.

By one-thirty she held her head in dismay, watching Cooper's score rise, leaving everyone else's, including hers, behind.

CHAPTER 10

He was winning. Sandra hit refresh—it was her hourly allowance of checking the voting results. After Monday, when Cooper's numbers soared, she had implemented damage control measures, and without bragging about her own prowess in promoting the many other candidates, her interviews had boosted the scores of most of the candidates by Thursday afternoon.

Her own numbers were abysmal. Well, she was third place. She might as well have been out of the running. What she couldn't figure out was why Cooper was so popular. He hung out at a smelly bar. His start-up business was flashy with its technological aspects, but small and only employed himself and his partner. His high school days were long gone, along with many of their old friends. This town was full of his fans—it was the only explanation.

There was tough competition in the contest list. She hadn't realized so many talented, respected people were living in Sycamore Cove and would give it a try. Although, beside herself and Cooper, the heavyweight contenders so far were: Mackenzie Stow, a single mother who ran an organic coffee stand on the promenade; Jason Walker, a fireman who looked particularly good in wet t-shirt pictures for fundraisers; Margaret Torres, a local wiccan and small shop owner who sold love potions among other oddities; Timothy Freeman, the beloved high school science teacher with a couple hundred teen supporters; and Ms. Medina, the feisty librarian. And by feisty, Sandra meant seventy-year-old book advocate fireball, who could and would teach anyone and their dog how to read.

It had taken most of the week, but she had met up with all the candidates for interviews. Ethan Carter was last on Sandra's list for an interview, although he was the businessman overseeing the competition, and not a competitor. He agreed to say a few words tomorrow on Friday afternoon, and she suspected he would mention being pleased with the start of the project.

Third place. The numbers hung heavy around her shoulders every time she refreshed her screen.

Across the open office space, several colleagues, including Brad, gathered at the snack table, laughing raucously. Her nerves along her spine crawled at the noise. Why wasn't there a fire or something she could go cover? Anything would be better than sitting doing nothing. She had a few things to write, but she couldn't concentrate on little stuff.

Then again, if nothing was happening, no one would miss her if she left half an hour early for a change. She scooped up her purse and suit jacket in one move.

Brad stopped laughing and closed his mouth as she sashayed by him and to the hallway. She could sense his eyes following her, but she resisted turning around to see if she was right. Of course, he would wonder where she was going and why she thought she could leave before five.

Because she had worked all weekend and she couldn't take the office environment a second longer. Fresh air and a view, it would be worth whatever Brad made her pay later. Plus, a bottle of wine was calling her name in her kitchen. A quiet evening of wine, sofa, and crocheting would be a balm to her soul.

And of course, her phone rang the second she was crawling into her closet to find her comfiest sweatpants. She debated briefly running to the kitchen and opening the wine before checking to see who it was. The tinkling chime pulled her eyes to the screen though.

Cooper.

Calling her?

Now she really wanted the wine. Biting her lower lip, she swiped. "Yes?"

"If you don't want to fall to fourth, I suggest you put on something hot and get over to Murphey's by eight."

"And hello to you, too. As if I'm dumb enough to believe that getting sexy and visiting that dive on a Thursday will make a difference in my votes." She had to roll her eyes, a move she reserved for idiotic things Cooper said.

"Under normal circumstances, I would agree. But do you know who has teamed up for tonight's karaoke battle?"

"Why don't you tell me?"

"Well it's not me and not you, but your place at third in the contest is in serious danger. Any ideas now?"

She puffed out her breath and sat back against her bedframe. It wouldn't be Ms. Medina—she went to bed by seven-thirty after an hour of yoga and meditation according to her interview—or the science teacher, since he had a newborn at the house.

No. The fireman and the coffee lady, an explosive pair if there ever was one. But how would team karaoke help them?

The same way that swinging four stories from the ground had helped Cooper.

"Jason and Mackenzie. Well, I wish them the best of luck," she said, picturing herself in the kitchen pouring the wine already.

"You could come and cover the show, don't you think? As part of your interviews?" he said. "I'm not telling you how to do your job or anything, far from it, but this place is hopping on karaoke nights. Only once a month, you know what I'm saying?"

"Eight tonight?" she asked. "Where's the trick?"

"No trick. They are on the roster. You can come and see for yourself."

He was hedging—there had to be a trick, and she had to be ready for it. But he was right. If Jason and Mackenzie were getting on stage, she had to at least put in an appearance.

"I'll see you there." She hung up.

Seconds later, Sandra was hip deep in her closet, desperate to find the perfect outfit for that evening at Murphey's. It had to say, 'gorgeous babe,' 'too good for you,' and 'I just threw this semi-professional, old thing on because I can get away with it' all at the same time.

Her phone rang at the same instant she put her hands on a classy jean-jacket from her college days.

It was her oldest sister. As the youngest of four girls, Sandra was kept busy babysitting nieces and nephews, giving accessory advice, and arranging times to meet up in town.

"'Sup?" she asked in a long, excited drawl.

"Hey, girl!" Noëlle said. "I just wanted to check in. You good tonight? Otherwise you can come with us to dinner. It's your favorite. You don't want to miss out."

"Are you going by Captain Jack's Shack?"

"You got that right."

"Oh," Sandra moaned into the phone. "So tempting. But I have to meet someone at Murphey's and then cover the evening for this contest."

"Is it me or are you going crazy for this contest?" Noëlle asked, sounding as though she already knew the answer. "All right. I'll tell the kids you're very busy. They'll be disappointed."

"Tell them I've got big, sloppy, wet kisses for their cheeks and I finished making their dinosaurs. I put them in the car, but at the latest, I'll pass by to give them to them this weekend and go to the park if they want."

"I'll tell them just as soon as Kaley stops pretending to be a Velociraptor chewing Noah's head off. By the way, voting's going well, don't you think? Third place behind a fireman and your old friend Cooper. It's kinda peculiar the way you and he are competing. Like old times, in high school..." Her voice trailed off, probably hoping for some juicy tidbits to share with the rest of the family.

Sandra wasn't fanning the flames of gossip, though. She *mm-hmmed*.

"Well," her sister continued after a baited pause, "I hope you have fun tonight."

"Yeah, you, too!" Sandra forced herself to sound cheerful. She hung up and threw the jacket on the bed. The outfit called for huge sunglasses, but it would be late evening by the time she left. A fitted top and butt-hugging skirt would have to do.

Third place in the contest. She would see about that.

Murphey's in the evening was the same cruddy dive she remembered from coming once last Christmas with Cooper for lunch, but times ten. The smell of food and alcohol mixed with too many bodies, and not all of them washed, was as thick as smog. The country music was too loud and people shouted over it, creating a cacophony of noise.

And it was only eight. What must this place be like at midnight? She shuddered to imagine, wishing she was at the Mermaid Dance Club. Which wasn't the smartest name for a dance club, now that she thought of it. Cute but paradoxical at the same time.

Cooper had a two-person table with barstools in the corner. He lifted his beer in greeting.

She squared her shoulders and marched in, ignoring the crunch of chips or pretzels beneath her feet.

"So," she said.

"So." He motioned for her to sit, friendly as could be.

She pursed her lips. There had to be something wrong with the chair. "Where is the karaoke stage? Are Mackenzie and Jason already here? Have you been sitting here since you called me at five?"

"Would you like a drink to go with your interrogation?"

"Not yet," she said. "I'm good. Point me in the right direction, Mr. Hall, so I can get set up."

"Through the arched doors, same as the toilets. But if you reach the toilet, you've gone too far and need to make a one-eighty."

She narrowed her eyes and walked toward the arch, wondering where the trick was lurking. The next room over was large with a small crowd forming. Mackenzie was there, sipping a cocktail, and Sandra waved. At the same time, a tall guy in faded jeans and a black tee clapped another man on the shoulder and turned her direction. Jason. Sandra smiled and nodded in greeting. So Cooper hadn't been lying, after all.

The stage stood at the far end of the room and on a table next to it was the song selection book and a fish bowl.

And Cooper thought there wouldn't be any pranks tonight.

First, however, she would make the rounds and tell everyone she was covering the fun to post on the behind-the-scenes of the news channel. Then it would be her pleasure to take care of Cooper.

A couple of minutes later, she perused the laminated, but sticky, instructions to participate in the karaoke.

One name and one song per ticket

Drawings start at eight-thirty pm

The jar only held a couple of paper tickets, and several of those would be the dynamite pair she was filming. That didn't seem right. What fun would tonight's karaoke be?

No fun at all, and it was her duty as a good citizen to rectify the situation.

Cooper Hall

She filled in his name hastily on several tickets.

Would twenty tickets be too many? Nah.

Songs. What songs would he love to sing for everyone?

Opening the book, she began flipping pages and choosing.

"Baby One More Time." Yes. "Barbie Girl." Yes. "I Touch Myself," Oh yeah. "Like a Virgin"? Sure. "My Hump." Absolutely. "All About that Bass." Yes, yes, yes. "Ice-Ice, Baby." For the groans, yes. "Just a Girl." Why not? "Sexy and I Know It." Isn't that his theme song?

She scrawled in the titles as quickly as possible and dumped the tickets in the jar. Wait, one more, for good measure. He would thank her later for all the exposure, no doubt. She stepped back to admire the bowl, much fuller now.

"Gotcha," Cooper's low voice filled her ear. "You couldn't resist it, could you?"

Sandra jumped, bumping her butt into the table edge, and a guilty wave rushed to her face. Getting caught preparing a prank was worse than fumbling one.

CHAPTER 11

"I was just…" Sandra waved her hand at the name bowl and mumbled something Cooper didn't catch.

"Hoping to sing a song or two? I know the feeling. And you see I wasn't lying to you about the karaoke. In fact, I'm glad you decided to come and stay a while," he said. Because how else would he pull off his next prank if she was lounging on her sofa at home all evening?

Not that he knew what she did at home, but he might, on the odd occasion, imagine her gracing her living room sofa like one of Leonardo DiCaprio's French girls.

A guy could dream, *n'est-ce pas?*

He snapped back to reality when she laughed.

"Me sing a song! You know me. I'm all for fun and games, but it's probably best if I don't. I came tonight on business. I need a beer." Wiping her hands on her skirt, she spun abruptly and hailed a server.

If he didn't know better, he would have assumed she was nervous. But Sandra? No way. Which meant she wouldn't mind the first surprise. Mackenzie and Jason thought they had a fun, thank you prank worked out for Sandra—they would call her onto the stage and then have her sing. But the real prank would be waiting for her in her living room that evening when she went home. Cooper hoped she liked her home decorated in pink. And that she always dreamed of a huge picture of himself.

A moment later, she appeared at his elbow, pad of paper in hand. "When does it start? Explain how this works again. One of the servers pulls a ticket from the bowl, or what?"

"Interrogation part two, commencing. Let me tell you everything before you get the nasty idea of torturing me with pliers or hot wax. First, the very lovely April will take the sta—" Sandra was jostled hard from behind as a drunk guy stumbled past. She would have fallen, but Cooper caught her and pushed the man upright and away from her at the same time. "Hey, watch it!"

The guy blinked, bleary eyed. "Yeah, sorry about the...so where's the toilet, I gotta take a...sorry ma'am. Where's the toilet?"

Cooper pointed in the right direction. "And when you're done, you might want to go home."

"Yeah, thanks, man."

Sandra gazed deep in his eyes as if she wanted something. She cleared her throat. "You can let me go now."

He was still holding her against his chest. Her notebook poked him uncomfortably, but her slim waist cradled in his arm was creating all sorts of problems in his jeans. "Sorry about that. Where was I? It's starting already."

"I wanted to get this from the back. Come with me." Sandra took his hand and led him past several tables to the back wall. She set up her camera in a tripod and focused. "You were saying."

"Too late."

"Why?"

"Ladies and gentlemen," April called from the stage. "It's going to be a very special evening tonight. We have a few local celebrities, if you don't mind me saying so. I want you to get ready to put your hands together!"

"This is a prank. A cheap prank to make me sing karaoke," Sandra hissed under her breath.

"Actually, I'm not pranking you."

"Mackenzie Stow, you goddess of the organic coffee, and Jason Walker, one of our favorite firemen and protectors of our town, come on up!" April waved for Mackenzie and Jason to join her, and the crowd cheered. Especially the corner with half the fire department.

"Good," Sandra whispered. "I'd hate to have to get even with you in a bar."

"I'm not pranking you here, I swear it." Cooper tilted his head until he touched her crisp curls. "They are."

"Hey, everybody," Mackenzie said, shielding her eyes from the spot lights. She shifted nervously. "To get this battle going, we wanted to invite another guest up. Someone who gives this town and us so much, and someone who recently reached out to all the candidates for the Townsperson of the Year Contest—go and vote, please, on their website. You'll see my name—and this special person wanted to give her competition the chance to say a few things about themselves and why they hope to win. However, Jason and I realized that she didn't get this same chance. So, please, put your hands together again, for the amazing Sandra Kelly from WCC 12. Come on up with us!"

"No, no, no. I don't think so." Sandra's lips pursed, and she shook her head.

"They won't make you sing, but they do want to say thank you." Cooper touched her lower back to urge her forward.

Mackenzie must have spotted her from the stage and gestured excitedly, her bleach blond braid bouncing. Sandra sighed in defeat and hustled to the stage.

She smiled and waved and whispered a thank you into the mic. "It was my pleasure to introduce the candidates for the contest to the people of this town. As Mackenzie mentioned, go and vote, please. Thank you." She would have exited just as quickly as she hopped up there, but Jason blocked the way. April took the mic to give a run down on the karaoke battle rules.

A man standing at the next bar table motioned to Cooper. "What is this Townsperson contest about?"

"Townsperson of the Year. This is the first edition, and the four of us are candidates."

"You, too? Really? And you're all giving the competition a big thank you on stage?"

Cooper tipped his beer. "Pretty much. I hate to brag, but it was mostly my idea to get Sandra here tonight."

"To make her look bad or good? I'm confused."

"Good. She's a dynamite reporter, and spent all week putting everyone else in the spotlight."

"But she's your competition. Don't you want to win?"

"Yes and no. To both comments." Cooper raked his hair from his eyes, thinking of how to answer the question. All he came up with was how would his asshole partner answer, because Cooper should say the opposite. "It's like in my business. I don't want to beat the competition by kicking them down. I'd rather win because even when they shine their brightest, I'm still better."

"Interesting. And what do you do?"

Cooper's attention was dragged back to the stage. They were trying to talk Sandra into opening the evening's battle with a solo of her own. She wasn't going for it. "Here's my card. Remember, have everyone you know in town vote. Can you watch the camera for a second?"

He took off without waiting for a reply and jumped on the stage in front of Sandra.

Hands on her hips, she glared. "You said this wasn't a prank."

"Please. This doesn't come close to the level of excellence to which I aspire in prankdom."

"But?"

"But you should do this. Because that crowd will tweet and post and praise you for it. Publicity, Sandra. Say it with me. Chant it."

"Hey," April shouted. "What's it gonna be, hun?"

Cooper glanced over his shoulder to answer her. "She'll do "I Will Always Love You," and she plans on throwing the name Cooper in the refrain." He winked at the waitress.

"I'm shocked by the number of delusions that run around unfettered in your head," Sandra muttered, grabbing a mic.

"I know you can kick this song's ass. You've got the notes, the lip shaking trick. I've been watching you for years. Scratch that. I haven't been watching you like some kind of stalker for years, but I know you. Have fun."

"Fun. At Murphey's. Singing to a room full of drunk people. Got it."

❧

What the hell was she thinking? Letting him, of all people, talk her into this shit show? She couldn't remember how the first part of the song went. The catchy, crooning refrain, sure, but the beginning?

Fake it till you make it. Or die on stage right now.

The music cued and the crowd went quiet. Her brain was coming up with a big, flat blank on the tune, and the opening instrumental didn't help in the least. Words rolled onto the screen, but no clues for the melody.

Seriously. I have no idea how this part goes.

Her pulse was already too high and breathing shallow. She'd never hit the big notes like this. She opened her mouth and whispered in approximation adding as much vibrato and air as possible. There were a couple of derogatory hoots and boos from the shadows.

Cooper tilted his beer glass at her. The first high notes approached. Several cell phones were trained on her and her stomach dropped. The performance was probably being streamed.

The main theme hit and she took a deep breath. Then she belted heart and soul her undying love. She had it where it counted. And yes, she added her Whitney-like trembling lips to go with the voice.

The crowd cheered as she reached the end. With a breathy flourish, she changed the last lyrics, adding enough grace notes for it to be hard to understand.

"I will always prank you, Cooper."

He would understand.

Done! She did it and Murphey's approved. She took a quick bow and jumped from the stage. Cooper, standing over her camera in the back, gave her a thumb's up. Mackenzie tackled her from the side before she could get any further, hugging her and bouncing up and down at the same time.

"That was unbelievable. I had no idea you were talented," she gushed.

"Thanks. I think. Looks like you and Jason are up, I'll be in the back."

She began wending her way between the tables. Cooper had disappeared, probably skipping off to the bar in between acts. Reaching her camera, she took a deep breath. Her hands were shaking.

A loud commotion broke out as the entire group of firemen, as well as Jason, stood up, threw some bills on the table and bolted. The room was stunned to near silence. Sandra frowned at Mackenzie. That wasn't a good sign at all.

The older gentleman at the next table said congratulations and started to ask a question. Sandra's phone rang at the same time, however, and Brad's name appeared on the screen. Maybe he knew what was going on. "I'm sorry I have to take this," she said to the man talking to her. Then she swiped.

"Yes?"

"Sandra, we need you to come in. There's an apartment building on fire out on 60th by the gas station. It could get ugly."

Adrenaline shot through her system. Ugly could mean

heartbreaking and she didn't want that, but she had to go and be the voice for the victims. Her chest ached for them already.

"I'll be there in ten."

She was loading her camera into the trunk when Cooper shouted her name across the parking lot.

"Wait up. Where are you going so soon? You're not going home, are you?"

"No, not home," she said and slammed the trunk. Sweet angels above. Hadn't she hoped for a fire or some emergency to cover earlier in the afternoon so she could forget her misery at only being third in the Townsperson contest? What kind of pathetic person wishes tragedy on others to make themselves feel better? "There's a fire. Work called, and I have to go cover it."

"I was afraid you were tired and ready to hit the hay already." He clapped his hands once, as if in relief. The next second, though, his eyes narrowed in worry. "You seem upset. Are you all right? Do you need me to drive you?"

"I haven't needed you to drive me to work for the past three years. I can handle it."

"I am offering, that's all." He put his hand on her car top, close but not too close. A friendly sort of close. She died a little inside. Once again it hit her—the sheer weight of their shared history through high school, how much their lives were twisted and tied up together, pranking and competing, laughing and joking. But most of all, just how impossible it was to be with him without wanting to both smack him and wrap her legs around his waist.

He tapped her car lightly. "I'm offering because obviously spending the evening in my presence has left you—"

Whatever infuriating thing he was going to say, she didn't want to hear it. Closing the distance in one step, she crashed into him. She stole the words from his lips and silenced his voice, except for a low rumble coming from his chest, more animal than human, more raw and needy than she'd ever expected. The roughness of his beard faded with the softness of his lips and the play of his tongue against hers. She had opened her mouth to his, without a thought, without regret.

His arms wrapped around her waist, lifting her higher and the teasing of a surprise attack changed to something more urgent and demanding. She bent back and he supported her, her head brushed the car, but the rest of her was suspended, trapped in his hold.

From toes to scalp, she tingled and wondered, distantly, what she was doing. One knee lifted to rub up the side of his jeans until it reached his thigh. He groaned in her mouth, urgently searching for something hidden inside of her.

She fisted his hair with her free hand. Damn, she loved the feel of his hair. And those lips, along with his beard. Scratchy, soft. Salty, sweet. More, more, more—she ached for more.

They kissed. She kissed him and damn, did he kiss back.

When a flash of heat hit her panties, she had a wild image in her mind of dragging him into her car and driving back to her place. And getting tangled up with him on her bed.

She couldn't do it, though. She shouldn't. But most importantly, she wouldn't. For one thing, work was waiting for her. She broke free of the kiss and cleared her throat. "What is it about Murphey's that makes me want to do the wrong things with you? I'm sorry. I have to go and we have a contest to concentrate on."

For another thing, life always went wrong when she and Cooper got too close.

He stepped back, dropping his hands and pressing his lips together. "Two contests actually. I intend to win them both."

CHAPTER 12

The scene of the fire was madness. Sandra parked her car well out of the way and rushed past the gas station and a row of houses, searching for the news van. Firefighting crews, trucks, and first responders had established a perimeter, but half-dressed people huddled in groups, stood alone, or hugged their children on the sidewalks nearby, staring with uncomprehending, zombie eyes. Most of the windows along the top of the four-story apartment building were broken open, and red flames and black clouds of smoke poured out of them. The whole thing glowed devilishly against the night sky. Sandra swallowed.

It was ugly.

Please don't let anyone be hurt.

"Sandra!" John hustled across the street, carrying a load of equipment. "Glad you made it. Brad is in the van with Phoebe. I'm supposed to get set up as close to the building as possible. Are you ready?"

She nodded and buttoned her jean-jacket nearly to the top. Her butt-hugging skirt was less than ideal for the situation, but it couldn't be helped. The attention would be on the fire, not her ass, anyway.

Brad showed up as she clipped her IFB in place. "What are you wearing?"

"A skirt and jacket. Where do you want us to do the shoot?"

"Jesus, Sandra. Stand over there. I'll have Phoebe go first for the building shots and then you can do interviews. Try to look as professional as you can. John!" Brad snapped for John, and he and Phoebe moved into position. The next instant, she was describing the scene in detail for the viewers at home, although, in Sandra's opinion, not much was needed. The fire spoke for itself.

The noise of breaking glass and popping came inside the building, making her flinch at each new crack. Several firefighters aimed additional hoses at the top of the building, and several others prepared to go inside, which reminded Sandra she had her own camera.

In a flash, she ran back to her car, pulled her camera bag from the trunk and returned, just in time to film Jason, of all firefighters, carrying out a tank. A little girl shouted.

He had saved her turtle. Sandra caught it all, her heart bursting.

Behind her though, another toddler was crying. She turned to ask what was wrong, but the baby mumbled something she couldn't understand.

"He wants his snuggly. We ran out without it when the alarms went off. He was asking why the fireman couldn't save the snuggly if he saved the turtle."

"Oh, sweetheart," Sandra said. "The firemen have to get all the living pets out and then they can put out the fire."

The little boy started crying harder.

Way to go, Sandra. She glanced up at the mom. "Where is your apartment, if it's far from the main fire, there might still be hope for the snuggly."

"See that window there, with the ten-foot flames shooting out of it?" the dad said, pointing. "Yeah. That's ours."

The mom shook her head, tears running down her face. "We've lost everything. Everything."

Tears threatened behind Sandra's eyes. Blinking them back, she rubbed the toddler's back. "I might have a new snuggly who needs a good home. Would you like to meet him?"

He nodded, sniffling. Sandra dragged her camera bag closer and found the hand-crocheted Triceratops she had made for her nephew. He would understand. She held it up for the little boy who threw his arms around the soft, green dinosaur. He buried his face in its side, wiping his tears away.

And now Sandra had to wipe her own tears. There was another boy in the family, several years older. Sandra pulled out the crocheted Stegosaurus complete with a double row of spikes in green and brown for him. A crooked-tooth smile lit his whole face. She put her hand on the mom's shoulder. "You aren't alone. Not in this town. We'll make sure everyone knows where to send help and donations."

As Sandra gave the woman a hug, John smiled firmly at her from behind his camera. He gave her a thumb's up. Her home had never gone up in flames, but she knew what it felt like to be a kid with nothing. These families weren't alone. Not on Sandra's watch.

❧

By the time Sandra arrived home, her feet throbbed from standing and pinpricks of pain tingled up her legs with every step. Everything else ached. Her knees, her lower back, her shoulders, her head, her heart. She coughed, the thin remnants of black smoke pouring from windows into the air becoming dislodged from her lungs.

It took her a while to get the key in the door properly and to creep inside. She leaned against the door as soon as she shut it, closing her eyes in the darkness.

But that was worse. Then she saw the tear streaked faces of an elderly couple who lost all their worldly possessions. Others who sat on the sidewalk past midnight, first responder blankets draped over their shoulders. The scorched, empty windows and doors to the apartment building.

But thank God no one was seriously injured. They even got all the pets out, thanks to men and women like Jason, who had bolted from the karaoke and arrived well before she did.

She stumbled forward, not bothering with the lights. Her foot kicked something heavy and it flew forward, knocking into something else that was maybe made of plastic. She yelped and jumped back, searching for the switch. Then something else toppled over with a hollow thud. And another in a chain reaction. The lights flipped on.

She screamed at the man standing in her living room. There was a psycho pervert standing in her living room. He was in her house. Right next to the sofa!

Still yelling, she scrambled for the pepper spray in her purse.

The man in her living room was holding a bouquet of flowers.

Wait. Hand on her heaving chest, she paused. Cooper, that cretin.

A cardboard cut-out of a life-sized Cooper leaned precariously on her floor, surrounded by an ocean of bright pink, plastic flamingos. The big, lawn decorating sort of flamingos. He had lured her away from home with promises of a party and publicity and even ran out in the parking lot to make sure she wasn't going home too soon. Well, she hadn't gone home after leaving the bar.

It was two a.m. and she was exhausted and heartbroken from interviewing victims of an apartment fire, and it really wasn't a good time for her to find fifty fucking plastic flamingos and a cardboard cutout of Cooper in her house.

Drawing her phone from her purse faster than a Western cowboy facing a wanted outlaw at high noon, she called Cooper's number. His picture smiled back at her from the living room. That creep.

Normally, burning this thing would be oh, so satisfying, but she really wasn't in the mood for any more flames that evening. She would save it for a special occasion, instead, wouldn't she?

After six rings, Cooper's sleepy voice came on the phone. "Heyo?"

"Cooper Hall, you are the biggest fuck in Sycamore Cove and believe me when I say you are gonna pay for this. I have spent the last four hours consoling families whose apartment building was gutted by the worst fire this town has seen since Schmidt's Baked Goods went up in flames in 1912. Tonight was really not the night. Goodbye."

She hung up to the sound of him apologizing. Almost instantly he called her back. She turned off her phone, took off her shoes, and tiptoed through the flock of flamingos to her room. There were another ten on and around her bed. Muttering under her breath, she cleared her bed and crawled under the covers. Had she really kissed him in the parking lot? Why would she do that to herself?

He would pay.

She had held onto his house key from Lauren for over a week, scheming and plotting for the perfect prank and a good moment to strike. But you made your moments, as Cooper had shown her, by ensuring she would be out of the house tonight for the massive delivery. Where did he get her key? Didn't matter.

He would pay, and she had just the diabolical prank to pull.

Sandra had permission to go in late to work the next day, which was convenient, since she had reconnaissance work to do. Despite knowing Cooper like a circling hawk knows all the habits of a field mouse, she didn't know what kind of coffee he drank, or if it was ground or in little aluminum cups or what. So she had to make a side trip while he was at work, on her way to the station.

The things she learned during her side trip—the lack of decorating skills, the sort of coffee and machine, the bare cupboards, the collection of chipped mugs, the hand-crocheted throw, and that it was true what Cooper said about his wine cellar.

Well, it was a normal basement, but the wine...the wine was impressive.

She spent so much time combing through Cooper's house that when John called asking if she wanted to meet for lunch, she went straight to the café. And what a relief it was to be in a self-respecting restaurant after that dive Murphey's from last night. The floors were clean, the tables weren't sticky, and no matter how she sniffed, testing the air, there were no insidious undercurrents of old socks or dried beer.

The waitress waved her to a table at the window with bar stools, and Sandra took a seat to wait. She was double checking her Townsperson score, which had leapt to second place during the night, when the door jingled and John walked in, laughing.

Cooper strode in after him. That sneaky, underhanded, low-down, broad-shouldered, gorgeous mess of a Norse god who sent panicky flutters to her stomach with his grin and who was now ducking his head in shame at the sight of her. Once again, he was setting fire to her panties and fraying her nerves ragged without saying a single word.

"Hey, Sandra," John said, pulling out a chair. "Look who I ran into on the way. I hope you don't mind. I invited him to join us for lunch. Since you guys are friends."

"How could you, John?" she asked.

"Eh, think nothing of it?" he mumbled in confusion.

"May I sit down?" Cooper asked. "I wanted to apologize, sincerely apologize for the poor timing of last night's incident."

He turned his warm brown eyes to hers, a wavy lock of hair hanging across his forehead. Nervous, he ran his fingers through it, but it fell again. And she wanted to grab his hair in her hands and hold it from his face while she kissed him again like last night, but then the memory of stubbing her toe on a flamingo crowded out the very wrong desire.

She motioned to the seat in front of him. "Don't worry. You'll make it up to me, sooner or later, in an unpleasant manner."

"Great. I'm looking forward to that." He raked his fingers through his hair again, even more nervous than before sitting down.

The waitress came by, smiling and greeting everyone.

Sandra dropped the menu. "What kind of drink can you recommend that won't make me sleepy or impair my ability to work this afternoon, but will take the edge off of life?"

"I know how you feel, hon. Let me suggest a Dark Moon—coffee, coke, and rum. It should kill any discomfort but also make you want to run in circles for three hours."

"Dark Moon, it is. And the tacos lunch special, thanks."

"Tacos," John echoed, "and a diet tea."

"I'll start with some fried pickles and then dive into the tacos, too," Cooper said.

"We don't have fried pickles, sorry sweetie."

"What kind of monsters are you?"

Sandra shook her head in exasperation. "Ignore him. We'll have some chips and guacamole."

The waitress tapped her pad and collected the menus.

"Will you excuse me a minute, guys?" John, still flustered, left for the restroom.

Cooper narrowed his eyes at Sandra. "Sorry again about the prank's timing. If you want to call this all off..."

"Not a chance. I can't help it if you're scared of paybacks, but my Townsperson ranking is moving up, despite the prank war. I will win. And you will lose. When that happens—donkey balls, there's my boss. As if it wasn't bad enough I have to see him at the station."

He turned in his seat to look out the window. "That guy is your boss? Wait a minute. I just figured it out. That's the guy who dumped you last winter, isn't it? You said you worked with him, right? What was his name? Brian, Brad?"

Groaning, Sandra dropped her head in her hands. Where was her drink? Sandra had been a wreck after the break up and by the time she bumped into Cooper, she hadn't wasted a minute trying to get him into her bed. "His name is Brad, and I have so many regrets right now."

"You know I can help you with your problems. A hot bath, a little wine, foot massage… Whenever you want it."

Suddenly, the most tempting thing in the restaurant was by far and away the man sitting across the table from her.

CHAPTER 13

The door jingled as Brad came in and spotted her. He had on a smart suit and his usual slick attitude that set Sandra's teeth aching. Of course, he sauntered right up to their table as the waitress brought them their drinks and the chips and guac. And of course, he helped himself.

"Sandra, I want to talk to you about last night. The clothes, the tears. Handing out random toys? Seriously. We need to review your performance."

"It's noted. See you later?"

Not taking her hint, he seemed to notice Cooper's for the first time. "Hey, wait. You're Cooper Hall, right?"

"Yes, I am." Cooper stuck out his hand. "And a big fan of San—"

"We just loved the way you handled that unusual situation at the light house last week." Brad shook his hand and clapped his shoulder, smacking it. "The short videos we posted on our Facebook page are extremely popular. Love that. Very impressive and the viewers are clamoring for more."

"I don't think there will be any—"

"Right," Brad said, cutting him off again. "Good luck for the Townsperson of the Year contest, and everything. Isn't it great how we sent Sandra out for the interviews? Nice outfit you had on for that, I might add. Anyway, we're very excited about the contest's outcome. May the best man win, I always say!"

Sandra had gulped half of her Dark Moon by that point and was seriously considering splashing the rest in his face.

He started rambling on about the station's ratings, a chip filled with guacamole in his hand, forgotten. Watching him carefully, she twisted the top off the tabasco and doused the chip liberally.

"We've seen our viewers getting more and more engaged on several social media platforms, which we are exploiting, naturally." Brad paused to eat his chip, blanched, but chewed as tears filled his eyes and sweat broke out on his forehead. "Would you please excuse me?" He bolted from the table.

"Well done," Cooper said.

"It was well deserved. Besides criticizing me for doing my job well, last December he forgot we were dating and started sleeping with someone else." Sandra propped her elbows on the table and whispered, "And that was nothing compared with what I have in mind for you."

He mirrored her position, their faces only a few inches apart.

She could smell the fresh scent of his cologne and see the streaks of gold in his deep brown eyes. What did she want more? Revenge for the scare and mess from last night, or that foot massage?

"Can I say I'm sorry again about filling your house with flamingos the same evening you had to cover a bad fire?"

"You can say it. I like the way it sounds."

"I'm serious, Sandra. I'm sorry." One finger came up to trace down her cheek and the contour of her lips, setting off fireworks in her nerve endings. "You've got a bit of coffee right there," he said. She doubted she had anything on her face, but then he rubbed the corner of her mouth with his thumb and she was lost in the heavenly sensation of his touch. He traced the curve of her top lip, barely touching her. "There. All better."

Both Brad and John reappeared from the bathroom, chatting,

but Brad headed for the take-out counter. He spoke with the waitress, who poured him a large glass of iced tea. Sandra was overheating, too, but for a much different reason. She grabbed her drink like it was a fire extinguisher and drank as fast as she could to cool off.

Cooper's fingers were the stuff of legends, and only his thumb had touched her. Thank goodness her clothes weren't flammable.

"Have you seen the voting results so far?" he asked.

She shook her head.

He tapped his phone screen a couple of times and then put it on the table for her to see.

Saints above and glory be—first place. First place.

That's right, baby.

"Between singing at the bar, rushing off, and talking to the victims from the fire, I'd say you did well last night. You won't need any more of my help, anyway," Cooper said.

Sandra relaxed back in her chair and crossed her arms. "Your help? Is that what all your sweet-talking apologies were about? You wanted to butter me up and get me to drop the pranks now that I'm in the lead?"

Brad breezed by with his take-away bag. "Sandra, my office when you get in. Oh, and Mr. Hall, feel free to drop by for a tour one of these days."

Cooper cleared his throat. "What exactly was the appeal of that asshat? You're over him, right?"

"Without a doubt."

John slid his chair out with a screech and dropped into it. "Hey, guys. Sorry about leaving for so long. I've got some sort of gastro thing going on."

Sandra tuned him out as he chatted on and on about sports, weather, his various ailments, and his favorite comic characters.

The waitress stopped to ask if everything was all right and if they were saving room for dessert. Only Cooper accepted. He was a bottomless pit, apparently, and Sandra couldn't fathom where he put the extra calories on his sculpted, muscular frame. Too bad all those lean lines were wasted on his personality.

She heaved a sigh of regret. The things she could have done to him if he wasn't such a pest.

There was a basketball game on the flat screen hanging not far from them and John was sucked into the action. Some big final game on replay. Dessert arrived, and Cooper dug into a gooey, chocolate and cream cake. He turned sideways to watch the TV.

His phone was on the edge of the table. All alone. Vulnerable. Just waiting to be taken. Prank revenge or a long soak in a hot bath? Somedays, she wanted both with Cooper.

She shouldn't take the phone.

He would turn and catch her.

But it would only be for a second.

She threw her napkin on the table, near Cooper's phone. Neither of the men noticed. Heart beating faster she put her elbows casually on the table and then stretched out her forearms flat. Cooper continued eating and watching while John groaned loudly at the screen.

Her hand covered his phone.

It would be so easy. She wrapped her fingers around it, careful not to make any noise and slipped it off the edge.

Taking it into her lap, she checked for a security code. Nothing. She was in.

"Whoa!" Cooper yelled.

She jumped, ready to apologize.

Cooper was pointing his fork at the screen. "Did you see that?"

She nodded, enthusiastically. He hadn't noticed his phone was missing.

She did a quick search using her own phone.

This one's a beauty.

She flipped through his contacts, holding her breath and pretending to watch the game, when she was actually watching Cooper from the corner of her eye.

Almost done. Her thumb flew over his screen, heart racing and prickles of sweat tickling her arms and neck.

Done.

He finished the last bite of his cake. The game was over, too. She reached for her napkin, knocking it off the table on purpose.

Instantly, he bent to grab it from the floor.

She set his phone down.

Cooper smiled, thanking her and John for the company during lunch. As he stood to go, he leaned forward, hand on her shoulder. "About last night. I am sorry for the flamingos, but not for returning your kiss in the parking lot. You know where to find me if you want that foot massage and wine. Lunch is on me. I'd like for it to be on me, *on me*, next time, but for now I'll tell the waitress to give me the check."

And the image of her licking guac off his stomach flashed through her brain. Hands on his bare hips, nails in his buttocks. Rippled abs under her lips. Dazed, she couldn't come up with a snappy reply before he was gone.

The waitress came to collect dishes. Sandra shook herself back into reality. "I'm sorry about him and that 'monsters' comment."

"Oh, don't worry about it, hon. I know Cooper from my shifts over at Murphey's. Such a ham. He always leaves the biggest tips, too. Have a great day, y'all."

Biggest tips? Of course he left big tips.

After leaving the restaurant, Cooper hit the sidewalk and strode through the lanes of the old town, low brick and wooden buildings with cheerful store windows and cafés at every intersection.

Finding John earlier and tagging along with him as he walked to lunch had been a stroke of genius. Sandra had refused his calls since waking him up in the middle of the night to berate him for the prank, and he hated to shrug it off. Sure it was war, but he wasn't a completely insensitive jackass. Close, but not completely.

And so much for picking things up where they left them after that kiss. His cock tightened at the memory of her leg going around his hip. He would have loved to reenact that move today and see how far they could go from there.

Not now, though. Understandably, coming home at two a.m. after covering a bad fire in town, and finding sixty-five plastic flamingos populating your house would put anyone in a bad mood. That prank had not been easy to pull off, either. Talk about effort and work. He was lucky he had a friend with a warehouse full of the things and another friend willing to make a shady delivery. Sandra really needed to find a better hiding place for her spare key.

Ergo, she was pissed. Which meant she would get revenge. He should watch his ass from now on and be more careful not to provoke her. It was worth seeing her today, though. Those wide, luscious lips under his thumb had caused serious problems in his jeans. Just seeing her perched on the stool in her loose, cream blouse, her dark skin glowing in the sun had started a hard on.

He would have to spend some time in the shower tonight, remembering their kiss and the touch of her lips.

That thought was going to destroy his productivity for the rest of the day, but he owed it to himself to go in that afternoon and get some work done. Vic's threat would loom over his head until he won the contest.

They were close to signing a deal with one of the larger real estate groups in Richmond, which would bring some relief to the state of their bank account. If they could get these guys on board to use their portal, it would help attract more customers as an added bonus.

When they were setting up shop in the beginning, Vic had tried to convince him to put the office in Richmond, closer to potential customers, but Cooper argued that it was cheaper and more attractive here.

But that was only half of the reason why he wouldn't leave the town.

His mom and sister were here, plus his crazy Aunt Jo (actually bat-shit, crazy-cat-lady Aunt Jo, but that description was too long), and they needed him. They would never admit it, especially since his mother had remarried years ago and Lauren had Gabe now, but someone had to have their backs just in case.

Hell, his dad was buried here. Most of his family were buried here. He had roots. He had...history here.

No way could he leave.

He'd spent the night with Sandra on his mind—when he should have more worried about his start-up and maintaining first place in the Townsperson's contest. Yesterday, as soon as Mackenzie contacted him with her idea to thank Sandra, Cooper had jumped aboard. It was too tempting to have an excuse to see her, not to mention the possibility of getting under her skin with the flamingos prank.

His evening had been one of missed opportunities, though. Usually, Cooper took advantage of every opportunity that came along, be it blonde, brunette, or redhead. Not last night. After Sandra abruptly left him in the parking lot, he posted the video of her song, added a short bit of himself explaining that karaoke night was canceled due to the fire in town, and went straight home.

For probably the first time since puberty, he wasn't in the mood to get laid. He stayed awake late, watching the ceiling fan spin and wondering if he had a terminal illness.

When she called, his heart had nearly stopped. He had jerked away, afraid she had been hurt or in an accident.

His damn prank.

But he had to win the contest, and this helped his chances, right? What the fuck was he doing with his life if this was all wrong?

CHAPTER 14

Cooper used a simple drip machine to make coffee at his house, which made it all too easy for Sandra to put her fiendish plan into motion. All she had to do was find his brand in decaf at the grocery store.

She picked up the package and took a deep breath. This was wrong. So very, very wrong. Could you harm someone by switching out their coffee with decaf? From what she knew, he had at least three cups first thing in the morning in order to be barely functional. He might fall asleep on his way to work, zone out and land in a ditch or on the sidewalk. He might not even make it to the front door without a major accident.

But it was so deliciously evil, she couldn't resist. Besides, she would get to spend some time in his house, putting sexy lingerie on two of the flamingos and arranging them in his bed. He deserved whatever he got, as far as she was concerned. This was all his idea to begin with. To think she couldn't handle a prank war, the contest, and maintain her cool.

Holding first place and staying strong, that's what she was doing. This was war and she was on a Blitzkrieg.

There was still the problem of getting him out of the house at some point during the weekend, though. The problem was real...and solutions were few.

A call from his landlord in his office building because of liquid coming from under the door? She could put ice cubes down to fake a pipe leak.

Email from the city morgue to come and identify a long lost, rich uncle?

Call and pretend she was an admirer with fluffy pink handcuffs who wanted to get to know him better?

Her thighs quivered as an image of him attached to her bed invaded her mind. No. There was no way she could call and keep her voice steady. Besides, he'd recognize her voice. Blowing a curl from her face, she beeped her car trunk to open it. She really wasn't having any luck with ideas.

"Sandra! Sweetie!"

Arms engulfed her, choking her. She craned her neck to see who was squeezing her to death in the PumpkinMart parking lot. "Hey, Val, how are you?" She would have said more, but another face appeared, scowling at her.

Clarence crossed his arms, steel studs on his jacket hissing a warning. "I knew I saw you at the Yarnucopia, Ms. Kelly. You bought yarn."

"That's right. On the odd occasion I get yarn." She disentangled herself and backed slowly away. Her butt hit the car.

"Then with the yarn, you crochet toys for kids." He glared. In fact, he didn't seem capable of any other expression. "I love that, Ms. Kelly. I'm your biggest fan now." He reached his leather jacket and she tensed, ready to run if things got weird. He pulled out a hand-knitted tube snake scarf in bright green. It had mismatched buttons for eyes and a ribbon tongue.

Sandra's heart melted into a gooey, pink puddle. Clarence tucked his scarf out of sight almost as fast as he had shown it to her. "I knit when I'm emotional."

"Amazing. Who are you and why have I never seen you at the yarn store? I'm sure I would have noticed the dog collar."

"Isn't he the best?" Val side-hugged his man.

It had to be fate. This was too perfect. "Are you guys busy? Right now? Because I have the most devilish plan hatching in my head and you could do me a big favor. There's someone I need you to call and invite to the park."

From her car fifteen minutes later, she watched Cooper pull out of his drive and head for town. Showtime.

She took several deep breaths to steady her nerves and climbed out onto the quiet street. Checking furtively for nosy neighbors, she walked around her car to get out the flamingos, cardboard cutout and shopping bag. No one came out as she hurried around the street corner to Cooper's front door and let herself in with the key Lauren had loaned her a week ago.

First, the coffee switch. She pinched her lips together. Was this all right? She threw her head back and laughed, diabolically. It felt so good to get back at him for her living room, which was still piled high with the plastic decorations. He thought she wouldn't be able to compete against him in the Townsperson's contest? Just wait until his brain shut down from lack of caffeine.

She dumped his regular grinds in a sack and refilled the tin. That accomplished, she took off for his bedroom. It was surprisingly neat and tidy, same as it had been the other day. So the man makes his bed? All the better for her to position her seductively dressed flamingos in it.

She pulled the covers up to tuck it under their black beaks. The front door rattled. She froze.

The door was opening.

No, no, no. She bolted for the hallway, thinking she could possibly escape out the back. She reached the back door. It was locked. She twisted the handle again, hopeful it would turn, and bit her lips. Maybe there was a window in the kitchen.

She spun to make a dash for it when Cooper's laughter rang out in the quiet house.

❧

"You know I actually got halfway there before I realized that Val calling me out of the blue to say he had my shoes at the park had to be fake."

Sandra pivoted to face him, grimacing. Cooper loved it when she looked guilty. "I was going to pick up my own shoes, actually. You said they would be here."

"The delivery is Monday."

"Right. Oops." She shrugged. "So, I'll be going, then."

"What's the rush? Stay for a glass of wine, if you want. It's Saturday afternoon, I've got nothing else planned, and this morning I stopped traffic for a mother duck and her ducklings to cross the street while at least four people filmed me. My work for the Townsperson contest is done here."

She pulled up sharp on her way around him to the door, nailing him to the spot with a glare. "And that's exactly why you don't deserve to win, Cooper. Believe it or not, some of the contestants want to give to this town because it's the right thing to do. You don't do a single good deed without expecting a return on investment. You help your sister with a fundraiser, you expect homemade cookies. You help a little old lady walk her dog, you expect to pick up chicks in the park. You save a duck and her family, you expect to rise to first place in the contest. When do you ever give without expecting something in return?"

"I can't believe you of all people asked me that." He crossed his arms and leaned against the wall. "Tell me, did I expect something from you last December when you came to me with your heartbreak?"

"You expected to get laid."

"Only after you offered. No, not even then. I hoped. Hell, yeah, I hoped. But I gave you a lot and didn't ask for anything in return."

"I really don't remember this version of events."

"You don't—" He scoffed, a sideways grin tugging the corner of his lips. "You don't remember the bathroom floor, the staircase, or the neighbor's garden shed when you wanted to get out of that horrible Christmas party?"

"Of course I remember. I wasn't drunk the whole time. I meant, you expected more from me." She waved her arms, flustered.

He had finally managed to knock her off balance. About time. "Such as a relationship? What the hell was I thinking? You're right. But the truth is, I gave and you didn't complain until you ran off scared. Tell me you don't remember that."

"I never ran off. You think I'm scared? Scared of you? Ha. Would you like to know why I called things off last December?"

"I would love to finally know. One minute you were dying to meet for a late dinner at the Seaside Bed and Breakfast, the next you insulted me and told me to get out of your life. But lay it on me, I can take the truth."

"Because you haven't changed since we first met. All you think about is whether or not you get what you want. If you win. If you look good. If you come out on top. That is how this prank war got started—I was standing in your way and still am."

"You started the war. You hung my tighty-whities on the summer camp flag-pole."

"Honey, you're lucky I didn't hang you on the pole for making fun of me."

"We were fourteen. You can't still be mad I laughed when you tripped over your own feet and got ice-cream from your nose to your shorts."

"I'm not still mad, but you haven't changed in twelve years." Hands on her hips, and crowded into his space, she fumed.

But he didn't care how mad she was. If she wouldn't listen to reason, he'd have to show her. "Sandra, if there is one thing I do where I don't put myself first, it's this."

"What? Fight with me?"

"No." His hands dove into her thick curls and he tilted her head, drawing her in for a kiss. For a second she stiffened, lips pursed, then she relaxed in his hold, responding to his silent urging. His lips on her wide, luscious mouth, she wound her arms around his neck. He switched their places, maneuvering her to the wall, the lengths of their bodies pressed together.

Every nerve buzzed. His heart raced. Heat rushed through his gut and hit his cock. He tangled his fingers in her hair and breathed in the perfume of her body. She kissed him fiercely, nipping at his lips. He kissed her back hard, thumbs at the corners of her mouth.

A leg circled his. He reached down to pull the silky thigh higher around his waist and leaned into her, the pressure on his erection through his jeans a sweet agony.

He had lied a little. He was absolutely putting himself first—the only person who could stop him from having her, was Sandra herself. He would do whatever it took, take as much time as she needed. He wanted Sandra so badly for himself, and had wanted her for so long, he couldn't bear going any longer without hearing her gasps and soft moans, without feeling her moving with him, on him, against him. Yeah, he was putting himself first. He needed her.

She tugged up his tee, and he reached over his head to yank it off one handed. Her blouse had a million fucking little buttons and he fumbled at them for a second. It fell open at the top. She arched her head back and he ran his lips over the dark, velvet skin of her neck, collar bone, and chest. The firm hills of her breasts were just out of reach. Time for a change of technique.

"Wrap your legs around me."

As he lifted her by the waist, she jumped up to cling to him with arms and legs. Her desperate lips searched out his again from her new position. Cooper carried her to the bedroom, perfect ass in his hands and the heat of her pussy against his stomach. He could swear she was already wet through her panties, and it drove him crazy. His erection ached, confined behind his jeans zipper.

He strode towards the bed, ready to throw her on it, when she suddenly twisted free and dropped to the floor.

"Wait, the flamingos," she breathed.

He shook himself, mentally not sure if he had her correctly. She started to leave, but he grabbed her hand and blinked at the two flamingo heads poking up from under the covers. They were nestled in with the cardboard picture of himself in the middle. A plastic and cardboard *ménage à trois.*

"I should go." Sandra tugged on her hand.

"Or we could get in there with them…make it a real party. I appreciate the effort you went to for your prank, but it doesn't have to stop us. Personally, I don't hold grudges."

"No? But you are the competition. I really shouldn't be sleeping with the Townsperson contest enemy."

"Frenemy. At the least. But if you really want to go, why don't I walk you to your car?"

She edged sideways for the door, twisting her tight curls in her fingers. "No, I'll be fine. Middle of the day, friendly neighborhood."

"Don't say I didn't offer. You wanted proof I could put you first, and I tried."

CHAPTER 15

Sandra's windshield was two inches deep in shaving cream. That rat. Carrying her off to his bedroom with sweet words and promises, and all the while he knew he had left a monumental mess on her car.

She stuck her hand in the stuff to wipe it off. A sugary, vanilla scent hit her nose. She sniffed her car. It wasn't shaving cream—it was whipped cream. She groaned. The fat would be impossible to clean off. Damn Cooper and his stupid war.

Muttering to herself, she scraped the whipped cream off and flung it on the pavement, thoroughly coating her skirt, arms, and the rest of her car at the same time. She was a sticky, sweet, goopy mess by the time the windshield was clear enough for her to try the wipers and windshield fluid. She dropped into her car seat. She'd have to clean the interior afterwards, too.

Her windshield wipers streaked back and forth, leaving huge white smears at each pass.

"He will pay. He will pay. He will pay." Too angry to do anything else, she took her phone gingerly from her bag and with grungy fingers, swiped to see her current status in the contest. She rolled her shoulders and loosened her neck muscles. *First place.* There was justice in the world. She might have been caught in the act of pranking his house, but he thought the flamingos and picture were the only little surprises she left for him.

The phone buzzed with an incoming message. Her email. She cackled and twerked in her seat. Talk about good timing. It was almost as if fate struck twice in the same day—she had a response to her Craigslist offer. *Blitzkrieg.* Cooper wouldn't know what hit him. Nothing was sacred in this war, as he was about to find out tomorrow afternoon. With the thought of his suffering lifting her spirits, she eased her car into drive and inched down the street and around the corner. At Cooper's drive, she pulled in and parked. At nearly the same time as she climbed out to stomp across his yard and get his garden hose, he strolled out his front door, a cup of coffee in his hand and a smirk plastered on his face.

"Beautiful day, isn't it?" Cooper hopped down the steps and sat down on one, watching her yank the hose free, as if he hadn't carried her to his bedroom only ten minutes ago.

"It is indeed, but forecasts predict that tomorrow will be even better. Nothing but blue skies." Sandra turned her back on him to first rinse her hands clean and after to spray her car.

"If you are ready to surrender and end this prank war, let me know. It doesn't have to be like this between us. Sneaking into each other's houses, leaving plastic flamingos, and you, denying your true feelings about me."

Sandra spun. "How's your coffee? Need to water it down any?"

He set the coffee down and in one graceful move, pulled off his t-shirt and strode towards her, shirt swinging at his side. "Why don't I wipe this off for you? You always seem to have a little something on you." He paused at her side and brushed her curls off her shoulder, and then rubbed her whole face with the t-shirt.

She squirted him with the hose, soaking his chest and jeans. The spray shot and arced, and came down on her head, getting her wet, too. She squealed and danced away, but kept the hose aimed on Cooper until the cold water forced him to run for the far side of the car. He sputtered and shook glistening droplets from his hair.

Laughing, he started wiping down her windshield and car body, while she pretended not to notice the rippling muscles in his arms and shoulders as he leaned forward to scrub.

Was there anything sexier than a wet, half-naked, well-formed man cleaning in the hot sun? He glanced up and must have seen her grinning broader than a Cheshire cat. He tossed his soaked t-shirt at her and she screamed, jumping sideways. Faster than she could blink, he tackled her, pinning her to the ground.

"Remember, I offered to walk you to your car. Hell, I would have gone back and cleaned it up all by myself if you weren't too stubborn to end this war."

"Never. Not even when I win, which I eventually will. I will leave you and everyone else in the dust," she said. Her chest heaved, but not from effort. Water dripped on her face and neck and she squirmed, trying to free her arms from his hold over her head.

"You can certainly try, Sandra. You can beat down everyone around you, but I doubt you can beat me."

"I guess we'll see." She raised one eyebrow in a challenge, and he had the good sense to rock back and help her stand. "Enjoy the rest of your coffee, Cooper."

※

Cooper shielded his eyes from the setting sun and then checked his front porch again.

There were still eight Austrian guys standing on it, holding coolers and backpacks and smelling like dead fish. One of them had on lederhosen.

It was not a myth. Austrians wore lederhosen.

"Yes, I'm Cooper Hall and this is my address, but I am sure this is a monumental..." fuckery cooked up by Sandra, "mistake."

It was Sunday, only the day after Sandra had put the flamingos in his bed as a half-failed prank, and already there was another prank standing at his threshold. This was her retaliation for the whipped cream—she had put out an ad that his house was open to needy tourists. A house swap but without the swap or him going anywhere else. His house. Two minutes ago, he had been working from the living room and was smack in the middle of tweaking access to his portal for one of his few clients. He didn't have time, energy, or the finances for prank fuckery.

This was an invasion of personal space, an explosion in his life. Too far.

The group's leader pointed at a printed paper in his hand. "But the Craigslist, it is your name, yes? It said up to ten visitors, we are eight."

"Craigslist. Yes. Sorry, but that was a typo. I didn't mean ten." Sandra had such a sense of humor. "I meant one."

Frustrated muttering from the crowd. *Scheiss, Richtig Schweingluck. Verdamt.*

"Your house is very big. I don't think it will be a problem. How many beds do you have?"

"Two, including mine."

"Good, and you have a sofa? And the floor? We will be so drunk, I, Jonas, promise you, we will not know if we are on the floor or in a bed."

"Yeah, but—"

"Hey, it is OK!" Jonas cried and clapped his shoulder. It nearly knocked him over.

The group of fishing tourists, as they had mentioned on arrival, took this as the sign they were staying. And Cooper realized he couldn't stop them at this point. A wall of massive bodies pressed forward to get through the doorway and for safety's sake, he let them by.

"Where is your kitchen? We need to put the fish and the beer in the... *Wie heist das schon, das Kuhlschrank?*"

Kuhlschrank... Endless hours of his ninth-grade German sank its teeth in his brain. Cooper said the first word that came up. "Refrigerator?"

"Ja! Hey, you speak a little German. What kind of *Bier* do you want? *Dunkel, Blonde, Weiss, oder...*" Jonas flipped up the lid on one of the coolers. A connoisseurs' selection of German, imported, and local beers was nestled in frosty ice.

So the situation wasn't all bad. He took a Doppelbock he didn't recognize and raised it to cheers.

Approximately five hours later, he was weaving unsteadily through the same sea of bodies but who were now stretched out all over his floor and sofas on his way to his bedroom. The room tilted first in one direction and then the other, and he wondered just how long the grilled swordfish he had eaten would stay down after at least six beers, five shots of whiskey, and a small glass of home-brewed schnapps. Apparently, one of the moms from Upper Austria made her own schnapps flavored with nuts and spices, and her son took a bottle of it with him wherever he went. It was very smooth. Cooper might have had a couple glasses, actually.

He put his hand on the wall. That was better. He had to keep his sea legs under him on this ship in the storm. Only a few more feet to go and he could go to bed. The hallway was clear and with the help of the wall, he arrived safe and sound in his bedroom. He peeled off his shirt and shucked his jeans in the dark, ready to fall on his bed and sleep instantly.

A snore stopped him cold. He flicked on the bedside lamp.

Two hairy men were snuggling with his pillows. He tried to close his eyes, but it was too late. He saw the drool and knew it would never be erased from his brain.

Sandra. He stumbled from his room. In the hallway, he pivoted to return for his clothes. Next, he went to the bathroom to splash his face with cold water and brush his teeth, then he got dressed.

This was her fault and she was about to take responsibility for his bedlessness.

CHAPTER 16

Sandra stirred, head swimming from deep sleep. There had been a noise. She waited. Men's voices and then a car drove off.

She fell back on her pillow and burrowed under her comforter. Just as she began drifting, her phone startled her with its tinkling chime.

Icy fear struck. It could only be bad news at this hour. She rolled from bed and lunged for the dresser to get the phone.

The hell? She pressed her lips together in anger and had to count three Mississippis before she could answer.

"Cooper, it's past midnight and I have an early shoot tomorrow. This better not be a misplaced booty call, or I'm gonna place my booty knee highs right where it hurts."

"I'm on your porch."

"Then get your ass off my porch and get it home!"

A distant thud sounded from the front room. The sound a head might make if someone hit her door with it.

The line was dead. She sighed in frustration and wrapped up in her fuzzy robe. "You have got to be kidding me," she grumbled as she headed for the door. "Showing up in the middle of the night. *I'm on your porch.* As if I care when I have to get up at 4:30 the next day..."

When she threw open the door, Cooper stumbled and nearly fell in. He blinked in confusion several times to focus on her and then rested his head on the casing. "Sandra, don't believe what they say about it being smooth. Propaganda and lies. I mean, it is smooth at first, but it sneaks up on you, ties your brain up, hijacks your thighs, and then suddenly the world as you know has disappeared in a smooth fog."

He sat down, deflated on the threshold.

Right.

Drunk as a skunk on a Sunday night. And he crawled here wanting sympathy.

"All right, Cooper, talk to me. Who said it was smooth and why are you complaining to me about it?" As if she didn't know. She was smirking triumphantly on the inside. So he didn't like strange people showing up at his house and taking over as if they owned the place? Bless his poor, Appalachian, mountain-man heart.

"It was you. It's been you since the beginning. First they showed up on my doorstep and I thought they've come bearing beer and fresh fish to grill. Hell, they've even got brats and schnapps they brought from Austria. Just the schnapps is from Austria. Fritz's mom makes it on the farm. So smooth. We started drinking. We ate. There was beer, so much beer. My glasses weren't big enough for the beer and they laughed at me."

Images of what his evening must have been hit her. She had to restrain herself from laughing at him, too. Her evil plan of revenge for Flamingapocalypse had come to fruition. She would have rubbed her hands together in glee, but she needed them to prop Cooper upright.

"Who laughed at you?" she asked, knowing full well who.

He squinted at her. "The Austrians. They came because of you. An army of eight. Because of Craigslist, and now they are passed out all over my floor, my sofas, and in my bed."

"I got confirmation they would be arriving today or tomorrow, and I wanted it to be a surprise for you. Which reminds me, I owe you the fifty dollars they paid to rent the floor."

"I have nowhere else. I'm crashing with you tonight."

She stopped laughing. "Like hell you are. You have family, credit cards. I'll give you that fifty in cash right this minute. Now go get a room somewhere else."

He closed his eyes, forehead and mouth in a deep frown. "It's your fault they came."

"It's your fault I still have to find good homes for forty plastic flamingos. I can only put so many up in my yard before the neighborhood watch knocks on my door. The only reason you are still alive after that stunt is because I think flamingos are kind of cute. If you had sent plastic tarantulas, your face would be printed on milk bottles."

"I would never send tarantulas," he slurred. "Never. I know you are afraid and I wouldn't do...all things considered...no arachnids. No spider things. Nope. None. I'll go. I just...I need a moment," he said, words jumbling together. He leaned too far forward and she grabbed him, thinking he had passed out on her threshold. In her arms.

All right. He was kind of disarming like that. She had to admit he cut a fine mountain man. Full beard and wild hair splayed across her arm. Eyes closed, she could forget how infuriating he could be and simply enjoy the relaxed lines of his strong jaw and fine cheek bones.

And of course, his bow-shaped lips, parted and soft instead of twisted up in some damn half-smile or smirk. She had always had one hell of a weak spot for those lips. When she was a kid and they first met, as a teen girl with too many emotions and not enough good sense, when she was far from him for four years of college, and last Christmas when she had run to him with her broken heart and then fallen for his charms and temptations—since the beginning she had wanted to kiss those lips.

To think, she never should have been at that summer camp. It was practically an accident, because both her parents had been laid off at the same time and for nearly a year the family had barely survived. The town had stepped in and offered her a summer vacation with meals included. What would things be like if she had never stayed in those bright green cabins and started the war with Cooper when he laughed at her? Would they have even met or interacted in college?

One thing was sure, she would have noticed those lips and wanted to kiss them when she was younger.

But not now. He was not on her list of healthy midnight snacks, and she had to be up before the crack of dawn.

Which meant she had to get her ass back in bed and Cooper off her porch. She could call a taxi. She could call...

No. They kept their pranks between themselves.

"Hey, baby, wake up," she said. She smacked his face a couple of times and he grinned, eyes still closed.

"Your robe is so soft. I could curl up in it. And it smells like... girly flowery stuff. God it smells so good." He snuggled deeper in her chest.

She smacked his cheek. "Wake up. You've got to get on the sofa, and I'm not carrying you."

He blinked up at her, grinning more.

He tucked one foot underneath him and then the next. With a groan, he managed to stand, but leaned on her heavily. She stumbled under the weight. His height somewhat hid the width of his shoulders, but this close, holding him in her arms, she could feel his true size and how much lean, hard muscle he was.

"Sofa." Her voice was stern, but he was nuzzling her neck and it sent shivers through her whole body. Her nipples decided to be perky right then, and she had to hope the bathrobe hid them.

He allowed her to guide him, turning to her living room, and they made the after-hours waltz to her pink three-seater. He collapsed on the sofa, pulling her down.

"All right, baby, I'm not part of the packaged deal," she said. There were too many body parts wrapped together with his. She wasn't sure how to untangle herself without falling on the floor or kneeing him in the stomach.

"You keep calling me baby and I'm a gonna do some dirty dancing for you," he whispered into her ear.

She groaned at the cheap line, but butterfly wings danced up and down her neck and shoulder.

Baby? Slip of the tongue and then some. She pushed upright, knees digging in the cushions. His face was at the same level as her breasts, and her breath caught in her throat. Her nipples grew painfully hard at the thought of him brushing aside her robe and kissing her.

She had to get out of there. This was not the time to cause more confusion—he'd get the wrong impression with her 'baby,' especially when he was already convinced he could show up uninvited at her house and crash.

"No dirty anything when you are drunk, Mr. Hall. I'll get you a blanket and a pillow, but that's it." She twisted to the side, freeing her leg from underneath his, but accidentally pressed her upper body into his face. He wrapped his arms around her, tying her to his warm body.

"Cooper!"

"I don't blame you for trying to take advantage of me when I'm in this condition, but you should know, I won't be any fun."

"Why, you—"

"You are fondling my moob."

"The hell I am. What is a moob?"

"It's a man-boob."

She jerked back. Sure enough, one hand was covering his pec. She pulled it away and leaned sideways to crawl off of him. He lifted her waist at the same time to help her, but it backfired, and her bathrobe rode up over her hips.

"Good God, those panties should come with a warning," he whispered, voice ragged.

Sandra tugged at her robe, flushing with embarrassment and something else. "Well, don't look!"

His arms should come with a warning, too. He would have lifted her again, but she batted away his hands. Then she tried to get up gracefully, not exposing any more flesh or underwear than he had already seen, but it wasn't possible. She twisted, flailed, and finally fell on her ass on the floor. He reached out a hand to help her stand.

"Are you all right?"

"A blanket and then sleep," she snapped.

Blankets and pillows were in the hall closet, her old rainbow sparkle throw would be perfect for the occasion.

By the time she returned he was resting on his side, watching her every step as she came closer. She tossed him the things from a safe distance.

He was too long for her sofa and the throw. His feet stuck out over the edge.

I bet he spoons like an Olympic champ with those long legs and arms. The kind you got tied up in and never really let go of again.

Her eyes drifted over him and she wondered what he looked like under his t-shirt and jeans. He had to have a massive V. All that muscle through his clothes couldn't be lying to her.

She could let him share her bed. As a frenemy. A frenemy with benefits.

What?

Sandra shook herself sane the second the thought of sharing her bed flitted through her head.

That wouldn't be any temptation. Her core tingled with treacherous warmth already. Her hormones had minds of their own and hadn't figured out that Cooper was a no-fly zone.

He would simply have to survive the night with no blanket for his feet.

Resolute, she nodded, ready to switch off the light.

"I gotta say, Sandra, sending the Austrians was a good prank. A good prank."

"I hope they make you miserable and leave you a nasty mess in the bathroom," she said.

He grinned, sitting upright to arrange the blanket. "I made popcorn and we all watched your bloopers on Facebook on repeat."

"Son of a biscuit eater." She shook her head, wishing she had found a group of nutty cult members theologically opposed to bathing to send to his house instead. "I'm only getting started."

"You love me when I'm salty, though, admit it."

"Love you, Cooper? Ha. Not a chance."

He dropped his head back and groaned. She assumed he was done for the evening and was walking out of the living room when he stopped her.

"Hearts are fragile things, Sandra, and our lives depend on them. Be kind to yours and protect it. It's a precious, beautiful thing. A fragile thing."

She gasped at his unexpected words.

Rumors from their earliest days of high school surfaced in Sandra's mind. There had been talk, tragic things mentioned between the slams of locker doors and whispered from one desk to the next when the teacher had her back turned. Dramatic events that made other students feel sorry for Cooper, but nothing that affected their own, safe lives.

His dad had died of a heart attack shortly before they had met at summer camp. Strange that she had never thought of the timing before. His father died, they met at camp, and she started the war. What was worse, if she could believe the rumors that had spread like weeds in the hallways and classrooms at the beginning of their freshman year, Cooper had been at home alone with his dad when it happened.

She padded up to the sofa and touched his arm gently. "Thank you."

He caught her hand and tangled his fingers in hers. "I'm sorry, but I didn't realize you were wearing see-through underwear and now I can't get it out of my head.

She rolled her eyes, exaggerating her annoyance. "Is that all you can think about? I thought we were having a tender moment."

"If you want the truth, I'm having a rather hard moment, but if yours is tender that's all right by me. It's actually pretty natural."

The most embarrassing part was that she *was* feeling tender towards him and knowing that he was rather hard was heating her up from head to toe. He winked at her, as if he could read her thoughts or had heat sensors to detect her temperature increasing.

Her lady bits had had enough of the empty wasteland that was currently her love life. She tingled, and her see-through underwear would soon be damp and even more see-through.

Cooper tugged gently on her hand. "How about a kiss goodnight?"

She poked his chest, bending over him. "You are drunk. You are crazy to think I would kiss you after everything you've done. You have nothing I want—"

With a wrestler's ease, he pulled her down and flipped her at the same time, pinning her between his body and the back of the sofa, her legs on his.

"Nothing at all?" He didn't let her answer. Protests and insults rushed to her tongue, but died before she could utter them, smothered by his lips.

CHAPTER 17

It took Sandra a full second to comprehend the collision of bodies was a kiss, and then she attacked him in a frenzy of pent up want.

His hand roamed up her thigh to her waist and loosened her robe. It should be a problem, but for some reason wasn't. He inhaled as she exhaled. They flowed together, fighting for dominance in a game of kiss-and-trick, with nipping, pushing and pulling. One moment she covered his hand to touch her harder and the next she was shoving against his chest to make space between them. She couldn't think or breathe with her chest pressed to his.

Then his hand was on her breast and she moaned, dropping her head back. He kissed along her collar bone and neck, a stone skipping on water, each kiss sending tiny ripples of desire through her body. He brushed his fingers across her bare nipple.

She fisted his hair, vaguely aware of her leg wrapped around his and that her hips were rotating into his. The solid mound of his erection pressed through his jeans and she moved into it, needing more of him. Wanting him closer.

He smelled of whiskey and summer nights by the sea. He tasted like trouble and every sugary treat she ever craved.

"God, I could fall in love with this," he whispered.

"Wha—"

He cut her off, kissing her deeply. Finally using his strength to his advantage, he pushed on top of her, running his hand over her panties and hip to the warm, quivering spot between her legs.

She jolted with the shock of pleasure. Fireworks were lighted, hissing and sparkling with tiny lights. She shivered against his hand and cocked her leg higher so he could continue his exploration.

The beard bristles on her neck tickled and scratched as he worked his way to her chest. He kissed her nipple, sucking it gently.

Sandra arched upwards into him. He cradled her, arm around her back. Then when she was about to beg for more, he rubbed his thumb across her sex.

"I could fall in love with you."

What did he just say?

Her heart jolted, as if he had dashed her face with cold water. She sat upright, hitting his face with her breast. He bit into her on accident and she yelped. Shoving him away, she tried to untangle her legs from his as he fell of the sofa and onto the floor.

He reeled in shock, muttering under his breath. She had forgotten he was completely hammered.

She groaned, face-palming the cushions. She had almost slept with Cooper Hall on her sofa when he was so drunk he thought he loved her. That was wrong on so many levels, she didn't know where to begin enumerating them.

"Can you help me up? The room just tilted out from under me," he said, holding out a hand.

"Goodnight, Cooper." She straightened her clothes, gathering what was left of her dignity and stomped by him.

He caught her ankle. "Sandra, don't go. Not yet. I thought we were having a moment."

"The moment is over. It's dead and gone. Better get sleep, sunshine, tomorrow is going to be rough." She swept out of the room, leaving him to turn off the light or not. As soon as she reached her bedroom, she shut the door and threw herself on the bed. His hands, his lips, his scratchy beard. Too wonderful to bear and too warped to allow. With a little luck, he wouldn't remember, though.

Her nerves continued to buzz with his nearness, despite the fact he was on the sofa and a closed door was between them. Frenemies. They were good like this. She couldn't stand the thought of losing even this connection. This might be the only way they could be together.

And there was still the possibility of frenemies with benefits.

An excruciating pressure in his skull, as if there was a huge hand wrapped around his head, squeezing him like fruit, was the first thing Cooper noticed.

His eyelids glared an angry red. His blinds must be open. He tried to open his eyes, but they were gummed shut. Why was it bright? He always closed his blinds. Rubbing his face, he managed to get his eyes partly open. In the blur of his surroundings, he made out something perched on his chest. His eyes popped wide open.

Lizard!

With a surprised cry, he swatted at it. It kept its claws in his shirt, teeth exposed and neck flared. He yelled and threw himself backwards, but the toothy reptile clung to his chest. A hard swipe knocked it to the floor, where it rolled to a stop in exactly the same flared, biting position as before.

Sandra had duct taped a plastic lizard to his chest. Nice.

He groaned, the pain in his head returning with reinforcements as the adrenaline in his system faded. Sandra's living room came into focus, flooded with the light of day. Sunlight pierced his eyeballs with tiny spears and set his brain on fire.

Sandra on the sofa last night. Great balls of fucking fire. He had rolled with Sandra on her sofa until she pushed him off, right when he dared to dream she would be his for a few minutes.

He thought he had said something stupid, but it was hazy after he started kissing her. And touching her. See-through, lace panties.

Fuck me.

He checked his watch.

Half past nine. He should have been at work an hour ago. Well, he could pick up donuts on the way and eat a couple for lunch, too, to make up for lost time.

There was a note for him on the back of the plastic lizard. He wasn't sure why she had such a great toy, but he was tempted to borrow it for decorating the inside of his fridge at work.

Cooper,

> *There's a care package for you on the counter. Sorry the Austrians took advantage of your wimpy tolerance for homemade brews from the Old World. Key to the door is on the table. Let yourself out and hide it under the pink quartz.*

Sandra

Care package? Well, well, well. Crashing here wasn't such a dumbass move after all.

She put together a care package for him.

It took a couple of tries, but he stood and found the kitchen. Sure enough, there was a bottle of aspirin, a drinking glass, and some odd-looking bread for the toaster on a plate.

It must mean she cared, *n'est-ce pas?* As Isabelle, the owner of Les Amis, would say. She must care and not be mad about whatever he had said or done that made her shove his ass on the floor.

He reached the counter and sank to his elbows. First problem— the bread was as plastic as the lizard. The glass looked clean, but suddenly he didn't trust it, and...there were Skittles in the aspirin bottle.

That was his Sandra.

If you wake her up in the middle of the night to sleep on her sofa and wind up with your hands on her breasts, don't expect any kindness in the morning. He tossed a few candies in his mouth for the sake of the sugar and checked the coffee pot. It was clean and ready to go, from what he could see. No hidden explosives or dirt in the basket.

He found a tin of coffee. A spoonful of grounds huddled around the edges. Maybe enough for one small cup. Barely. It would be weak, at best.

She had not only replaced the aspirin with Skittles, she had emptied her coffee tin to deprive him of the necessities of life. Her cruelty obviously knew no bounds.

Well, when life gave you a teaspoon of coffee grounds, you made an Americano with it.

He poked though her cupboards and even stole a peek in her fridge for other edibles or caffeinated drinks, but they were pretty bare bone. She must eat out more than he did. Or judging from the childish drawings and pictures of laughing kids on the fridge, she spent a lot of time with her family.

The percolating machine hissed that it was done, and he poured the half cup of thin coffee in a cup. Her sugar bottle was on the counter and he measured out three heaping spoonfuls, more than usual to make up for lack of caffeine.

He took a thankful sip. And spit it out in the sink, coughing.

Coffee made from the Dead Sea could not be worse. He could float a nail in that coffee, it was so salty. He dropped his head to the counter top. She had replaced her sugar with salt, the evil vixen.

Steps on the back porch alerted him to someone close by. He swiveled and pressed his back to the wall so whoever it was wouldn't see him. A burglar? On Monday morning? A key turned in the lock and the door swung open before his hungover brain realized that Sandra herself was walking into her home.

He peeled himself off the wall, heartrate going back down. Today was not the day he would have to fend off fiends breaking into his...what was she to him? His competitor? His enemy? His not-quite-one-night-stand-but-he-still-held-onto-hope-one-night-stand?

Sandra screamed and brandished karate chop hands upon seeing him. The next instant, she relaxed. "You. What are still doing here? Don't you have an office to go to?"

"Of course. I was grabbing a quick cup of coffee on my way in. Thanks for switching out the sugar on me..."

"You should know me better than that by now. You should pick up coffee on your way to town, and considering it's nearly noon, I imagine you are having heavy withdrawals."

"Noon?" He closed his eyes and his jaw tightened. "Shit. Yes. I'm going. Right now." He ran his hands through his hair. That would have to be good enough. He had a travel toothbrush at work and no dress code, so his jeans and Hawaiian button-up from the day before would be fine. Shit. An entire morning wasted after not finishing his project yesterday when the Austrians showed up.

Not to mention, he had done nothing to improve his contest scores in several days. A cold rock formed in his stomach. He was perilously close to losing it all, and he was wasting time drinking with strangers and sleeping on Sandra's sofa.

Sandra frowned at him. Her hand touched his arm, but then jerked away as if burned. "It was mean of me. I hid the coffee and sugar in the bathroom if you need a quick cup."

"Thanks, but I really need to go." There was nothing else to say. He patted his pockets for wallet and keys, then remembered he had taken an Uber. He nodded to Sandra as he stepped past her on his way out, and he found his phone.

Walking from her house would be nearly as fast as waiting for someone. And it would give him time to clear his mind. He was about to shove the phone back in his pocket, when he remembered that among the many things he was neglecting, he had to check in on his mom once a week or so, or she sent Lauren to find him. He should invite her for lunch. Scratch that. Lunch was now. He should invite her for dinner one of these evenings.

He pulled out his phone and found her name as he set out at a quick pace for downtown.

"Hello, there." She must have had a cold, her voice was throaty and deep.

"Hey, Mom, just calling to check in. How's it going on this beautiful day?"

"Oh, baby, I'm so fine. I was hoping you would call. Now I want you to tell me all about yourself. Please, don't skip any of the dirty details."

"Mom?" he asked, strangling.

"Yes, keep calling me momma. You know I love it. Have you been a naughty boy? Does someone need to be spanked?" she asked, ending the question in a fake growl. "Why don't we get together in my chat room? What do you say, big boy?"

What the? He took the phone from his ear, staring at it in horror. How? Oh, sweet angels above, this was so wrong.

He swiped the screen. Contact details, contact details.

A 1-900 number. Those numbers were free, right? A prank. Damn it, he hadn't seen a thing. How did Sandra do that?

Last night? Or the restaurant from the other day. Probably while he was watching the game.

In the refined art of prank war, this retaliation was small fry, used in order to exhaust the enemy. Not quite petty, but definitely small. When he counted this one with the other pranks, Sandra was seriously ramping up her game.

But replacing his mom's phone number with a sex worker was beyond the pale, much worse than inviting tourists to stay at his home. He wouldn't let her off this time. He turned around, took a deep breath and dashed down the street for her house. He pounded on her back door.

"Sandra! This has gone too far—"

She jerked open the door and fisted the front of his shirt to pull him inside. And into her arms. On tip-toe, she pressed her lips to his.

Cooper had no idea what the hell was going on, but he wasn't going to stop and ask questions. Kiss first, kiss more, and talk later. Talk about something that had made him mad, but he couldn't say what.

This was how it had all started last time over Christmas, Sandra arriving from nowhere, dragging him into a corner and showing him how badly she needed him. It was like holding a volcano in his arms. They had both been burned in the end.

He was willing and ready to try it again, though. He was giving all she asked for, and he stumbled inside and kicked the door closed. She tipped her fingers up his chest to the bare skin of his neck. If this continued, he would have a problem with his pants.

No. No problems, no interruptions this time.

CHAPTER 18

Sandra was the same force of nature he had always known and got too close to last Christmas. But Cooper wasn't holding back this time, taking things carefully. He had his hands on her firm ass, and he crushed her to his body, the pressure a delicious torture on his growing erection.

She pulled back, breathing hard. "This doesn't mean anything. We are two people blowing off steam in the middle of a work day." She ripped his shirt off, buttons popping off and clinking across her hardwood floor.

"Absolutely. Totally for fun." He grabbed her for another kiss, thrilled the only thing she was tearing up was his clothing. He tried to pick her up, get his hands under blouse, and kiss her senseless at the same time, but failed.

She saved him by hopping up to wrap her legs around his waist, and he held onto her as she nipped at his lips. Fingers raked through his hair, and nails dug into his shoulders. He growled. This was the way he loved her best.

"Because I could use some fun," she breathed into his ear.

"I can give you fun for as long as you want."

"To make up for the drama last Christmas. I never got my fill of you."

He carried her to the hall and paused. "Where is your room?"

"Last door on the left." She bit his lower lip, sucking, and he tightened his grip as he made his way. "Other left. Your left."

"Right." He burst through the door and they fell in a tumble on her bed. "Today is Christmas. In June."

"But's it's just casual sex between frenemies," she said, twisting to her knees to unbutton his jeans.

"Exactly. We can be casual. Sex between frenemies, whatever. Sounds good." Her blouse was a nightmare of small buttons. Where did she get her evil shirts? "Just sex. Fuck, I need to put my tongue on you now. Now."

"God yes." She shimmied her pants over her hips and then eased backwards on the bed so Cooper could pull them all the way off. "No-strings sex today, and the Townsperson contest continues as normal. No big deal, right?" Her hands fled over the front of her blouse, and as soon as it was loose, she let it fall from her shoulders.

Cooper could barely breathe. Lace panties and a see-through bra were all that stood in his way of Sandra's gorgeous body. His heart pounded like he was swimming the 200, trying to break a world record. "No strings. No big deal. We're both adults." He hooked his thumbs in her panties and locked eyes with her. "This changes nothing."

His erection strained painfully in his half-zipped jeans, but he couldn't waste time on it. He began to slide off the frilly panties—no, thong. Shit, he had only now noticed she was wearing a thong, and he almost regretted not seeing her walk across the room in them, and he slid it down the length of her long legs.

Then he bent forward to taste her. She was exactly as he imagined. During their almost-fling at Christmas, things had never progressed past frenzied kissing, first in the staircase of the club they were dancing at, next the bathroom floor of his Aunt Jo's when Sandra tried to interview her but had to lock herself in there to avoid the cats, and finally when she dragged him off to the garden shed in near freezing temperatures to avoid a horrible office party.

He ran his mouth over her soft, tangy folds, making her jump and shudder until she wrapped her legs around his head and squeezed. He could barely breathe. It was amazing. He lifted her up, hands under the small of her back, and continued to explore her sex, every gasp and moan from her throat was a drug he needed more of.

Sandra shuddered and planted her feet on the bed so she could lift herself, and Cooper plunged his tongue into her nubbed, wet depths. He wanted to drink her every last drop. He was addicted.

"Yes, like that, Coop," she gasped.

He moved his tongue in her again, this time using his thumb to keep a circular pulse on her clit. Her knees tightened against his ears. He continued his movements, back and arm muscles flexed to hold himself in place against her growing agitation.

"Coop, I..."

She didn't finish her sentence, so he kept going, drinking and tasting her, and loving every second of it. She dropped her hips, but her hands in his hair dragged him down with her and she moaned his name again.

He slipped his thumb inside her sex, licking upwards to flick her clit with his tongue. She writhed as if she would move away. "Coop, I can't...I—"

"You can, Sandra," he whispered, and traced the outline of her sex before sliding in two fingers. She whimpered but grabbed his hair hard and bucked her hips in rhythm to his fingers and mouth. Her sex fluttered and a new wave of moisture came to his lips. She cried out, digging nails in his shoulders.

He was relentless. He knew she hated losing control and letting him give her what she needed, but he wouldn't let that stop him. She arched her back, scratching and bucking as an orgasm ripped a final cry from her mouth, and she was completely submerged by pleasure.

When Sandra climaxed, she brought the house down with her, and Cooper wouldn't have it any other way.

He kissed his way from her sex to her belly button and stomach and then to her chest, where he suddenly realized he had forgotten to take off her bra. His hands circled her back to unhook it.

She locked eyes with him and, like a predator, wrapped her legs around his waist. "I'm not done with you yet."

"I'm not done with you, yet, either. You said you needed fun, and that was just the beginning."

"I want you to fuck me now, Cooper."

Her voice wasn't convincing enough. He pulled her bra straps down her copper arms and exposed the dark brown of her puckered nipple. He rubbed his bearded chin on it. She yelped and swatted at his shoulder. With a quiet chuckle, he covered it with is lips and drew the bud into his mouth, sucking gently. She moaned. He sucked harder and her legs gripped him tighter, drawing his pelvis to hers.

"What did you want?" he asked.

"Give it to me, Cooper. Give it all to me."

He rasped his tongue across her sensitive nipple and nipped his way up her chest to her neck. Her hands fumbled at his jeans to push them all the way off and, finally his ill-treated erection came free of its confinement. She ran her hand along his length and cupped his balls.

His world nearly stopped.

"Are you really going to make me beg?" she asked.

"Yes." It was one of the hardest things he'd ever done. She had to want him, though.

"Please, Cooper, just this once." She squeezed his erection and gently tugged upwards. "No more games."

No more games—agreed. He found his jeans at the bottom of the bed and flipped through his wallet. The ground opened up and he was plummeted into a cold, rocky pit. He couldn't go any further. Sandra was begging him for more and he couldn't provide.

"I don't have any condoms," Cooper said, voice rougher than he intended. Shit. Major fuckup and no one but himself to blame. He'd taken an old condom out a week or two ago, meaning to change it for a new one, and forgotten. There was a box in his bathroom—a whole box—for all the good it did him now.

"I do." Sandra reached to open the drawer of her nightstand.

"That is so fucking hot." A woman who knew what she wanted and how to get it? Scorching. She put the corner of the package in her teeth and with a slow, careful pull, tore the side off of it and then handed him the condom. Her eyes continued to bore into him as he rolled it on his cock.

"Tell me how you want it," he said, on his knees in front of her.

"Make it count, so I never forget."

He hooked his hands around her thighs to tilt and lift her hips up to meet him, and eased into her. He wanted to do the work for her—which wasn't work at all, but was pure pleasure—but to keep the effort for himself to show her how much he had to give when she let him.

He moved slowly in and out, building up Sandra's excitement and frustration, which were clearly visible in her expression. In that position, her hips too high to use her feet for leverage, she couldn't make him change his pace. She bit her lower lip and curled her fingers in the tussled bed cover. "You're still playing games with me."

He grinned and thrust hard, making her gasp. As he began to move faster, driving each thrust as deep as possible, her eyes fluttered. She moaned his name, voice breaking, and grabbed his forearms.

He needed a position that gave him more strength. He paused, pulling out. Turning her knees to face the edge of the bed, he stepped to the floor. Just as he had estimated—her bed was the perfect height.

Sandra propped herself on one elbow. "This isn't over, I hope."

"You should know I never quit until I have what I want, Sandra."

He placed his hands on her hips and drove his cock in to the hilt. She wrapped her legs around his waist and gasped for air as he continued to pound into her wet pussy. As her moans became higher pitched, he licked his thumb and rubbed her clit.

This pushed her to a climax for a second time, exactly as he wanted. Watching her thrash, eyes closed and mouth open in ecstasy, set off his own orgasm. As she shouted his name and planted her nails in his arms, he was lost in own pleasure coursing through his body from his balls up to his gut and stomach and through his chest and the top of his head.

He shook as his erection spent itself, with Sandra's sex clamped tight on him. She drew a quivering breath and released her grip on his arms. He crawled to her side, and twined his limbs around her possessively, allowing himself to enjoy her presence without worrying about a fight for a change. "If that wasn't a good time as per your request, let me know and I'll try again in ten minutes."

She laughed, rolling first towards him to kiss his chest and then away from him to grab her underthings from off the floor. "It was exactly what I needed." Before he knew it, she was dressed and scrunching her hair into place, although he didn't see a difference. Her curls were always wild. And perfect.

"I don't know if this was a Holy Hot Tamales or a temporary truce, but remember, this doesn't change anything," she said.

"Not for the Townsperson contest it doesn't, but if you want a truce, all you have to do is say the word." Actually, a truce would be a welcome relief. She was killing him with the pranks. As for this not changing anything between them...he didn't want to point out that this could change things between them. It could change everything. But she was already edging for the door, gathering her things as well as her calm, collected attitude at the same time.

"Honey, I won't be calling truce anytime soon. Not since I'm in first place despite your pranks. But, thank you for this time together. You have no idea how much it helps."

"I'm always here for you." He leaned back on her pillow, arms crossed under his head. It was true she was still first place, and he needed to win that contest. For his job. His mom and sister. His father's grave at the cemetery. More than that—this was his home, where Sandra lived, as well. He couldn't fail. "You know how to get in touch if you want me. Should I let myself out using your spare key? I have to call an Uber. My shirt seems to be in tatters…"

"I ruined your shirt, didn't I? I'm so sorry. Yes, let yourself out. Wait, I have a few things from my dad for my gardening work." Sandra shoved her closet doors to the both sides, rummaged in the back, and tossed a pile of faded, well-worn shirts and tees on the bed next to him. "I have to go or be late getting back to the station. See you… I'll see you around."

She waved awkwardly and practically sprinted from the room.

Had she just run scared from him? Cooper scoffed, replaying how she left with lightning speed from her own bedroom, moments after they…

He rolled to his feet, groaning, and picked through the pile of her dad's old clothes. This was all wrong in so many ways. What had happened before she ran out was not wrong, however.

Among the long-sleeved wintry shirts, there was a grey t-shirt with white dots in swirls and the words *the galaxy loves you* across the chest. He pulled it over his head, the thin cotton infused with Sandra's scent. He inhaled, mind caught in a whirlwind.

No more games.

Had she meant more by that phrase than him drawing out the moment? Because he was afraid the whole thing meant more than he intended.

CHAPTER 19

The deadline for her piece was a few hours away, but after her tumble with Cooper, Sandra's brain wasn't cooperating with the rest of her body. It refused to think about anything else. Her brain wasn't batting for Sandra Mercy Kelly, that was for sure—it wasn't even in the stadium.

No, wait. Actually, her body seemed to be conspiring with her brain to keep her from productive work. Every time she thought about Cooper—his hands, his arms, his lips—her whole body would spark and flush in different places.

After a furtive glance over her shoulder, she pulled up the Townsperson contest website on her phone. She shielded her phone from view of anyone passing by her cubicle and scrolled down for contest voting results so far.

He was gaining on her. Her solid lead was melting away, quite like her panties had practically evaporated at the sight of him charging through her door, passion blazing in his eyes. She fanned herself discretely. It would be something to remember on cold, winter nights. Nothing more.

Right now, though, she had to get her ass in action. She had to win. Despite her recent lead, Brad seemed more and more smug every day, convinced he was right that she couldn't win and shouldn't have tried. With Cooper in the lead, Brad would take advantage of it.

She placed her phone face down on her desk, determined to work on her latest fluff piece that Brad was forcing her to cover. It would be a crowd pleaser, at least. Everyone loved happy stories about kids, and knowing which activities would be the most popular during the Seagrass Summer Camp for pre-teens was sure to be useful to parents sending their kids there. It would get her votes from parents and grandparents alike.

Funny—the Seagrass Summer Camp was where she first met Cooper. A hot rush of blood flooded her chest and face. Pranks and tricks aside, he had turned out to be a magnet.

But she wasn't going to think about him. She faced her screen, telling herself to think about the camp. That summer camp had changed her. The town had sponsored her camp fee, three meals a day and as many activities as she could fit in from sunup to sundown, and marshmallow grilling on Friday nights. She would never forget. It had been the first time she understood what it meant to be part of a community and had set her feet on her path to her career.

Brad might try to drive her out or keep her down in her reporting, but she still had plenty of time to win and get her promotion. This was Monday, and the contest finale was next Sunday, which meant five more days of voting.

As if her thoughts had summoned him, Brad himself emerged from the hallway and walked by. He paused to lean on the cubicle divider, arms crossed on the top.

"I'd like to invite you for a drink later, tonight if you are free. I think we should talk. There are some upcoming events you should know about, and I would like to be the one to tell you."

Her stomach flipped, pinching her heart. That sounded like bad news. Was the network making them lay people off? Was someone in the office diagnosed with cancer? But he wanted to tell her over a drink. That made it personal.

If she was getting fired, it would be in his office, no frills, fuss, nor fuzzy alcohol.

Her mind raced, but she couldn't think of a single thing to say in reply. "Events?"

"Let's say Casa del Pasta at eight-thirty. We can meet there or I can pick you up at your house. You don't have to worry about a thing."

Don't worry? As if that was possible. She was on the verge of panic. Going to a fine restaurant made it sound as though he wanted to get back together. And he would pick her up? So if he had horrible news for her and she drank herself under the table he could drive her home?

She frowned at her screen, pushing for information. "You know, tonight doesn't work for me. I'm not sure when I'll finish this. It could be late. Why don't you just tell me what's going on and we can get drinks some other time."

"I'd rather not do this at the news station. It's private. We were very close once upon a time, and I would like some time alone to talk. That's all." Brad used his velvet persuasion voice to perfection when he wanted something, like right now.

Her hands went clammy and her mouth dry. This was getting scary. They had been close. She thought he would ask her to marry him and then he suddenly lost interest before dumping her without explanation. When she noticed him sniffing around the receptionist, it was enough to make her want to set his car on fire.

John sashayed his booty along the cubicle corridor and put an arm around Brad's shoulders affectionately.

"Has he told you the wonderful news?" John asked.

Sandra fixed her gaze on Brad. He hunched his shoulders and darted his eyes, not looking at her.

"He was just about to tell me something," she said.

"Ah, then I'll have to beat him to it! Congratulations are in order, Brad. You and Sandy are going to be a great couple."

She stood up slowly. Brad shrank back, lips pressed together.

"Well, congratulations on your upcoming marriage, Brad. I never would have guessed that was your news. Not in a thousand years."

He hadn't even waited six months after cheating on her and breaking things off to get engaged. The rat. On the other hand, she had skirted disaster and fate had saved her from him.

"Thanks. Let's get that drink sometime and catch up on stuff." Brad cocked a finger gun at her as if shooting the invitation her way.

"Absolutely," she said. "Just as soon as the sun swallows the Earth in a blazing ball of fiery death. I should be available by then to have a drink with you."

John's eyebrows shot up in surprise and he pivoted to waltz off.

What a bunch of lies Brad had been feeding her. He couldn't have actually cared, but she had let herself be convinced.

"Well, I'm sorry you feel that way," Brad said. "I wanted to be mature about it and discuss."

"There is really nothing for us to talk about. My congratulations and best wishes are yours. I need to get back to work." She dropped her gaze to her screen, trying to remember where she had been in her project. But Brad didn't leave. He coughed and leaned further in.

"Since you don't want to do this privately, there is something else I wanted to talk to you about. You have been giving me problems for every assignment this entire past week as well as today. You have dedicated more time and energy to winning this stupid Townsperson contest than you ever spend on just doing your job. The attitude is obvious and I'm not the only one who has noticed." He held out his arms. "The network management has been asking questions about you, and quite frankly, I don't know how to respond."

She steepled her hands. "Have you tried using unbiased facts? I've heard they work wonders."

"Unbiased facts would get you in seriously hot water. Fall in line, Sandra, or start looking for a new position at another station."

"I'm trying to work on my latest assignment this very minute, but so far you've interrupted me to announce you will be marrying the station's receptionist you cheated on me with and to threaten me by making vague statements about network management. Are those facts unbiased enough for you, Brad?"

He clamped his mouth shut and shook a pointed finger at her. A blood vessel throbbed at his temple and she could practically hear his teeth grinding. "I better not get any more attitude. You work for this news station, which means you work for me. And speaking of, I'm having Phoebe follow up on the fire victims, including the family you gave toys to. Apparently, they've found a nice situation with a retired teacher. I want her to do this one. You were a disgrace the last time."

Sandra's breath exploded from her chest in shock. "My story is going to Phoebe? How do you think we know they found a home to stay in?" She pointed at herself. "Because I've been making calls to find out!"

"Yeah. And Phoebe can take it from here. You have summer camp to tell us about."

"Brad, I—"

"You don't get it, do you? Your job, as Junior Reporter, is to do the stories I give you and be a good girl about it. Period. Don't like it? Complain to the network. They want to know more about you and why you are running around in non-professional attire and involving city citizens in your behind-the-scenes preparation."

She gave him a wide, fake smile. "Well, then, I'd better get to work."

There was only way she would escape this and make him pay. Win that contest. Get the promotion. Rub his nose in it until he suffocated.

He sauntered off as if he hadn't just threatened her career and flaunted his sparkling happy life.

Phoebe was going to report on the family she had helped. Would the boys show her hand-made dinosaurs to the folks at home? Sandra's stomach turned. She'd made those for her own niece and nephew—the two little boys were like family, too, since she gave them the toys.

Plus, a feel-good piece like that would earn her a ton of votes.

Covering her mouth with one hand, she shook her head. She was turning into a cold-hearted mercenary, worrying about votes when that family had lost everything they owned in the fire. She barely recognized herself that day.

She walked from the cubicle, furious at Brad but also herself, and headed blindly down the row. She had to hide, and there was only one place to go.

Ladies Room.

The stall door clanged shut and she flipped the lock in place, slumping down on the toilet. Her head fell heavy in her hands.

She didn't care about his upcoming marriage. She hated the bastard anyway. She'd known for six months he was a worthless cheat. But having to stay here under his controlling thumb was unbearable.

Her phone was in her jacket pocket. She felt the old, familiar tug of turn-to-the-devil-you know in response to the aching hollow in her chest. And her devil was Cooper. Her cure for the evils of the world was a bearded trickster. Her poison. Her craving. Her sugar-laden treat.

She was bringing up his messages before she realized what she was doing. To her surprise, there were several from him that afternoon she hadn't read.

Cooper: your new shoes are on your table plus a bottle from my wine cellar

Cooper: for letting me crash on your couch

He had delivered new blue suede pumps and a bottle of wine. Bless him. She kept scrolling.

> Cooper: the Austrians drank the rest
> Cooper: but I'm not mad because they talked me up to everyone near the port and in all the bars since this morning and now I'm first again

She groaned, her voice echoing audibly in the small restroom. She had lost so much ground in the last day, but she could be an adult about it.

> Sandra: Congrats. You must have made a good impression on your house guests

Several seconds ticked by, becoming a minute, maybe more. He must not have noticed the message.

Then a ping.

> Cooper: Why yes I did. Not just them—I'm the town's golden boy
> Cooper: Come have a donut. They are on me. Literally. I will feed you donuts from my chest

Apparently, he'd already forgotten their fling at noon was a one-time thing and was trying to get in her pants again. She shivered at the thought, chuckling. That would be bad. But it would also be terribly fun. He was nothing if not a consummate flirt.

No. It would be meaningless sex and the longer she kept it up, the more risk she ran of getting in a painful situation.

> Sandra: Tempting #nottempting
> Cooper: I gave the Avon lady a call

Sandra had to think a moment before she realized who he was

talking about—at River Crossing park, when he dressed in drag, an Avon representative had parked next to them.

Sandra: how much did you spend?
*Cooper: I'm not saying. Isn't it priceless to have women want to
    chew on your lips?*
Sandra: So you're set for skin care?
Cooper: I'm a deep autumn
Sandra: congratulations
Cooper: I need to wear earth tones, like berry and wine lipstick
Sandra: dear lord
*Cooper: I know. I'm trying the Plumping Divine Wine first. Not
    sure what it plumps, but it must drive chicks wild because wine
    and divine rhyme.*

She put the phone to her chest a moment and shook with laughter until tears slipped free from her eyes. Only Cooper Hall.

No one else could make her laugh like him with his quips and quirks, but things always wound up skewed sideways when Cooper was involved. It didn't have to be that way, though, did it? At Christmas, she was the one who was spooked. She had started feeling things she didn't want to feel, not right after the debacle with Brad, anyway.

That had nothing to do with Cooper, though.

Sandra: getting some work done now.
Cooper: have a great afternoon

She gnawed her lower lip a moment, staring at the beige walls of the toilet. The simple act of texting a few messages to her arch-nemesis had given her new energy for the battle. She would get back to her desk and finish her piece on the summer camp. Then she would start making some calls. One family might have found a safe situation until a permanent solution could be found, but there were dozens of apartments in the building that had burned. She was going to find those people, because this was her superpower. Maybe Cooper could play monkey bars three stories up, but she amplified voices to make the truth known and stories heard in her town. Once upon a time, this town had helped her family, and this time around it would save the victims of the apartment fire.

She would make as many phone calls and pound the pavement as much as necessary to save anyone still struggling to get on their feet after the fire. After that, she was going to win the contest. Who said you couldn't have it all in life? Career, justice, and maybe even Cooper Hall.

CHAPTER 20

Cooper stared at his last message to Sandra, wishing her a great afternoon, and wondered if she would send another little bubble to join his wholly inadequate platitude. Nothing came. He rubbed his stubbled chin, scratching and thinking.

Sex with her had been everything he hoped and dreamed except for Sandra's hasty retreat. Something had happened or had spooked her, but he had no idea what. It was going to drive him fucking crazy until he figured it out, too.

After he left her house, his Uber driver had taken him home, where her new shoes were on his porch, his house guests' clothes and extra fishing gear were flung about in every corner, and enough beers were in his fridge for two more parties. Half a dozen wine bottles lined his counter top, too. He hadn't remembered drinking wine the night before, but it was possible Austrians drank wine for breakfast.

He didn't mind, though. He was in first place thanks to the Austrians staying with him.

No more messages were coming from Sandra, so he had no excuses to not get his ass in gear and finish going through his emails. There was one last one he wasn't sure how to answer. Of all the random people he'd talked to about his start-up business, he hadn't expected the laid back, older guy with the retired-in-the-Caribbean look from karaoke night to write and ask for more information about his portal platform. But Gregg said he was in real estate and was intrigued. Cooper pulled up his standard letter for potential clients and plugged in the correct name at the top. His cursor hovered over the send button.

He ruffled his hair in frustration. He'd already lost so much time that day, there wasn't any more to waste on a personalized answer, but on the other hand, the guy didn't strike him as the standard response type. He'd shown up for karaoke in a Panama hat. Then again, he didn't drop any big company names, which meant he was most likely small fry, and Cooper shouldn't bother wooing his business.

Fuck it. With an attitude like that, he might as well sell his baby and move to the nearest major metropolis. Cooper rolled his shoulders, deleted most of the standard text and started typing.

Of course I remember meeting you, and I'm still bummed the rest of the karaoke battle was canceled....

The afternoon flew by with more emails, another request to tweak part of his platform for his one large client and several negative responses from potential customers. No sign of life from Vic, though. Lauren called, asking if he wanted to come over for dinner, but he told her he was too busy. He ordered pizza delivery and stayed at the office long into the evening, and by ten o'clock that night he had an epiphany. He needed an assistant.

He called Lauren.

Her drowsy voice answered after five rings. "Cooper? Are you all right?"

"I'm good. Good. Let me talk to Gabe."

"Wait." He could hear her shifting in bed. "You woke me up to talk to Gabe?"

"Yeah. I know he doesn't answer this late. Can you put him on?"

"Sure. But first, I need you to take your phone, put it to your left nostril and push it upwards firmly until it hits your brain. Then massage gently while repeating 'don't call your sister late at night unless you're about to die' over and over until you pass out from the pain."

The phone went dead.

He called back.

"Cooper! I'm telling Mom to never fix lasagna ever again!"

"Wait, I've got a temp job for Gabe. Just put him on. And please don't ask Mom to stop making lasagna. That's cruel and unusual punishment for the small crime of calling late at night."

She took a deep breath, huffing into the phone.

He cringed.

"Gabe," she called. "It's for you."

"I love you, sis," Cooper yelled, not sure if she was listening.

"Hey, Cooper," Gabe said. "Coming over for dinner this evening wasn't an option, but calling at ten and putting me in the dog house with your sister is fine?"

"Are you busy?"

"Short answer is yes. I have to placate my raging girlfriend who has to get up at five tomorrow morning and go to work."

"Good. Meet me at the office. I have something to discuss with you. Bring some beer, too." He hung up before Gabe could say no. Sometimes, you just had to get things done.

He cracked his knuckles in satisfaction. Being single had definite advantages. In fact, he loved being single. No doubt. Because, for one thing, he didn't have to worry about his schedule interfering with any relationships. He didn't have to go home at any particular time or arrange his days and nights to suit someone else.

It was ten at night, and he could keep working until two a.m. on a new project and then work twelve hours the next couple of days in a row if he wanted.

This last-ditch effort might not be enough to save his business if he didn't win, though. He rubbed his face with his hands and squinted his over-strained eyes at his screen, but it was impossible to focus for more than a few seconds. He would need more caffeine for the night ahead. The coffee pot was in the far corner, along with the mini-fridge, hidden by a panel divider to create what he called the 'kitchenette.' Other than that, the office was an open space.

The light above him flickered from faulty wiring. The paint on the walls was peeling in a few patches, and the carpet was shabby and worn thin. Vic would have them out of here the minute the winner was announced if he didn't win. Cooper didn't mind the lack of luxury, but investing in a nicer office would be his first move as soon as he could afford it. He sighed, watching the carafe fill with fresh coffee.

Gabe buzzed at the intercom from the downstairs door, and Cooper unlocked it to let him in. It was good to have an unemployed friend who was an expert in big data, and who was willing to show up for odd jobs late at night.

His phone buzzed on his desk with an incoming call. He nodded a greeting to Gabe as he walked in and swiped to answer.

Gabe snorted and pushed past him, a box of beers in hand, and made a beeline for the mini-fridge.

"Hey," Cooper said. It was Vic. So the man was alive.

"Well, did you finally make an appearance at the office today?"

"I've been here since shortly after lunch. I'm still here, in fact. Were you looking for me, because you've had over eight hours to find me."

"Wow. Yeah. I wanted to talk this morning about a potential client out in Durham, but you never showed, so I drove out there to meet them on my own. Funny fact, I would have saved an hour if the office was in Richmond. Anyhoo. We had a nice chat over dinner and I'm staying here tonight. Company bill, of course."

"Of course. Did this client sign anything?"

"Not yet, but we had some excellent steak and wine."

Anger flooded Cooper's system like an electric storm. Flashes of adrenaline in his spine set off the thunder of his pulse in his ears. The swine was feasting on steak and wasting an entire day.

"Considering the company bill is paid in part by my money, it's only fair," Vic said, continuing. "I see you are back at number one in the little town contest. I hope you stay there."

"Thanks. Who is this potential client? What kind of specs are they looking for?"

"I wouldn't worry about any of that. We'll see if they sign, then you can get involved."

Cooper clenched a fist as his heart rate spiked. "I have to worry about clients before they sign, to ensure we can deliver."

"Nah, I covered the basics. You just keep plugging away at what you do, so you win. Otherwise, we relocate."

"We have an agreement to move if I don't win, but there's no reason to move if we sign a few clients in the next couple of days. I'm not going to waste money for nothing."

"If you don't win, I leave. One way or the other, Cooper. See you later."

Vic hung up, leaving Cooper fuming at the crackling paint on the wall.

Gabe handed him a beer. "Since when do you let dickwad make all the business decisions?"

Cooper tipped his beer back for a long drink before answering. "I don't."

"Yeah. I only had half the conversation, it's true, but it sure sounded like he's calling the shots now. So? What's going on?"

"He's found an *out* to our partnership. Shit, Gabe, the money isn't exactly rolling in, but our position on the market is moving in the right direction considering we've only been at this for two years. We are right where we are supposed to be, literally and figuratively. Vic wants to move the office to Richmond so we are closer to clients. Except clients are all over the state, as well as the whole coast, which is my target for the real estate platform. If I don't win the Townsperson contest and get a breather for my baby, he's either pulling out, which will sink me, or I have to agree to move the office."

Gabe crossed his arms, then leaned against the edge of the counter. "Screw that shit. This is your company. You created it, you coded the platform, and did most of the marketing. All he did was show up with his parents' funds. Does he even do anything else here?"

"Not sure, but without those funds, I won't make it long. I'm not going to lie—things could be better, and winning that contest could be a game changer for me in a whole lotta ways. I can't...I can't move. Not now—there are people in Sycamore Cove who need me, but if he skips out, I'll be bussing tables."

"You'd make more pole dancing. I've been told it's quite lucrative."

"Oh, yeah? Who told you that?"

"Your sister." Gabe winked.

Cooper mimicked a hacking sound, like a cat with a fur ball. "If I lose my business I might consider it. Hell, we could even form a team, but keep my sister out of it and away from the audience."

"Speaking of Lauren, you know you don't have to stay in town for her sake. Not anymore. She's mine now and I'm not going anywhere, ever."

"I know you'd take care of her no matter what. And my mom has my step-dad, but there are other reasons..."

"Other people, you mean? One other person in particular?"

"No. Just in general." Cooper swigged back his beer, acting as casual as possible.

"In general, my ass. I know you. This other person you can't leave wouldn't happen to be Sandra, would it? The same Sandra who dumped you last Christmas?"

"The hell are you talking about?"

"Come on, Coop. I know all about your strange history with that hottie. Summer camp, high school, your prank war. You have issues, man, and I think she's the solution."

"How do you know... Lauren. Lauren told you. She talked shit about me and you never told me?" Cooper gestured to himself. "What about the bro-handbook?"

"Girlfriends before dudefriends. Everyone knows that. Besides, Lauren doesn't talk shit, and I don't report what Lauren says, not to anyone, not for any reason. It's called a relationship built on trust for a reason."

"Except now I know. And I'm hurt. I'm deeply wounded." He tilted back his beer and finished the bottle. His own sister... "Holidays will never be the same, just you wait."

"If we could keep Lauren out of the conversation for a minute, I think I mentioned your problems with Sandra."

"I have no problems with—" Cooper's voice broke. He coughed a couple of times as if he had swallowed the beer in the wrong tube. "With Sandra."

Gabe didn't look convinced. He shook his head and scoffed. "You know you could always try to tell her how you feel. I have it on good authority you should always try it when dealing with a woman."

"Yeah. Right. It's not quite that simple." Cooper couldn't admit to how complicated things had become with Sandra. "Shit. All right, she's part of why I have to win this contest and keep my business here in Sycamore Cove. I can't leave this place, or I'll never figure things out."

"So how do I fit in as unpaid labor for you to figure things out with Sandra?"

"Your brainpower. I could really use the help for a couple of days to keep my start-up afloat."

"Fuck it. Fine. I'll work for beer for now. Where do I start?"

"Big data, my friend. Your specialty." Cooper ushered Gabe to Vic's desk (clear of any clutter or actual work in progress), and Gabe set his laptop up. "Thanks for this. I owe you." He would have said more, but his phone buzzed with a message. "Weird. She just sent me a message."

"Sandra wrote to you this late at night? On a Monday?" Gabe laughed and relaxed in his chair. "Maybe you don't have as many problems as I thought."

CHAPTER 21

Sandra: so u think ur hot

Cooper squinted. This was not like her—she didn't do textese.

"Hey," he called to Gabe, "I think Sandra is drunk texting me. Do I get any coolness points for that?"

Gabe rubbed his face and sighed. "No, she just loses points. So many points."

Sandra: Just want to remnind you of all you cant have
Cooper: have you been drinking?
Sandra: maybe. A little
Sandra: our one anfternoon stnd is over but this is what yor missing
Cooper: call uber and come to my office. I have pizza
Sandra: i'm not that drunk
Cooper: I promise you won't regret it.
Sandra: what kind of pizza?

Cooper grinned. She was toasted.

Cooper: pepperoni and pineapple. You know you can't resist when it's salty and sweet

There was pause and Cooper wondered if she had fallen asleep. Too bad. He was having so much fun. He would definitely splurge on pizza if she agreed. And kick Gabe out.

Sandra: feast on this instead

"Oh, shit!" Cooper yelled. He started to stand but fell from his chair instead. He stayed on the floor, hand on his heart and eyes glued to his tiny screen.

"What? Coop, what the fuck, you ok?" Gabe asked.

"I'm…" He pointed vaguely at the screen. Sandra had sent him a picture of herself standing sideways in her new blue suede heels and showed off her legs all the way to her hips. By all appearances, she wasn't wearing anything else.

Gabe rushed over and grabbed the phone, but Cooper wrested it from his hands and cradled it to his chest. "Keep your eyes off my legs, man! These are for me."

"Your legs? You have a picture of your legs on there? Jesus, I thought there was some real problem. You're on the floor like you're having a fucking heart attack."

"I might still have a heart attack. They're Sandra's legs…"

Gabe groaned and stalked off to the fridge for another beer. "You don't pay me enough for this crap. Big data. Explain what you need and stop drooling on her. You know if she's drunk she'll regret sending that pic tomorrow. This isn't fixing anything."

Cooper ignored him and answered Sandra instead.

Cooper: why don't I come tuck you in? Keep you warm.

If she answered yes, he would go to make sure she was sleeping on her side, because if she said yes, she was too drunk to do anything safely.

Sandra: pffffffft. C u latear

Too bad. Cooper stood up and shifted his pants to be more comfortable. How the hell was he supposed to concentrate on big data with Gabe now? The only thing he could think about was his big, urgent need to get over to Sandra's house and explain just how sexy he thought she was. Preferably with his tongue all over that body. Why did she do that to him? And in the same messages remind him their one-afternoon-stand was a one-time thing? He had to convince her otherwise. That was the only solution.

"Cooper?" Gabe snapped at him. "Man, I could be with my girlfriend in bed right now. Are we working or not?"

"Yeah," Cooper said, trying to motivate himself. He shook himself mentally. Getting his business rolling in the right direction was his backup plan if for some unforeseen reason he didn't win the contest. He couldn't afford to fail. The image of her silky legs flashed before his eyes, skin shining like copper, toned curves winding upwards to her high ass, and his mouth almost started watering. He could not afford to fail and leave town. "Yeah. We're working now."

❧

Cooper woke up to a sharp pain in his neck and an aching throb in his back. He blinked and glanced around. The office. He'd fallen asleep on the two-seater, his neck propped up on the armrest. Groaning loudly, he twisted to his feet. How many hours had he slept? Three? Four? It was seven in the morning and he was a disgusting slob who needed coffee and a shower, preferably at the same time.

He grabbed his wallet and keys off his desk and headed for the door.

Sandra was on the other side, hand raised in a fist. He ducked reflexively and then realized she probably wanted to knock on the door. He stepped back, scratching his mess of tangled hair, and grinned sheepishly. She bit her lip and shifted nervously on the tops of very high heels. She was stunning in a blouse and skirt, professional and smooth as satin-coated letterhead paper.

And he was a rumpled newspaper, fit for the recycle bin.

"That picture I sent you last night—it never happened," she said.

"Morning, Sandra. You look great. Off to the news station?" he asked as innocently as possible. The mention of her picture was warming his lower half, as if it needed encouragement that early in the morning. "What picture are you talking about?"

"Exactly." She crossed her arms and tapped her fingernails on one arm. "There was no picture, and if for some reason you see something from me on your phone, you go ahead and delete it, right?"

"Absolutely." As soon as hell froze over. That picture was going with him to the grave.

"Right. Good. We understand one another. I can get on to work now and you can get to..." she waved at his disheveled appearance, "whatever it is you are doing this morning." She pivoted to go.

"Your new shoes are amazing by the way," he called.

She turned on him faster than a cat pouncing on a ray of sunlight. "That picture does not exist, and if you ever, ever show anyone—"

He took her hand and kissed it. "I would never, ever show anyone."

"If you prank me—"

"I wouldn't," he promised. "Ever."

"Well, all right. I have to go now. The florists will be setting up shop. Goodbye, Cooper Hall."

He watched her go, savoring every moment of the sight of her long curves and her scent in the hallway. That goodbye had sounded entirely too final. What had she meant by florists setting up shop? He sent off a quick message to Lauren, who knew everything going on in town, and strolled out of the building into the fresh morning air. Time for coffee and a quick shower at his place.

By the time he was done—drinking coffee while taking a

shower, although it sounded like a great idea, was actually awkward and counterproductive when shampoo wound up in the cup—he had his answer from Lauren. The opening for the wedding arrangements expo was today. It would go on all week in the historical district on the corner of 12th and Emerson. A chance to get cheap flowers for his mom and see Sandra in action was too much temptation to resist. He poured another cup of coffee in a travel mug, asking himself why he wasn't feeling the least bit of caffeine in his system after two cups already, and headed out the door.

The corner of 12th and Emerson was a florists' paradise. At eight-thirty in the morning, the sidewalk was already swarming with young, dewy-eyed women vying for the best arrangements and clamoring for more information on delivery. Flowers exploded from every available surface. Cooper was suddenly very aware how out of place he was among all the females and flora. He was terribly alone in his masculinity.

Sandra was positioned at the host flower shop's entrance, getting ready to start a report. He sighed in relief. She had John and a young guy juggling equipment with her, plus Phoebe, the anchor from the station. Two other men were with him in this jungle of femininity.

"Can I help you?" a voice at his shoulder asked. A perky, older saleslady smiled at him.

"I really hope so. I'm feeling a little bit lost."

"With the language of flowers you can say anything you want. What would you like to say to someone today?"

"I wanted to say..." He hesitated. He was sure that saying *forget the pranks, forget the competitions and arguments we've had since high school, forget the contest and most importantly, forget everyone but me, and I'll do the same for you* was going to be difficult to put in a bouquet. But that was what he wanted to say. Instead, he ducked his head when Sandra looked up. "I wanted to say to my mom that I'm sorry I haven't been calling home on a regular basis."

"Ah," the lady said. "We'd better go to the large floral arrangement table."

He followed her past the front entrance of the store to a sidewalk table practically groaning under the weight of massive vases filled with flowers. She started pointing out the different ones she thought would do the trick, asking about his mom's favorite flowers and colors. He had no idea. Plus, he was only paying attention with one ear as he strained to hear what Sandra was saying to the camera. She was several feet away, though, and inside the entrance's recess. The saleslady held something up in pink, white, and purple. Like springtime fireworks.

"Perfect," he said. Another bouquet on the next table caught his eye. Smaller and refined, it immediately reminded him of Sandra. "I'll take this one, too."

"That's a bridal bouquet. Are you sure?"

"Oh, yeah. To show my…sister. It's perfect. She can't come today. Or the rest of the week. I recognized the roses, but what are these other flowers?" He pointed to the crepe petal puffs of pale pink among the off-white roses.

"Peonies. I'll wrap those for you over at the cash register."

He let her go first, and as she wrapped the bridal bouquet, he snapped a picture of himself to post in front of the tables. He posted it with a quick, "Men, don't neglect your moms."

Although the table was near the entrance, Sandra must have gone around the corner. He tapped his leg for a moment and then carefully peeked around the brick corner. Sandra had her back to the building, her arms crossed and one hip out. She was shaking her head at her boss, the ex-boyfriend. Cooper pulled back, not wanting to be caught listening.

"That'll be $185.45."

He almost choked. It was possible he should have asked the prices first. With a wry smile, he gave her his credit card. A man's voice approached, and he realized Brad was coming around the corner.

"Fine, Sandra. Go do your interviews with whomever you like. This doesn't change anything. You don't get a promotion for nothing, so you can either win the contest, like we agreed, or you can buckle down and do what I say. These family interviews you want to do are on top of your other assignments. And you need to get in touch with the network. Someone is sending you an email today."

"Yes, sir." Sandra stepped into view, anger brewing in her expression. Cooper had an overwhelming urge to tackle Brad and rub his face in the pavement for upsetting her, but he only clenched and then relaxed his fist.

"Here you go, and thanks for stopping by," the saleslady said, handing him the two bouquets.

Sandra's eyes whipped in his direction. She frowned and then nodded as if she found him tying her bra to a flagpole. Which, for the record, he had never stooped to doing. She approached, anger brewing like a cloud around her.

"Did you overhear my entire conversation just now? What is this? Are you spying on me?"

He cleared his throat, briefly debating on whether or not to deny everything. "I heard some of it, yeah. In my defense, I didn't intend to, but he was speaking pretty loudly."

"Well." She paused and licked her lips. "Well, now you know why I am going to win this contest."

"Something about a promotion?"

"For a promotion, yes." Her face was cold and unreadable. "And to pick my own stories."

"Those are two good reasons. A promotion. That jackass off your back. I'd be motivated too."

"Yeah. I want him off my back, but more than that, if I don't win, I'm out of here."

"Out...out? What do you mean by out of here?"

"I mean, I am leaving this town. It might break my heart to leave my mama and sisters, their babies, everyone, but I cannot stay here like this. Not with him—"

"I understand. I'd leave, too." Cold swept through his chest. He stepped away and remembered the smaller bouquet in his hand. "This is for you, actually." He set it on the edge of the nearest table, unable to get closer to hand it to her.

"A bridal bouquet? Are you serious?"

"Think of it as a souvenir of your day today. You deserve flowers, and this was a special wedding expo. It doesn't mean anything else. And there you have it. I'd better get back to work, so I'll see you later."

"Wait," she called and hurried after him. She caught his arm. "The contest competition is still on. Right?"

"Absolutely. You and me. Only one can win. I have to go. See you later." He forced himself to walk away. He had to walk away and not look back at her, or he would lose it.

Now he barely had a handful of days to figure this out.

CHAPTER 22

A man posts a picture of himself buying flowers for his mother and the world stands still to applaud him. Unbelievable. Annoyed, Sandra blew off a curl of hair that kept falling on her nose. Maybe she should head to the nearest hardware store, fill up a basket with duct tape, WD-40, and a couple of hammers, and then post it online saying, *I love you, Dad!*

But it would never have the same outpouring of love and attention as Cooper reminding the guys of the town to buy flowers for their moms. Still. She should troll his post with a picture of her and a wrench. Actually...

Maybe she should. He'd been avoiding her since they ran into each other at the flower expo two days ago on Tuesday morning. It was only Thursday afternoon, but his absence left a strange hole in her life. Although she kept looking over her shoulder and double checking her car for pranks, she had the odd feeling he wasn't planning anything. And his lack of pranks was far worse than anything he'd ever done to her before.

What she couldn't figure out was why he was avoiding her. He didn't answer his phone when she called once and didn't text back when she congratulated him on maintaining first place. That one really stung. He was winning *and* ignoring her. No jokes, no tricks, no insufferable taunting. Who the hell did he think he was? He finally got her in bed and then drops her like trash?

Wait a minute.

Sandra smacked her forehead. He was a player. It wasn't a secret, and she knew perfectly well he was allergic to commitment. Then again, she was the one who had said their fling was for one time only, to make up for missed opportunities in the past. One time, then move on.

Except he was moving on a bit too much.

All right. She was going nowhere with this obsessive analyzing. Was Cooper sitting in his car somewhere with a burger worrying why she wasn't pranking him? She scoffed. Doubtful. She wolfed the last bites of her lunch and turned the key. The engine sputtered to life. As she pulled out of the shady spot at Sycamore Cove Park, her phone jangled with a call. The number was from out of state and she didn't recognize it.

"Sandra Mercy Kelly from WCC 12. Can I help you?" she said.

"Hey, this is Joan from Coastal Connections. Is this a bad moment or can we chat?"

Sandra slammed on her brakes. The person from the network—Brad had warned her someone would email, not call. She took a quick breath and swallowed, hoping her voice would be steady. "I'd love to chat, but I have an appointment for a story and I'd hate to be late."

"I understand. Priorities, right?"

"Can I call you back? This evening, or—" Damn it, she had another story for Brad to look into and then the chili meet and greet...

"I am going out of town later today, actually. I'll be close to your neck of the woods in fact. I'll try to send a message and set up a time, maybe even meet in person. Sound good?"

"Of course. Of course. Let me know." Her voice had turned breathless. Management from the network was contacting her directly. Was that bad? Brad made it sound bad, but if they wanted her fired, then all they had to do was tell him.

"And Sandra," Joan said, "I like that the story is more important than me calling out of the blue. Go get 'em."

"Thanks. Have a nice day." But Joan had already hung up.

Wait. Joan who? Had she given her last name? Sandra huffed in frustration and checked her watch. She didn't have time to do any digging now. Thinking about Cooper had already put her behind schedule by making her eat more.

You gotta get that man out of your head.

Besides, she'd see him tonight at the get-together for all the candidates. In fact, she'd interview him along with anyone else she could corner for a few words in between trips to the chili buffet. Until then, she had to meet two more people from the burned apartment building to find out how they were doing, track down an insurance agent because Brad told her to, call the former maintenance man because he might have information she needed, and get cleaned up for tonight. Plus wait and see if Joan sent her a message. So, really no time to play.

She had to look to her best so he would know exactly what he was missing out on.

On the evening of the chili buffet—the Townsperson of the Year organizers wanted to give the contestants a chance to get to know one another and discuss the ups and downs of the contest to improve future ones—Cooper alternately swirled the champagne in his glass, pretending to listen in on conversations, or prowled the length of the ballroom, looking for Sandra.

The presentation was about to start, but she was nowhere to be found. Usually, she would arrive an hour early for something like this to talk to people as they arrived. She would pounce on them while they were fresh and cheerful.

The ballroom where the organizers for the Townsperson of the Year were hosting the buffet was filled with the myriad of contestants and their spouses or partners. All sorts of people from every walk of life (or at least the walks of life found in Sycamore Cove, which was surprisingly varied) milled around the appetizers table or stood in groups, chatting and clinking glasses together.

A judge mingled with a librarian and a car-shop repairman to talk about education. The gossip columnist listened to a former mayor and the coffee barista argue about zoning. A dozen people he didn't know were laughing at fishing jokes, discussing the weather, or swapping survival stories of when the last hurricane hit.

Even Sandra's idiot ex was there, schmoozing the other guests.

He heard their voices as he paced, like annoying insect buzzing that he could understand but wished would disappear.

It was hot and stuffy in the room. They must still have the heaters on at the end of May. He set his champagne, which was warm and flat, on a table and loosened the top of his shirt.

An organizer took place behind the podium and hit her glass with a fork. "I believe the buffet is ready, so come and help yourselves, then take a seat. There's no arrangement, sit wherever you like. Thank you! We'll start the presentation soon."

Where was she?

He rounded the drinks table again as people lined up for the chili.

At the double doorway, Sandra appeared in a beige, sleeveless dress with a red belt and a row of brown buttons down the front, and red heels. She hurried in, exposing too much leg for Cooper's physical comfort. He groaned under his breath again, but not from impatience, sternly ordering his cock not to get any ideas. Goddam. Somebody drench him with a bucket of ice water now.

She stormed across the ballroom like a gust off the Atlantic, sweeping aside contestants and organizers as she searched for someone.

He grabbed a champagne glass and downed it in one go, set the empty flute on the table, picked up two full ones, and strode towards her.

Another man intercepted her. Brad. Son of a monkey's ass.

The head of the organization, Ethan Carter, chose that moment to call again for everyone's attention. "I was supposed to tell you earlier—there are surveys at each seat for you to fill out, or not, so we have some written feedback on how the contest was handled this year. That is all. Carry on." He motioned to the chili buffet, where the guests were forming a long line.

Apparently, Brad had been first, and he had taken a second bowl of chili for Sandra, which he pressed into her hands. Then, insistent, he escorted her to a nearby table that was rapidly filling up.

Cooper, skipping the chili for now, strolled over to take the last available seat at the large, round table. There was a petite blonde several seats down and opposite them. He recognized her as the barista, Mackenzie, and he gave her his most charming smile. "Excuse me, would it bother you to exchange seats?"

"No problem," she said and hopped up.

Sandra watched his maneuvering with a deep frown. Brad put his arm around her chair.

"Hi," Cooper said to them.

An odd expression flitted in and out of Sandra's face, as if she was happy to see him. But whatever it was, she wiped it off and replaced it with disdain.

"I'm surprised to see you here, Cooper," she said. "You've been missing in action so long, I thought they'd have search parties out looking for you."

Brad ducked his head and hissed, "Sandra, you have zero chill. Can we not antagonize the contestants who are also your opponents?"

"You're worried about my chill?" She curled her hands on the table. "Reporters don't need chill, you know that. They need answers." This last part was shot at Cooper, and it stung.

"It's been a rough couple of days. I've been pulling twelve- to fourteen-hour shifts trying to get a new component ready on the platform for better data analysis. Gabe has been volunteering quite a bit of his time to get it rolling and, hopefully, I'll be able to pay him back soon. Literally, pay him soon."

She opened her mouth to say something, but paused, lips parted. She must have changed her mind—her expressions softened slightly.

"That's all cleared up?" Brad asked her, tilting his head over her shoulder. "Good. So, where the hell were you? You were supposed to be here an hour ago."

"I was stuck at Safe Home Insurance, digging up a non-existent scandal as per your instructions," Sandra snapped.

"And where's John?"

"He dropped me off and went to visit an uncle at the hospital."

"That figures," Brad said, shaking his head.

The glance she gave him could have withered a full-grown oak.

One of the judges called for everyone to watch a short presentation at the front of the room. The lights dimmed, and a panoramic, touristy view of the town appeared on the white screen.

Cooper tapped his foot impatiently while everyone watched a short overview of what being the Townsperson of the Year should mean and the positive influence the contest should have on the town and for tourism and business.

It was worse than being stuck in class when you knew there was a fight waiting for you behind the building as soon as the last bell rang. He didn't know if she wanted to fight this battle or could use some backup, though.

Cooper's phone was in his jacket pocket and he took it out to hide it under the table and write a quick message. Sandra didn't react when he hit send, though, and he didn't hear her usual jingle.

The presentation continued, and he half listened, trying to catch Sandra's eye as people got up to quietly wander back and forth from the buffet. She didn't get up, though, so he wasn't able to get in another apology or ask if she was all right. He'd seen her call and her message from a couple of days ago, but was in so deep with his project, he kept telling himself he'd answer her soon. This Hail Mary to make his platform sexier to clients might be too late to save his business—but he had to try. If he got his financial worries out of the way, he could drop out at the last minute and let Sandra coast into first.

It was time for desserts, and Ethan stood up. He explained how this year was on a shorter, more intense schedule than the following years would be, as there was less time for the candidates to prepare themselves. They were especially looking for people who contributed to the community through business, activities, volunteer time, and more, and overall he was overwhelmed by the positive responses the contest had produced.

Voting during the last two days, Friday and Saturday, would be blind, so no one would know who held what position. Plus, the judges would evaluate the candidates again to cast their votes to validate the top three. After that, they would host the grand finale and hand out the prizes.

Cooper processed the information in the back of his mind, but his senses hummed with Sandra's every movement. The stiff posture, the way she jabbed her food, her nostrils flaring every time Brad got too close, and how she avoided his eye contact.

Sandra stood up the second she was done with her cake.

"I'll drive you home," Brad said, tossing his napkin. Another judge was presenting companies who offered prizes, and Cooper had to concentrate to eavesdrop. "That way we can discuss what has happened recently at the station."

She rolled her eyes. "Please, there is nothing I care to hear you say."

"This childish behavior has to stop. You need a ride and we need to talk."

"I assure you, I don't need to talk."

"Just wait for me—"

Cooper stood up, his chair screeched out from under him. "Holy Hot Tamales."

Sandra shot him a startled look, a crease forming between her eyebrows as she frowned at him.

"Holy Hot Tamales, right now," Cooper insisted.

"Right now, right now?"

"No, not now." Brad took Sandra's elbow.

Cooper's vision blurred for a second as adrenaline spiked. Brad was really pushing his luck that evening.

"Excuse me, Brad." She pulled free and stepped briskly from the table.

Cooper walked with her the rest of the way through the ball room and out to the hotel lobby.

"I can't wait to hear this," Sandra muttered. She placed a hand on her hip and raised her eyebrows. "This had better be good, Cooper Hall. You would not believe how tired I am of games tonight."

He allowed himself one grateful second of silence that she had allowed him to use the old code word from their junior year in high school. They would temporarily stop bugging each other to prank a nasty-tempered bully making Sandra's life miserable. Cooper's broken nose was his lifelong souvenir from it.

"If I had to listen to him try and coerce you into his car one more time for a talk, I was going to punch him, and I've been working very hard to control impulses like that." He took a deep breath. "Listen, you need a ride home and not with that putrescent piece of garbage, and I need out of here before the self-congratulating judges bore me to death." He cocked an eyebrow, waiting for her answer.

"Holy Hot Tamales?" she asked.

"You'll have the standard thirty minutes." Not exactly true—he wouldn't be pranking her whether or not the truce was over.

She visibly relaxed and even broke half a smile. "Let's get out of here, then."

CHAPTER 23

Sandra dropped into Cooper's passenger seat and promptly took off her heels with a sigh of relief.

"If you need help taking anything else off, I'm here for you," Cooper said, bringing his car to life with a quick twist of the key.

"Keep dreaming, Mr. Jealous." She massaged her aching toes, not caring what Cooper thought of her. Just to be mean, she gave a soft moan of pleasure.

Except now he was staring at her instead of watching the road.

"Red," she said.

"What?"

"Red! The light!" She pointed frantically at the traffic lights and he slammed on the brakes right at the intersection line.

"Would you mind waiting to do that until I'm not driving?" he asked.

"Why?"

"It's distracting—I might have a toe fetish for all you know. A car accident would be bad."

"You don't have a toe fetish. Someone would have posted that juicy detail online by now if you did. How distracting can it be? I was just rubbing my feet."

"You make that same little noise when you want to be kissed more."

Electric flutters came to life in her chest. He noticed things about her she had barely known herself. The light turned green, and he faced the road, turning his dark eyes away from her.

"Well, I think we are all done with the kissing, re our agreement. Remember?"

"I remember. One and done. Unless, of course, you change your mind..."

Heat swarmed through her veins and landed in her most southern regions, and flushed her skin. At the same time, she had goosebumps and shivered with cold. Hell yeah and hallelujah, she wanted to change her mind. But she had to have some self-respect since he had tossed her aside like a candy wrapping. "Want the truth? I almost changed my mind when I called you Tuesday night. Too bad you never called back."

"It wasn't that I didn't want to," he said. "But to take the time you deserved, I would have had to drop—"

His voice broke off.

"Drop...what? The project at your office?"

"You're right. All work and no play is not good. So am I to understand by your little foot massage noises, that you want me to kiss you again? You probably need my kisses. I understand."

She crossed her arms and clamped her lips closed as he navigated the backroads out of town and through waves of neighborhoods to her house. He was back to his quips and conceited self-delusions. Why did he have to be this way? She tried to ask what was wrong and he tried to get her in bed.

They rolled into her gravel driveway, which curved around to the back of the house and she got out without a word.

He pushed open his door and stood. "Deny it. Deny it to my face that you don't love it when I kiss you. Try and deny it, Sandra, because I don't believe you."

She stormed back to him until only the car door kept them apart. "I deny it. And listen closely, because I'm only going to explain this once. We had a connection the other day. A real connection for the first time. And for the first time in my life, I made the mistake of thinking maybe there was more to you than jokes and pranks. You say you pulled twelve to fourteen hour shifts these last couple of days? That's why you didn't have time for me? That's why you couldn't call me? I have never met a more immature, attention-greedy man-boy than yourself."

"I can't claim to be better or worse than other people you know, but believe me, I'm…" He paused.

She crossed her arms, determined to wait for him to talk. Finally, talk to her.

"I'm sorry. Every hour I spent at work I regretted it wasn't with you. But in order to be there for you, I had to stay away."

"Mmm. You had to stay away in order to be there for me. Why? What's really going on with you? You've never been like this to me before."

"I've never been this close to your naked feet twice in the same week before. It's done things to my head. To my body. Things you wouldn't believe."

"That's it, I'm out." She slashed her hands through the air as if she could cut through the bullshit. "Like I said, there is nothing I would rather do than give your inner-fourteen-year-old a good smack upside the head."

"My inner-fourteen-year-old would love to be smacked."

"You better—"

He reached over the door with both hands to cup her head and draw her face an inch from his. The surprise stopped her words stopped mid-sentence and she widened her eyes. If he moved his thumb just a little, he could stroke her lower lip. If he leaned forward he would kiss her.

If, if, if.

If only she didn't burn to kiss Cooper again. If only he wasn't so damn hot. If only she wasn't dying in slow increments to have Cooper to herself for a few seconds.

But she hated the turmoil in her soul and wished she could yell at him to leave her alone once and for all. Or to stop the games and be serious.

The muted light of street lamps gleamed on his forehead and cheekbones, and created black pools of shadows in his eyes and neck. The whisper of his cologne and warm, summer scent spun her head. She had to break this spell he could put on her with a snap of his fingers.

She arched her neck and narrowed her eyes. "Were you planning on doing something?"

"You see?" he asked. "You like when I kiss you, but you can't admit it. No one shows you how to have fun like I do."

"I wouldn't call the things you do to me fun."

"Oh, Sandra..." He closed his eyes a moment. "That only makes me want to rise to the challenge."

"If you are up for a challenge, then be honest with me. Tell me if you want more than another casual get-together. That you aren't interested in a second one-night stand. You offered to bring me home for a reason, and not because you were bored at the buffet."

"When you say honest, do you mean don't lie to you?"

"Cooper Hall." She stepped out of his reach, shaking her head. "I appreciate the drive home. But I won't be needing anything else tonight."

"Sandra—"

"Wait, I'm not done. Not only am I good on my own, but I'm going to win this competition. I hate to stomp on your ambitions and your heart in the same evening, but that's the way it is. I don't know if those hours you spent at the office were in preparation of your win, but it won't happen."

"In that case, Sandra, I wish you all the luck in the world. Of course, I intend to win, too. The prize at the end is too good to pass up."

"Bye, Cooper. Drive safely."

He gave a lazy salute and slid back into his seat.

A thought occurred to her.

She checked her watch. Since he had hit the table and called the truce, half an hour had passed.

That was exactly the official length of time the Holy Hot Tamales truce was supposed to last. Twatwaffles, they had been such idiots in high school.

The pranks could start again any second now. Or anything she wanted could start. That was how it was with Cooper.

He was staring at her, eyebrows raised in a silent question.

"What?" she asked. "Aren't you leaving?"

"You are holding my door."

She glanced at her hand. Sure enough, she had a good grip on his car door. She jerked away, but Cooper caught her other hand before she could go. He placed a kiss on her knuckles.

"Don't," she warned.

His lips hovered a hair's breadth from her skin, the down feather tickles of his breath sent shivers up her arm. No, she couldn't trust Cooper, but worse, she couldn't trust herself around him. "I'm going inside now."

"You should," he whispered.

"I am." But her feet weren't obeying. Her whole body was on standby, awaiting instructions her brain was unable to give, not while his breath was teasing her hand and the warmth of his long fingers enveloped hers.

"About that prize," he said gruffly.

"I know, that's all that matters to you."

"More and more, I think...this wouldn't be another one-night stand." His lips brushed her skin while he kept his eyes locked on hers. He was pushing her, seeing how far he could go. When she didn't pull away, he kissed her again, an inch higher.

"Which proves what I've suspected for the longest time," she said. "You'll say anything—"

He turned her hand over and kissed her wrist. The flare of sensation cut off her voice. She was about to insult him. She should insult him.

But that electric shock of lips and rough beard was all she could think of. The skin was so thin there it was practically transparent, half a dozen dark veins pulsed narrow as threads, and the lines of tendons pushed up in miniature ridges. The nerves quivered with the scratch of his beard bristles as he lifted his face.

"One time will never be enough," he whispered.

"Sweet talking, son of a—"

Then he kissed her again, a few inches higher on the inside of her arm. Dizziness that had nothing to do with the wine from dinner hit her head and she was spinning without moving. She was falling while still standing on her feet.

The tip of his tongue touched her just below the inner bend of her elbow. And he pressed his lips down. She gasped. That spot was much too sensitive. She had weaknesses she never imagined before and he was exploiting them. She let him. He pulled her slowly around the car door until nothing separated them anymore.

Her body shook and a hot pressure built in her core. That ache was rapidly becoming a need that only Cooper could fulfill. The infuriating and irresistible trickster who caught her off guard at every turn now held the key to what she wanted again and again.

He put his hand to her waist to draw her near, and dropped to the driver's seat, leaving his head level with her waistband. She let herself take a step towards him, heart pounding like a bird trapped under a cat's paw. He drew up her shirt hem. Her skin prickled in the cool air and he grazed the little bumps with his thumbs before tracing a line of kisses around her navel. Each kiss left a hint of moisture that made her shiver and need him more.

"Cooper, say it again."

"One time will never be enough."

CHAPTER 24

He was right. Sandra had been fooling only herself, thinking one time with Cooper Hall would be enough to satisfy her after all those years of circling each other. He probably knew her better than she knew herself, but she barely knew him at all. It was time to fix the imbalance.

A flood of moisture descended to her panties and heat flushed her cheeks. Her nipples ached, pressing tightly against her bra. The hand around her waist pulled her downwards. She raked her fingernails through his beard along the strong line of his jaw bone to reach his hair. He dragged his rough chin up her stomach to her breastbone, kissing and licking lightly until he reached the front snap of her bra.

She shuddered, sliding one knee across his lap. The space was too tight to be comfortable, and the steering wheel dug into her back. She pressed forward against Cooper, reveling in the hard feel of his chest and roped muscles. This was where she wanted to be. Arms wrapped around his neck and arching backwards.

The more his mouth covered her chest, the more she wanted him to explore her. When he tugged back the edge of her bra, she leaned into him, offering herself up to him. Whenever, whatever he wanted.

His wet mouth on her nipple sent waves crashing through her body, until her legs straddling his lap went weak. He supported her weight, nipping and sucking at her tender breasts.

She pulled at his shirt. He tore it over his head and she ran her hands across his back.

He was beautiful, like a mirror image of the moon, gleaming pale with dark secrets in the mountains and valleys of his body and a hidden side he never showed the world. She showered him with raindrop kisses that should never be his.

Shuddering, he gripped her hips hard enough to leave bruises and she moaned into his silken hair. Sweat broke out on her skin, leaving her shivering although burning hot.

Pants. She undid the button on Cooper's, and yanked at the waistband, but she couldn't get them off in this cramped position. The wheel hit her back as she lifted off him to kneel on the seat. He unzipped his jeans, pushing them down along with his boxers. His cock stood proud and free.

Her skirt was riding high on her hips and all she had to do was push aside her lace panties. Wet, velvet skin hit her fingertips and touching herself made her jump, her sex quivering with desire. She touched herself again to move the crotch of her panties and Cooper's hand covered hers.

"Show me," he said, breath hot in her ear. His hand moved with hers, circling the valleys of her sex, every stroke a flame heating her core and burning to ash any thought but having more of him.

His finger dipped in. Once. Twice. Three times and stayed, searching deeper. She gasped and moved her hands to his shoulders to sway against him, begging without words for him to continue.

Don't stop. Don't stop. Don't stop.

Her legs trembled from crouching over him and she couldn't wait any longer. She tilted her hips and moved towards him, aching to have him press inside her.

"Wait," he whispered. He reached for the glove box, popping it open and digging inside, the glaring light an unwelcome guest. He found a square condom package and used his teeth to tear it open.

She lowered herself onto him as his fist rolled on the condom. They moved together. Each thrust was limited in the cramped seat, but urgent and needy. Sweat beaded on her chest and he licked it off as he kissed his way across her collar bone and then down to her breast.

He sucked first one nipple and then the other, the cups of her bra shoved underneath them. She held on to his arms and shoulders, and he guided her hips to meet each thrust. Caught in the power of his grip and the maelstrom of her own needs, she flowed with his movements, bucking her hips to take him in. And he filled her completely. Drove her wild.

She couldn't hold back from crying out and didn't want to. When he thrust faster, she arched back and grabbed the dash for support. His moonlight skin contrasted with her dusky night skin and she marveled at their bodies, flowing together but perfectly opposite. An orgasm started to grow in her, like the beating of a bird's wings. The beats rose through her, one after the other, and she was lifted by them until she soared.

Cooper carried her through the orgasm and held her tight when she fell forward. He cradled her, hands in her hair and on her wet skin.

She hadn't even noticed his orgasm. It must have happened, the way he was breathing hard for air and relaxed in the seat.

The uncomfortable angle of her knees and the wheel in her back became unbearable. She leaned back as far as she could and closed her shirt as best she could, then pushed the door open.

"That would have been more comfortable inside," she said, laughing.

"I was being polite and waiting for an invitation. Can I come in? Stay a while?"

She climbed out, less gracefully than she would have wanted, but

Cooper lifted her hips to make sure she didn't fall on her ass at least. She took his hand. "Come on."

"Let me get my pants before I stand up." He grinned, hiking his jeans up and zipping them closed. When he got out of the car he smothered her in a hug and they stumbled towards her door, glued together like teenagers.

"Last time I ask, but it's still bothering me," Sandra said as she opened her back door. "The project you're doing for work and this contest…"

"You cannot make me talk about work. Not tonight."

"I don't want to make you talk, but I feel like I'm missing some piece of information. The second I explained why I had to win, when we were at the bridal flower expo, you clammed up and took off."

"Maybe I don't want to you leave if you lose." He turned her around to face him. "Have you thought of that?"

"I wouldn't leave the next day."

"Not good enough."

"You want me to win?" She frowned at him. She had wanted Cooper to stop joking around, but this was beyond anything she had imagined. "Are you thinking of dropping out? How serious is this?"

"Fairly serious."

She couldn't speak for a moment. "Why were you putting in so many hours all of a sudden at your start-up?"

"I usually put in about ten hours a day. Will you stop grilling me about work now? There are other things I'd like to do right now." He waggled his eyebrows at her, but his heart wasn't in it. Something lingered in his expression—fear or worry. In the near dark, it was hard to say.

"You have to win the contest, too. Don't you?" Her heart hammered in her chest. He had to win. That had to be the reason.

"I don't have to win the contest. I have to make my start-up profitable, that's all. And it's my problem."

She touched his cheek. "But if you won, it would be easier. There's money, support, and publicity from other businesses in town. Prizes look good to prospective clients. Shit. How bad is it?"

He closed his eyes, lips pressed together hard. With a sigh, he pulled away to cross his arms and lean against her door frame. "Bad, but only because my partner is threatening to pull out and take his investment with him. Strategically, we are where we should be after a couple of years. We have a solid product, several good clients, plans to expand, and lots of potential. But if he goes, I either have to go with him, which is unlikely, or find a job at a bar, which is more likely."

"God, Cooper, I had no idea your start-up was on shaky ground."

"Well, it is. Have I talked about work enough? Do you have any other questions? Would you like to see my business plan or the coding for the platform?"

"Don't be like that," she said, shaking her head at him. He had slaved at his start-up since graduating, building it from nothing. This was his dream, his creation. She couldn't let him walk away from it. "If you need this win to keep your start-up, then fight for it."

He wouldn't look at her. "What I need..."

"What do you need?"

"I needed you to not ask me about work, so I wouldn't have to think about it for at least the night."

"Coop," she whispered, "why would you hide this from me? Besides the stupid pranks and this contest, we have history. You can talk to me."

"Not about this. You gotta win. You're gonna win. I'm going to lose. So, nothing to talk about."

"No. You need to win just as much as me." He started to turn from her, and she grabbed his arm. "Don't walk away. We can figure this out. You don't have to lose everything—you can't lose everything because you won't fight for yourself."

"What do you think all those hours were for?" His voice was rough with frustration.

"But is it enough? You don't seem too optimistic, but that doesn't mean we can't figure something out together."

He covered her hand with his—so warm and strong. She realized she was trembling. "*We* aren't doing anything for my business. It's enough if you don't lose everything because of me."

"Stay," she said. "Come inside. We'll look at this together."

"Together?" He stepped back, out of her reach. "This isn't your problem, Sandra. It's mine. And I'll figure it out."

"Don't you dare you drop out of the contest. Not for me. Not if it costs you your dream."

"I'll call you," he said. "Or text as soon as I can."

"Don't do this." She reached for him. "Stay with me now."

"You'd be ready to lose?" He spread his arms in a question. "So I could win? And you think that's all right with me? When I could fix this with a phone call?"

"Don't you fucking do it, Cooper. You have never seen me mad, not mad like I would be if you did that."

"Funny thing is, I get to do what I want."

"Honey, it goes both ways. You think the pranks and contest stuff was bad? Just wait. I will make you so miserable, you will have to leave town, anyway," she said, jabbing a finger in his chest.

"I will be leaving town anyway. The second I don't win, Vic is out of the partnership unless we move the office." He hunched his shoulders. "But I don't deserve to win. Not like you do. The things you do for this town, always reaching out to others, digging for the truth. So here it is, you got my vote."

She was tempted to take off her shoes and throw them at his head as he walked to his car. "I swear, I will prank you until you die, Cooper Hall. If you drop out of this contest, you will regret it. I will never forgive you."

She sounded like some idiot kid throwing a tantrum. But he kept walking away. He climbed in his car and drove off. Hands shaking, she unlocked the door and rushed inside, sick to her stomach.

He would lose his start-up if he didn't win, but he was going to sabotage his chances for her sake. No. She couldn't let him. He had family here, too, and had poured years into his business. She hadn't planned on any more pranks, but that man could drive a saint to start kicking the furniture. She leaned over the kitchen table, hand pressed to her stomach, and tried to think.

Cooper had been a part of her life since that long ago summer camp the summer before they started high school. He had saved her from ennui, complacency, and the school bully. While the pranks stopped when they signed the contract a few days prior to leaving for different colleges, he was still a part of her life whenever she returned home.

His presence filled this town and haunted the back of her mind. His trickster smile and Appalachian mountain man style stirred up longings and grated her nerves raw until the only thing that would ease the frustration was more of him.

And they had been so close to starting something good together. She doubled in half, remembering his body moving with hers. They had almost made it.

Where not even the pranks could make them stay mad at one another, this stupid contest had wedged itself between them and crushed their chances of being together. How were they supposed to find happiness on equal terms now? It was horribly simple—if she won, he lost his start-up, and it would be her fault. Four years of dedication and work for nothing. If he won, she'd never stay here under Brad's micro-managing thumb, even if it meant leaving her family behind. If they both lost?

Sandra headed for her bathroom, peeling off her dress and underthings as she went. She stepped under the nozzle while the water was still cold, a shock to her hot skin.

If they both lost, they'd head off to different towns, full of regret and spite. Cold water ran off her feverish face and chest, warming by the time it reached her legs. She didn't move. She let the spray pelt her skin while she broke the problem down to its simplest parts. She could try and win and if she succeeded, get her promotion. Or she could try and lose and possibly Cooper would win and keep his start-up. Either way, she was losing him.

CHAPTER 25

"What do you mean it's too late to withdraw from the contest?" Cooper rubbed his face as Ethan Carter's secretary, who was handling administration and questions for the contest, babbled about rules, commitments, and responsibilities on the other end of the phone line. She paused and he continued his argument. "But doesn't my calling and asking to not be in the running kind of guarantee I won't win?"

She stammered out some vague niceties and he thanked her for her time and hung up.

Although it was nearly nine in the morning, he'd been up since six and working from home for over an hour. But there hadn't been any emails from new or existing customers throwing money at his business. He'd tried and failed to turn things around with a last-minute project.

He couldn't fix his problems. So what made him think he could fix things with Sandra, or for her? He couldn't even back out of the contest, apparently. She said since this was Friday and the finale was on Sunday, it was too late.

They wouldn't have much choice, though. You couldn't force someone to accept prizes.

This had Sandra's signature all over it. She must have contacted them and somehow made them promise to keep all the candidates in the running until the finale. Plus, the voting was blind the last couple of days, so he didn't know if someone else had moved to first place. Maybe this was all for nothing. He'd been going strong, but Sandra or one of the others might have caught up.

It was practically the weekend, for fuck's sake. He should be planning his drinking binge. Come to think of it, why was he even bothering with the emails or work today? Even if he played nice with Vic and moved the office to a larger city, he was the only one putting in the real hours, and he couldn't make this a profitable business on his own.

Yep. He was going nowhere fast today.

True to his word about writing her, the second he hung up, he sent Sandra a message. She complained when he ignored her. Maybe she'd start complaining when he was honest.

Cooper: your prank is not impressive
Sandra: you don't like it?
Sandra: wait until you see tonight's broadcast

What the hell was that? A threat? A promise? Or a prank. Damn it.

He poured himself another cup of coffee—his fourth that morning, but they weren't waking him up—and wondered what the hell she had cooked up to make it impossible to quit the contest.

His phone buzzed, jittering on the counter.

Lauren: this thing Sandra asked me to plan should be great
Lauren: can't wait to see you there

She added a line with a bunch of hearts, smiley faces and a castle.

Awesome. A castle. He was still working on coffee and now he might need a whiskey instead.

Would it be worth swallowing his pride and calling Sandra? To ask her not to do whatever the hell it was she was going to do? He might as well head to the beach and yell at the tide to turn. He would know soon enough. She had said to watch her broadcast that evening, and he had to put in as many hours as possible until then at the office. His patch he had made with Gabe for the platform was good enough to plug in without bugging the rest of it. Which meant clients could start using it soon as an added service to have better input on their potential sales data.

As he crawled into his car, he caught the faint scent of her perfume. The lingering hint of warm vanilla and fresh citrus was like a slap to the face, but he paused, breathing her in before the morning breeze carried her off. Whatever he had to do to help her win—tricks, schemes, manipulation, whatever—he would do it. It wouldn't be his fault if she didn't get that promotion. The answer for now was to keep fighting.

He picked up a fifth cup of coffee on his way to the office, a large one, but he swore it would be the last one of the morning. By the time he sat down at his computer, the fog in his head was definitely clearing.

He cracked his knuckles and loosened his neck. He could do this. Ten hours of concentration. Answer emails, make some calls, do some coding and some marketing stuff to spread the news about his —wait, what the...

His jaw dropped as he read and reread the subject from the most recent email.

Townsperson of the Year beauty pageant and fundraiser fun before the finale!

What had she done? Beauty pageant? That wasn't like Sandra. He scanned the contents of the email the judges had just sent to all the contestants.

Sweet angels above, let there be icing on the cake...

And there it was. Apparently, there would be a swimsuit competition. All right. It was true. She was doing this to torture him and she knew his weaknesses like no one else. Even if there was only one one-thousandth of a possibility she would actually don a swimsuit at the park on Saturday for a last-minute fundraiser, he would go. He steepled his fingers and tapped his chin. There had to be a catch.

He reread the email.

Dear contestants,

We cordially invite you to a party tomorrow on Saturday and ask you to forgive us for the short notice. We understand perfectly if your schedule will not allow you to come, and this will have no influence on the final judging for the Townsperson Contest. However, it has been brought to our attention that the contestants could perform one last good deed for the town as a group. We were informed the victims of the recent fire in the Green Hills apartments on 60th are still struggling to get their lives back in order. With that in mind, Lauren Hall from the mayor's office, with help and news coverage by Sandra Kelly, has organized a donation list, a silent auction, and beauty pageant style contest for fun in order to raise money and awareness for our citizens in need. Festivities will take place at Sycamore Cove Park, beginning at four. There will be introductions, interview questions, the chance to slip on some evening wear costumes, a talent show, a blow-up bouncy castle for kids, and yes, there will be a swimsuit competition. So bring the family and your musical instruments, prepare your beauty pageant answers to life's most important questions, and be ready to have some fun. To RSVP or if you have questions, please reply to this email. Hope to see you tomorrow!

Sandra had convinced his sister to host a fundraiser, organized the event with the Townsperson committee, and got permission from the city in less time it took him to drink his five coffees?

Maybe he should have partnered with her two years ago instead of that limp dish-rag Vic.

Speaking of…

He called Vic's cell phone to ask why he wasn't there yet, but after three rings it turned over to voice mail. He tossed the phone.

This was great. He'd never be able to concentrate now. He started to filter through the other emails, hoping to get some easy stuff out of the way until his brain stopped picturing Sandra in a bikini. The worst of it was, they were completely incompatible. He had no idea what she wanted from him. He would give up his business for her sake and that pissed her off. For three days, he'd tried to find a last-minute solution to fix his finances so he could drop out *and* keep his baby afloat. Now she was pulling this stunt—this public prank. Because that was what it was. A huge prank on him to force him to stay in the running. And if he won? On accident?

Brad's ugly faced reared up in his mind and he wanted to punch a wall. That was what she had to look at and would have to keep on looking at unless she left. Why was she doing this?

Cooper, concentrate, or you'll send your baby to an early grave.

Next email. It was from Gregg, the karaoke-slash-maybe interested in his platform guy. He had a few general questions and a technical one and Cooper shot off a quick response.

He was half-way through the next email when Gregg sent him a thank you. Cooper hesitated for a second.

> *If you aren't busy on Saturday afternoon, and would like to see the town in action, we are having a fundraiser at the park. See the WCC 12 News broadcast tonight for details if you are interested.*

There. It didn't cost anything to be nice.

It didn't cost anything to sabotage a prank, either. Not much anyway. She wanted a beauty pageant style fun-filled afternoon? He could do beauty pageant. He had an ace up his sleeve and just the thing to knock himself off the judges' list.

They would finally see that Cooper Hall didn't do serious. Nope. *Not a serious bone in my body, except for the one that counts.*

Sandra would drop her crusade to promote him, see that her own career and life were more important than him, and he could live his life—his happy, single life—in some other city. Done. Easy.

His phone rang. It was Vic. He drummed his fingers on the desk a second, wondering if it would be worth ripping him a new one for the pleasure of cussing him out. Then changed his mind and answered civilly. "Morning."

"Yeah, you called?" Vic drawled.

"I was wondering where you were. This data patch is nearly ready to go, and we need to get word to the clients."

"Remind me why, again."

Techno-moron… "Because investors will want as much data at their fingertips as possible. So we're giving it to them. That's why. This is a new selling point in our platform portal and we need to market it."

"Yeah, about our platform portal. I've been speaking to my lawyer and my banker. I think I'm ready to make you an offer to buy you out."

"You want to buy Homeward Bound from me?" Cooper stood, knocking his chair over. His whole body tensed. This could be good or bad.

"Yes. Not so much buy it from you, though, as pay compensation for what it's currently worth and take over your half of the business. This latest patch, untested and untimely as it is, won't be taken into consideration."

"So you plan on offering me compensation for *part* of my half?" Trust Vic to be an asswipe to the end.

"Fair compensation. Of course, at this point Homeward Bound isn't worth much." Vic paused. "But relocating with your dead weight on board is going to be too much for me. I am prepared to offer you six thousand dollars."

If he had been drinking milk, it would have shot out his nose. "That's a load of shit. I decline your offer."

"That's the best you'll get. I have a clear argument for unethical promotion of assets by your part. This will kill your baby, as you like to call your business. You can sell it or kill it."

"What does unethical promotion even mean? You don't have jack on me or our contract, you signed up in perfect understanding of the risks—"

"I gotta go. Let me know your decision as soon as possible."

He hung up. Cooper pounded a fist in his desk. This didn't change things, it just was a reminder of how big a dick Vic happened to be. Forget work. He had a beauty pageant to prepare for.

Now the question was, how could he find his good friend Valentino il Grande?

What else was Google for? When he found the phone number, he took a deep breath. And called.

"Val, hi. It's Cooper Hall. Remember me from the park interview? You serenaded me."

"Oh, darling, of course I remember you." Val growled like a big cat, and Cooper went cold with fear. He almost hung up. Val continued right away, though. "What can I do for you?"

"Would you happen to know where I can get a mankini for not too much? I have to look good and stay in budget."

"How good do you want to look?"

Cooper scoffed. "So good, you'll have to scrape the librarians off the ground and the city maintenance workers off the poles."

"I knew it. You're such a bad boy at heart. Where can we meet for a makeover?"

CHAPTER 26

I am a kung fu ninja reporter queen. I have trained to be poised in heels, under hurricane rains, in the blinding sun, when interviewing emotionally devastated people, and when bigots insult me to my face. I am strong. I am powerful. I am Woman.

And if someone doesn't get that bouncy castle to inflate and let the kids start jumping in the next five minutes, I will lose it.

Sandra shook her hands and rolled her shoulders to relieve the tension. It wasn't a defective bouncy castle that was the problem, and right before she scanned the park again to see if *he* was there yet, she forced herself to focus. She could do this. She had already accomplished the impossible, and there wasn't much more to do but let the festivities begin. As promised the evening before during her time slot, the city and contest committee were hosting a small fundraiser for the victims of the fire, a reminder that some people still needed help, in the form of a fun beauty pageant for the Townsperson Contest participants.

Complicated and ambitious? Yes. Would she waste her time with anything less? No. Not when getting Cooper Hall to face her, and his commitment to his own business was on the line. So far half of the one hundred chairs they set up were taken.

"Hey," Lauren called, beckoning her to come, "For the swimwear part, do you want the mermaid and merman costumes together or in the men's and women's tents?"

"Better put them in the separate tents and do the same with the king and queen evening wear. Then we'll coordinate before people come on stage."

"Great."

Lauren trotted off, still fresh and full of energy after starting to decorate and set up material at seven that morning. Sandra could never have pulled this off—the city permits, the organization, finding contributors—without Lauren's help. Which begged the question, were she and Cooper actually blood related or had he been switched out at birth?

Someone realized the blower for the bouncy castle wasn't plugged in, explaining why it wasn't working. With a shout of victory, the volunteers switched it on, and stood back to admire the inflating tubes. There were two minutes to spare before Sandra would have lost it. Meltdown avoided, good. City maintenance workers wandered back and forth to inspect, keeping a professional eye on the proceedings.

Sandra took a deep breath and allowed herself to take a look around, but not because she was hoping to see Cooper. The silent auction table was ready, complete with six of her hand-crocheted toys, coupons and gifts from local shops they secured at the very last minute, and some fun coupons to win, like dousing Jason the firefighter with a bucket of water while he wore a white tee-shirt. The donation list had been posted and bags were already piling up. There was a face painting stand, concessions, including Mackenzie's organic coffee, and some extra costumes for kids a former drama teacher had dropped off. But there was no Cooper. Every other contestant who had RSVP'd was there, either mingling or putting on costumes for the pageant.

I am strong. I am powerful. I am Woman.

There he was.

Sandra's legs went weak at the sight of Cooper strolling into the park in flood of sunshine. His grin was as cocky as she'd ever seen it, as if nothing in the world mattered to him. She didn't know whether she wanted to slap him or kiss him.

Neither. She couldn't let him into her heart and mind anymore. They would always be in a competition, always pushing and pulling each other, but never together. She could accept it or fight it. However, the facts would never change. Their whole relationship was built on pranks and tricks. It would never last. And that was why he couldn't throw away his chance at staying in this town with his start-up for her sake.

This was going to hurt. She whipped out her phone to text him.

Sandra: Meet me behind the men's changing tent.

He chatted with a couple of the other contestants, head high and hands in his jeans pockets. He hadn't seemed to notice his phone. As she glared at him over a pond of white folding chairs, Brad came wending through the Sycamores and down the path to the side of the gazebo. There was a woman with him.

The woman's gaze nailed Sandra to the spot as the two strolled to where she stood.

"Sandra, this is Joan, regional manager of Eastern Virginia for Coastal Connections," Brad said.

Ice formed in Sandra's veins. Brad's frown said it all. The network had caught up to her.

"Nice to meet you face to face, Sandra," Joan said, shaking her hand. "You are one hard journalist to pin down. I've been going through Brad here for several days, to no avail. Well, I called, as you remember, but you were busy. Then I saw your announcement last night and decided to come and see what is going on here for myself."

"As for what is going on, we are hosting a fund—"

"Our little Sandra is quite the enthusiast," Brad interrupted. "Hopping from one story to the next. I was intrigued myself when she wanted to combine two events, fundraiser and pageant for the Townsperson contest. The finale is tomorrow, Joan. I believe I mentioned Sandra is a contestant? We are certainly proud of her."

Why did his praise sound like he was making excuses for a child's bad behavior? "I'm so glad you could stop by in person to visit Sycamore Co—" Sandra started.

"Yes," Brad said. "We usually run a very tight ship. It's necessary. This weekend is a bit hectic for the all of us, though. Sandra is certainly keeping us busy."

"How did your interview go the other day when I called? I didn't see any mention of who it was or what happened," Joan said.

Sandra coughed. She had sent Brad a message but was trying to keep it under wraps. "I'm sorry, I can't really say. I met with a source who gave me a lead about the fire."

"You did what with who?" Brad asked.

"Do you ever check your email?" She raised her eyebrows at him.

"Haha. Such a joker, our Sandra. Why don't we talk more about it later?"

Joan smiled. "Following up a lead? Interesting." She took Sandra's arm to lead her a few steps away. "I can see you're busy now, but we do need to talk. I'll find you before I go to set up a time. Oh, and I can't wait to see this pageant."

Sandra nodded, mouth dry. That didn't go well. Brad wasn't finished, though. He leaned in to whisper, "Try not to embarrass the station too much for a change."

"If you think I'm not putting on any costumes, you are dead wrong."

She waved goodbye, but he turned his back to her. Her phone buzzed.

Cooper: I'm here. I'm alone. I have an agenda.

Sandra growled, too impatient to bother texting him back. She stomped off through the grass and around the gazebo. They had created a makeshift theater at the front of the gazebo with a few decorative curtains and put up two green room tents in the back for the contestants if they wanted to change clothes.

Cooper leaned against a tree behind the men's tent. His arms were crossed and his foot was kicked up on the trunk, in classic bad boy style. And that messy, glossy, dark hair…

Sandra growled again. He smirked as she approached and would have stepped forward, but she shoved him against the tree and pressed her hands on his chest. It was to keep him still, obviously. Not to get in a last feel of his pecs. Damn, he had great pecs.

"I don't want to discuss anything," she said, ignoring the swell and fall of his chest. "You will listen to me."

"Do I have to do what you say or just listen?"

"Both. Stop interrupting. These are the facts: you need to win in order to keep your start-up, and you need to play along to be considered for a win."

"Sandra, I don't need to win—" He tried to push free from the tree.

"Shush!" She pressed down harder. Muscles bunched and hardened under her fingers. *Concentrate.* "Life isn't a joke to be handled carelessly. There are consequences and we have to accept responsibilities for our actions, honor our commitments. Now you will get your ass to the men's tent and put on the king's costume for the evening wear, so people see you are here to win. Clear?"

"Yes."

"All right." Cautiously, she stopped pushing on his chest, not sure if he had truly absorbed her message. Orders. Fine, she was ordering him around. But for his own good!

From the corner of her eyes, she caught John sneaking around the tent, creeping up on her. Sandra held up a warning finger, and he jerked to a stop, mid-step. "I know you aren't trying to film private, behind the scenes drama that involves my personal life so you can send it to Pavel for posting."

"Sandra, please, this is current events. It's my job," he wheedled.

She waggled her finger no. "Go. I'm serious. Or no more donut breaks for our morning shoots, either."

He signaled defeat, holding up a hand and stepping backwards.

Sandra cocked an eyebrow at Cooper. "Your move."

"I appreciate what you're trying to do," he said. "You want me to stay in the running, but you are ignoring some other facts: I shouldn't be your competitor. We both know it. I've fared well in this contest because of luck—I'm popular, I have my own start-up, and every time Lauren worked on a charity project she twisted my arm to help her. She even tried to blackmail me once. People vote for me because I look good on the surface." He paused. He was going to make a cheap joke—she could see it coming. "Even you can admit I look good on the surface, right? Am I right?"

And there it was. The cheap joke. She shook her head in silence at him.

He crossed his arms and lowered his voice. "So I shouldn't be here, and there is only one thing I can do to fix this. And you know what it is."

"Do I look like I care? On my face, do you see anything resembling *I-give-a-shit*? You got yourself into this, and you will see it through to the end."

"You want me in the pageant?"

Was this a trick question? She hesitated, then nodded. "Yes. Give it your all."

"My all?"

Their eyes locked, but his face was unreadable. He was infuriating when he played dense. "Yes," she snapped. "Your all."

She was breathing hard. Harder than she should be. His eyes were still fixed on her hers as if he was searching for something. He reached forward at the same second she leaned towards him.

He kissed her. His arm was around her waist to crush her close, and she tilted her head back, melting into him. He had her completely caught in his grasp. Hellfire and brimstone, he kissed her, and heat was spreading like magma up and through her body.

CHAPTER 27

Fireworks screamed and sparked to golden explosions in her heart.

"I am not here for this," Sandra said breathlessly between kisses. "I am here to bring people together."

"We're together."

She bit his lip until he groaned in pleasure. "Not for much longer. We are finished. You walked off when I tried to work things out."

He bent her further backwards and ran his lips over her neck. "So long as you win that promotion you've earned and can stay in town."

She pushed him upright, hand firmly on his pec. "You think you can make me hot with your sacrifices?"

"If it doesn't work, I hope you tell me what does make you hot."

His grip around her waist tightened and her nipples prickled, sensitive and hard in her bra. If there had been a room nearby... But no. "Cooper, I hate it when—"

Lauren called her name, and they both jumped apart, straightening clothes and facing in opposite directions.

Lauren rounded the gazebo, smiling. "There you are." Her smile turned to frown. "Did I interrupt something?"

If we don't look guilty as sin itself, eating ice-cream in church on a Sunday...

"Hi, Lauren. It's all good. You said the men's tent is that one?" Cooper asked Sandra. She nodded. Was her lipstick smeared? "Like we agreed, I'll give it my best try. After all, I have to make sure the judges notice my performance today to take into account tomorrow."

Lauren must have figured out things weren't as good as Cooper said and her eyes dropped downwards. She kicked at a tuff of grass as her brother headed for the tent. Sandra couldn't say anything.

"I think we're ready to start the pageant. We've got lots of bids on the prizes and people are starting to sit down. We passed out the score cards to a dozen volunteers. All we need now is your opening statement," Lauren said.

Sandra swiped at her thighs as if brushing them off. "I'll make sure John is set up and rolling."

§

"Are you sure these heels are my size?" Cooper studied the rhinestone-studded, silver shoes squished onto his feet. "My toes are wedged in that tiny triangle part in front. That can't be right."

Clarence grunted, cracking his knuckles. "It's right. Stop complaining."

Kneeling at Cooper's feet, Val rocked back to nod in agreement at him. "They are sublime. But, honey, I think we should shave your legs and wax your jungle. I can have you squeaky smooth in ten minutes."

"Not a chance." Cooper had limits.

"But it's all so messy," Val whined. "Look, there are leg hairs touching your heels."

"I said no wax. And I've done my time shaving my legs for swim meets." He held up the straps of the slinky black thing Val brought. "Will this dress make my shoulders look soft?"

"That dress was made for you, darling. Quite literally. I finished sewing last night. You'll be the belle of the ball, trust me."

"All right. According to the schedule, we all go on stage for intros and then come back to change, and go up one at a time for the evening wear and then the swimsuit. I have to go last on the intros, so I am last for evening wear, but first for the *swimsuit* part." He winked when he said swimsuit and Val smacked his own cheeks.

"You are going to be incredible."

Clarence grunted, possibly in agreement, possibly to threaten him, Cooper couldn't be sure. Plus, he was opening and closing a fist while staring at him.

"Did you bring the shirt?" Cooper asked.

Val tossed him a ragged, black bundle.

"It's starting." Clarence said, head cocked to the tent's entrance.

Right on cue, Sandra's voice came through the loudspeakers by the gazebo. "Welcome and thank you for coming! WCC 12 News is thrilled to be here today to support the community on this gorgeous Saturday afternoon..."

"You can still beat her, you know," Val said under his breath.

"I know. That's the problem."

"Humph," Clarence muttered. "You don't have an ounce of her class. She uses merino wool for her amigurumi. Merino. Fucking. Wool. Do you know what kind of person crochets toys in merino wool?"

"No," Cooper said warily.

"The best. What can you do better than that?"

"Nothing. That's the problem."

Cooper's phone buzzed to life in his back pocket and he stepped back, relieved for the interruption. Another friend promising to show up at the park in a few minutes. He paused, reading the name —Gregg. He had a friend named Gregg? It was possible.

Wait—the karaoke guy. Well, even if he signed up for the platform it was too little, too late by now. Too bad.

Cooper unbuttoned his shirt and tried to put on the 'sexed up' tee-shirt Val had promised to provide, but there were too many holes. "How do I get into this thing?"

Smirking, Val helped him get it over his head correctly and down his torso. Stripes of his skin appeared through a dozen vertical cuts.

"Good?" Cooper asked. But what he meant was bad. It was all part of his image.

"In those jeans, you're devastating. Grrr." He pawed at him like a tiger, which Cooper took as positive.

A few seconds later, the handful of male contestants who could make it there for the afternoon headed out for the gazebo and filed onto the stage with the ladies. There were at least one hundred people in the park, lots of families and parents. In the back were groups of his friends, from high school days or Murphey's. Most of the people were sitting in the seats provided, but a few wandered around the two concession and coffee stands, or put in their offers for prizes at the auction stand.

One by one, the Townsperson contestants stepped forward to the mic to give their names and say a little about themselves in case anyone in the small crowd didn't know. Then they answered a question. These were written by local second graders, and Cooper's favorite as he listened was, 'What was it like growing up as a kid with no electricity?'"

Cooper hung to the back, watching Sandra. She stood silently, ultra-focused, next to Lauren who was doing the questions. John was off to the side, filming. It wasn't clear whether he would edit, so the news could present a few clips later, or if the show was being live streamed to the station's site. He hoped it was live. He didn't want to be edited out by anyone.

Sandra flicked her gaze towards him, as if hearing his thoughts. She blinked and then frowned briefly, staring at his chest. He rolled his shoulders back, stretching the ripped-up tee. Her eyes widened.

"What?" she mouthed.

He blew her a kiss in reply, and even from that distance he could see her muscles tense and nostrils flare. She was pissed. With a little luck, the judges would not be impressed, either.

Maybe he should have shaved and let Val wax his jungle.

Blargh. Too late now.

He was the last contestant on the stage and he stepped forward to the mic at the front near Sandra. Only then did he notice her hands were trembling. Scenes from their past flashed through his head—Sandra at thirteen, skinny and colt legged; at fifteen, haughty and her hair straightened, arms full of books; toned curves and inky-black-brown eyes that caught everything in their sight at eighteen. Flash forward to the smelly club at Christmas when she raked her fingers through his hair. He didn't care if all she wanted was a one-night stand, until suddenly he did want more, but only got it a few days ago.

She would never forgive herself if she won—got the promotion she deserved and kept her place in this town—and he lost everything. Unless he could make her mad.

It was really time for her to move on. This never could have been more than a rebound fling, and her crap boss wasn't the one who was holding her back.

He grinned and leaned down to the microphone. "Who else showed up today to support the person they love?"

CHAPTER 28

Her ears buzzed with blood pounding through her veins and her skin tingled like she was in an electric field. Sandra knew what she had heard, but she didn't want to believe it. She couldn't. This was, after all, Cooper. Trickster, joker, bane of her life. If he said *love*, he meant something else.

Details came into sharp focus. There was a soft breeze on her back, stirring her hair, and it smelled of flowers, fresh dirt, and the nearby restaurant. The breeze flowed past her and teased Cooper's wavy hair on his forehead, lifting it from his eyes. When the crowd applauded and cheered for his introduction, he grinned and white flashed between his bow-shaped lips.

"And your personal question," Lauren said. "Name your first, second, and third favorite desserts and if you didn't pick bacon covered donuts, why not?"

"An excellent question, indeed." He pondered a moment, a line forming between his eyebrows. "So, first favorite is apple pie à la mode, second favorite is cookie dough ice-cream, and third favorite is brownies without nuts."

Someone in the crowd shouted, "And what about the bacon donuts?"

"Breakfast food, my friend. While some desserts, like cake, can be switched in for breakfast, not all can do the honors." He paused for applause, but he didn't leave the stage, yet. "Before I go, I would like to draw your attention to one of the contestants who isn't joining us for the fun, because she is working today. Give it up for Sandra Mercy Kelly, the sharpest shooter in Sycamore Cove."

He stood aside and clapped while the crowd cheered for her as well.

"And after this, folks, those of you who can, should join me at Murphey's. Best bar in Sycamore Cove. See you there later. Much later!" He waved goodbye and jogged off the stage, leaving her stunned.

Love.

He could have meant Lauren. He could have meant someone else. This was a game to him, nothing more. She pivoted and scanned the crowd. The people were smiling, carefree and happy as though nothing important had happened, and the applause died down. But she was rattled, like a blow had knocked her through to the bone.

"Ready for the evening wear?" Lauren asked her. Sandra nodded. She risked turning from the crowd to wipe her forehead quickly and take a deep breath. So long as he played the part, the judges would keep him in the running. If she won, it was fate. If he won...

She would deal with Brad and her problems at the station if and when she had to, not before. Besides, if he lost...how could he stay in the town if he lost his start-up? Get a job cleaning tables at Murphey's? Did they even clean the tables there?

Mackenzie bounced onto the stage in cotton pajamas, her three-year-old daughter propped on one hip in a matching onesie. They both smiled, her daughter showing crooked baby teeth, and waved.

"As you can see, only the finest evening wear for me and my mini-me! This is how we spend pretty much every evening, just me and her."

Sandra took another deep breath and hitched her chin at John, in a silent question. He gave her the thumbs up to show that they were still filming and sending the live feed to their website for the viewers at home. She adjusted the IFB in her ear in case anyone at the station needed to contact her. She could do this.

What felt like an hour later, but was actually fifteen minutes, each contestant came on in their version of evening wear—besides pajamas for Mackenzie, there was a royal couple in RenFest costumes, Jason in his firefighter gear, a Santa Claus costume, the librarian was a cat-burglar dripping in fake diamonds and pearls, and more.

No one showed up in dress, though, until Cooper strode onto the stage in six-inch bling-bling stilettos and the tightest black dress she'd ever seen that wasn't made of rubber or paint. She stepped forward involuntarily as though to stop him or make him change his mind.

But this was evening wear and all the contestants had a fun time with it. Maybe that was all he wanted to do—have fun.

He swayed his hips wide enough to change the tide and tossed the end of his white and black feather boa over one shoulder before striking a pose at the end of the gazebo stage. The crowd, of course, loved it, and they yelled and whistled. His hairy legs and ragged beard juxtaposed with his sexy clothes, smoky eyes, and deep maroon lipstick, and he pouted, giving a wink to the audience.

"Let's give it up for the members of the LGBTQ community who helped me get ready today," he said, bending way down to reach the microphone. His voice was low and gravelly. More whistles and cheers.

Sandra shivered at the sound of his voice, nipples tightening despite his drag costume.

Stop being so needy.

He was there to support people, to represent groups who were often ignored and dismissed, or worse. She shook her hands loose. He was playing along.

Or was he?

Something was wrong, besides the stilettos, lipstick, and slinky evening dress. He was smiling too much. He was too happy with himself—which meant he wasn't finished, yet.

"Thank you for your appreciation of my evening wear. I have to admit," he said and paused to toss the feather boa higher around his neck. "I borrowed this dress. Never let your budget determine who you are or how you express yourself. Agreed?"

The crowd cheered louder than even before. Sandra's hands were slick with sweat. What was he going to do?

"And with that in mind, I do believe there is a swimsuit contest as well! Children under eighteen might want to avert their eyes."

Avert their eyes?

Sandra's heart dropped. From across the gazebo stage, in the back, Val stuck his fingers in his mouth to wolf whistle and waggled his eyebrows at her. Oh, no. This was going to be bad. So bad.

It clicked in her mind. She knew what he meant by making the judges notice his performance. There were a couple of judges in the crowd having fun today, and he wanted to make sure he would be struck from the winner's position. At the same time as Cooper reached up to his shoulders and started to unhook the dress striptease style, she grabbed the nearest decorative curtain and raced across the stage.

She threw herself in front of him the instant he held his arms up in victory, the flimsy dress flapping in the breeze at the corner of her eye. Face to the crowd, smiling, she whipped the curtain around his middle.

"Nothing to see here, folks," she cried. She'd never smiled wider in her life. "Absolutely nothing to see."

The crowd booed and hissed. They waved at her to move, and someone yelled, "We want to see his swimsuit!"

"Sandra," Cooper hissed. "What are you doing?"

"What's it look like? I'm trying to keep you from being arrested?"

"For showing off my mankini?"

"Your man wha—?" She turned and dropped the curtain enough to get a peek at his chest and abs, all the way down to... Where his V should have been, was a leathery black, sling-shot suit that cupped his package. Two thin strips rose from his abs over his shoulders, just wide enough to cover his nipples. "God, my eyes, it burns! What are you wearing?"

"Get off the stage. Let us judge his suit," an older woman shouted. She had a pen and pad of paper and everything. She shooed at Sandra as though to swat her aside.

"Due to a small wardrobe mishap, we can't expose his suit," Sandra announced. "In the meantime, Jason will present his white tee-shirt. Remember, one silent auction winner gets to douse him later with a bucket of water. Thank you!"

She dragged Cooper across the stage and down the second set of stairs on other side. Val moved to join them, concern knitting his brows in the middle of his forehead. She glared at him until he changed his mind and stayed back.

"What do you think you are doing, Cooper Hall? You think if you flash enough skin, the judges will kick you off the roster?"

"You think I should flash more skin, is that it?"

"No. For a second there I thought you were doing a Full Monty thing. But I'm not sure the—" she snapped his strap "—is much better."

"It's much better, believe me. I don't get arrested, but I do get left in peace if I flash this."

"This was your idea of sabotaging your chances, wasn't it." It was a statement. She didn't need to ask the question. "Being over the top today and discrediting your name."

"If you think I should give more skin, my mankini is a thong. What do you think?" He started to turn in order to show her his buns and she rolled her eyes skyward.

She already knew how amazing his ass was, but he shouldn't try to show it off in the park.

"Val," she called, since he was lurking nearby anyway. "Find Cooper's jeans and shirt, would you please?"

"Could you grab my bag, please?" Cooper asked. "Everything's in it."

She frowned at Cooper's face, thick eyeliner and dark lipstick marring his natural features. "This has got to go."

"Why? Why does it have to go? So it fits what they might want? What about what you want for your life, Sandra? Could you stop and think about yourself for a few seconds?" Cooper twisted the ends of the curtain to knot them at the side of his waist like a towel after the shower.

"This isn't the time or place. I organized this afternoon so people wouldn't forget about the families who lost everything in that fire. I forced my petty-minded boss to come so he would see there are more stories than the ones he wants me to cover. This is the last chance for the Townsperson contestants to have some fun with this contest and do some good before only one of us wins tomorrow, and yes, I twisted your arm by not letting the committee accept your resignation so you would stay in the running. I know you want to keep your home in this town."

"Before the voting numbers were hidden, I was ahead of you. I was in the lead. I know you don't want me to win."

"But I don't want you to lose, either. At least, not by throwing it away."

"Because you need to win and not feel guilty."

"How dare you say that? You have no idea how I feel. That is not the way my mind works."

"It's all right to admit you would rather win. Don't you understand that's what I want for you, too? You have to stop worrying about what other people might lose. Get your priorities straight for a change."

She crossed her arms and glared at him.

Val coughed. "Can I interrupt you for a second? And there you go, Cooper. By the way, you rocked the hell out of that dress. Here." He set the bag on the ground and backed away slowly. There were several other contestants and onlookers watching them from the tent.

Sandra took Cooper's arm. "Come with me. I'm not done."

He kicked off the heels, which fell with heavy thumps to the path, and pawed after her to the public restrooms. She rounded the small building and put her hands on her hips.

"You're right, Cooper Hall. I don't care if you lose everything you've ever worked for, and let me tell you exactly why I don't care. After you coated the insides of my only pair of jeans with toothpaste at summer camp, I have never liked you. Your tricks, your jokes, your blasé approach to life that everything is your due and everyone should love you by virtue of just being you, has been the bane of my existence. You and I are finished. Done with. I will be happy when you lose, because like I said, I have never liked you. I will never like you. This prank war, and all my problems are your fault."

"Everything is my fault?"

"Yes."

Cooper crossed his arms over his mankini suspenders. "All right. Let's do this."

CHAPTER 29

"You want to put the blame on me for everything that has gone wrong between us? Fine." If Cooper had to completely ruin any hope of a relationship with her to make her see she had to win, he'd do it. "One accusation after the other. First, the jokes and my approach to life are my way of keeping my priorities straight. Like you should be doing. Next, the prank war is my fault? Not a chance. Sandra, you know it's not true. I only pranked you after you had the brilliant creativity to run my tighty-whities up the flag pole, plus you wrote my initials in them with a sharpie."

"Because you laughed at me, heartlessly, when I tripped and got ice-cream all over my face and clothes."

He pointed at himself. "I was fourteen. You started the prank war because I laughed a little. Which I probably did because I was nervous."

"Oh, you jumped all over the prank war like a kid in a candy store," she said, huffing.

"That makes no sense."

"You kept it going after camp when we went to high school. After the toothpaste, you rigged my Bunsen burner to pass gas."

"You put cauliflower dipped in red dye in my trombone so it looked like it was spraying brains all over the floor."

She rolled her eyes. "Please. You had a taxidermied tarantula jump out at me from my locker."

"Sandra, it was dead. You put a goat—a live goat—in my bedroom. It chewed up my feather pillows and pooped pellets on my Led Zeppelin CDs." The mess of feathers, goat poop, and one obnoxious, hungry goat had been epic.

"At prom, you gave my date garlic bread toasts piled high with fresh garlic and anchovies to eat."

"He was an idiot. He didn't deserve to be kissed if he ate that stuff. Besides, you filled my car with ping-pong balls and lured me to the park only to handcuff me to a bench with fluffy pink handcuffs."

"The only reason I did that was because you had a clown deliver flowers to me in the hospital after I had appendicitis. A clown! Who does things like that? Clowns kill people," she said, waving her hands in frustration.

"That was better than how you ignored me after I got my nose broken by the bully who wouldn't leave you alone, the whole reason we invented Holy Hot Tamales." His nose was still crooked. Didn't that give him any brownie points?

"Ignored you? I did an article on you and the game you programmed. It was a really nice article that didn't mention a single one of your faults."

He shook his head in disbelief, chest constricting suddenly. "I got an article for beating up your bully. Did it never occur to you I wanted more?"

"Did it never occur to you that pranks are not a way to a girl's heart?"

"Have you never noticed that the times we stopped pranking each other it was my idea?"

"Have you never noticed that whenever I try to have a real conversation with you, you run away scared?"

"The first time I asked if you wanted to sign a peace treaty, you sent me an asparagus-flavored candy-gram. These things tend to scare a man."

"You just did it again. I tried to talk to you about something real, and you turned it into a joke. Well, you want to know what's really funny?" she asked. "I switched out your coffee with decaf a week ago." She shimmied her shoulders in a mini victory shake.

He staggered back. "That's low. That's cruel even for you, Sandra. I've been a zombie for days." That explained so much. "How did you get the keys to my house?"

"I never name my sources. Suffice to say the person was not part of the prank."

"It was Lauren, wasn't it? Betrayed by my own family." He had to drop his head a moment to process.

"And what about you? Who betrayed me to help you? I never could figure out how you knew I'd be at the lighthouse that day for the broadcast. You knew the exact time and place. Who told you?"

"I never name my sources?" he suggested, still reeling from the coffee prank.

"Only a handful of people from the station knew about it. I'm guessing it was John—you two were awfully friendly when you met up on accident and he invited you to our lunch."

"Sandra, don't be mad at him."

"Oh, I'm not mad at him." She shook her head, glaring at him.

"Be mad at me if you want. Hate me if you want. Here are the facts, though. When I suggested we sign a truce before leaving for college, you handcuffed me to a park bench before finally signing it. When this contest was announced, you practically begged me to start the prank war again. Sandra, I have wanted to stop this back and forth since I made that first mistake of retaliating at camp. We were stupid kids, and I want something so different with you now. I know it won't happen, that I'll never have this thing I want. But I will do whatever is in my power to help you reach your goals and dreams, no matter the cost to me. If I can help you win by making you hate me, or by dropping out of this contest, then that's what I'll do. Sabotaging my chances today was my last prank. I have something for you." He dropped to one knee.

She gasped and stepped back.

He dug through his bag and then handed her an envelope. "This is for you."

"What is it?" She flipped the envelope to see if the answer was on the back.

"Read it. It's yours." He stood and shouldered the bag to go.

"Cooper, wait. I want you to know that what we had together, the time we spent, it wasn't just sex. I wasn't with you just for the sex, even though it was great and if I had to do it again—"

"Whoa!" John shouted, rounding the corner of the bathroom. He raked her thumb across the front of his neck for them to cut. "Hold up. I'm going to interrupt this conversation and this *broadcast*, if you know what I mean, right there. No more discussing any hanky-panky. Not that anyone is having any."

"What are you talking about?" Cooper asked.

Sandra's face went from surprise to volcanic rage. Her hand flew to her IFB and then she studied the mic she was carrying. She switched a button. "He left it going live to the website."

"Yeah," John said, huffing for breath. "I swear it wasn't me. Well, I was the one who told Cooper about the lighthouse, you were right about that that, but he bought me breakfast at the French café. But I told Pavel to cut the feed. He said he had orders from up above to let it roll."

"Wait a minute," Cooper said. "Who did what?"

"Your conversation was on our website and Facebook. I was looking all over for you."

"I will tear him to pieces and feed him to the pigeons," Sandra said. Cooper stepped in front of her, blocking her way. "Out of my way, or you'll be first."

John juggled with his camera, bringing the viewer up to eye level and focusing on Sandra. "Let me adjust this real quick before you go. I wouldn't want to miss it."

"Not now, John!" she said, her eyes sparking dangerously.

"This is my job," he whined in reply.

"Wouldn't you rather keep your life?"

Cooper held up a hand for peace. "John, I'm sure Lauren would love for you to go back and film the rest of the show, all right? Sounds like the talent show is going on."

John grumbled something under his breath but lowered the camera and shuffled off around the bathrooms and back towards the gazebo.

Cooper took a deep breath and faced Sandra. "Trust me, it would be my pleasure to punch Brad for you. But don't throw away your career because he tricked you."

"The only throwing about to happen is me tossing that jerk onto a busy highway. This is personal."

"Sandra, calm down and think for a moment. You are out of control." He crossed his arms to keep himself from shaking some sense into her.

"I'm out of control? You're wearing a slingsuit and a feather boa."

"You will destroy your career if you run out there throwing actual punches. Brad will fire you and you'll have to leave town for another job without a reference, or worse, he'll press charges. Stop. Stop right now."

"Why are you the only one who gets to sabotage their career for someone else? When you do it, it's noble, but when I do it, I'm crazy? Maybe I feel just as strongly as you do about..." Her voice stopped, catching sharply in her throat.

"About what?"

"Maybe, and I'm not saying it's true, but maybe I care about you as much as you care about me."

Cooper shook his head. "What are you saying? Exactly?"

"When you introduced yourself on stage, the first thing you said was that you came out here to support someone you loved. You meant Lauren, right?"

"Lauren?" He blinked in confusion, trying to remember who that was. His sister. "Of course, I love Lauren. But it sure as hell isn't for her that I'm wearing a mankini."

"You're doing it again. Everything is a joke. Can't you be serious for one minute?" she asked.

"You want serious? All right. Here's what I would do for you. I would face Brad and thousand other asswipes like him to fight for you. I would drop out of this race and let the entire town think I am only here to party. I would let my business be stolen from me. I would take a job as a bartender, a janitor, or a pole dancer in order to stay near you. And if you read the letter, you'll see I will never retaliate again."

"Why? Why would you do all that? What could possibly be worth losing everything?"

"You really have to ask?" He stepped forward and before she could debate or handcuff him to anything, he cupped her face, tilting her head gently to look at him. "You have always been the only one for me. I just didn't know it until too late."

"Make a joke. Make a joke or run away, or I'm going to start believing you," she whispered. "Where's the trick? There's a clown or zombie that's going to come for me any second now, right?"

"You asked me to be serious for one minute. That's a short Holy Hot Tamales, but it's yours. I'm yours."

She wrapped her arms around his shoulders, pulling him down to press her forehead to his. "I don't know how to fix this. Or us. All I know is that I don't want you to lose everything because of me."

"That's what I've been saying for two days, but if I'm here with you. I haven't lost anything at all. Read the letter if you don't believe me."

"Wait," she said, hand going to her stomach. "I can't..." She backed away from him and, with frantic hands, ripped open the envelope.

He didn't have to reread it. He watched her eyes devouring the lines.

Sycamore Cove Peace Treaty

The Terms:

I, Cooper Dwain Hall do agree to end as of today, June 2nd, 2018 any and all of the following activities:

- *Pranks*
- *Tricks*
- *Boasting of pranks (past, present or future pranks)*

The Conditions:

There are no conditions. I will respect Sandra's person, mind, heart and soul, from this day on. And her property.

Forever.

Whether or not she loves me in return.

Cooper D Hall

Cooper Dwain Hall

She reached the end and tore her eyes from the page to look up at him, shaking her head.

CHAPTER 30

Whether or not she loves me in return. What the hell was happening to her chest? Sandra was the one who had started the asinine prank war, but here was his offer of peace. A one-sided truce to end it.

But it couldn't end with him leaving her forever.

One thing became clear in the whirl of conflicting thoughts and memories—her life would be empty without Cooper Hall in it. Empty and meaningless. "How do you always do this to me? Turn everything upside down until I don't what to do or say?"

He started to answer, but she pulled him down to shut him up with her lips. It was the only answer she wanted. They stumbled sideways, locked together and frenzied for more. Elbows and hip bones jabbed him and her hands tugged at his hair, but her needy lips sought his and he pressed harder against her.

"Earlier," he said, running small kisses up her ear and temple, "you said you might care for me. Is it true?"

"I care more about you than is healthy, is that what you want to hear?"

"Yes. Say it again."

"Cooper, I have fallen for you. I don't know when or how it happened. I did everything I could to stop it, but it happened anyway. I—" She couldn't quite bring herself to admit more. Instead, she dug her nails into his shoulders—his bare shoulders, she realized with a thrumming of pleasure—and kissed him again. His tongue darted in and out of her mouth, exploring and teasing. A flood of heat hit her core and she ached to take him some place very private. She lifted her chin and nipped his earlobe.

"I love you in return," she whispered.

He cradled her in his arms, not speaking or kissing her. His whole body shook with tension. "Then I win. Everything I want is here."

She nuzzled her cheek in the warm crook of his neck and shoulder. The feathers from the boa tickled her nose and she blew on them.

"If I crack a joke about my outfit will you hit me?" he asked.

"Too late." She pretended to smack his shoulder but laughed. "We should get out of here."

He stood straight, taking a step back. He glanced down at himself and took the end of his feather boa to toss it over his shoulder again. "Should I get the heels and dress for a private show?"

"Jeans and shirt. You can change in the bathroom. Make it quick!"

Grinning, he grabbed his bag and headed for the front side to change in the men's bathroom. The second he was out of sight, her stomach dropped and her mood changed. They couldn't go yet. She had unfinished business.

"Ready. Where to?" he asked, stepping out in his jeans and an unripped tee.

"Question." She took his hand. "You would be willing to lose your business, and take any job to stay here with me, so I have a better chance at winning?"

"Do we have to go over this again? Of course—"

"Right. Got it. Come on." She led him across the grassy park lawn behind the rows of chairs and the audience facing the gazebo.

The show was nearing its end with Lauren saying thank you again to everyone who had come out that beautiful day. Sandra saw the person she was looking for and made a beeline for the silent auction table.

Brad had the nerve to actually pick up one of her dinosaur toys to inspect it. She took it out of his hands and set it back on the table, then crossed her arms.

"Sandra, surprised you are still around." He shoved his hands deep in pockets and rocked on his heels as though thoroughly amused. "I would have thought you'd be gone by now. But since you are here, apparently, your little silent auction has brought in some big bucks. Unofficially, I've been informed your dino is going for two hundred dollars so far, and most of the requested items for the fire victims have been donated already. You did a pretty good job."

"Brad, I quit. I'm done with you, done with your news station," she said. "And what's more—"

"Quit?" he asked, sputtering.

Cooper took her arm. "Wait, that's not what we talked about, Sandra."

"I refuse to be harassed and belittled by you anymore," Sandra continued, glaring at Brad. "Keep your mouth closed, because I have some words to tell you—"

"Can I interrupt?"

A woman's voice cut through the haze of anger that was building in Sandra's head. Joan. The regional manager.

"Joan, I'm sorry, but I'm about to cuss out my former producer. I would have loved to have had that discussion with you, but—"

"Whoa, wait a minute. Let's just wait a minute," Cooper insisted, stopping her. She glared at him. And at Brad. What was wrong with these men? "I'm sorry, who are you?" he asked Joan.

"Joan Callahan, Regional manager from Coastal Connections. I stopped by today to see how Sandra handled this impromptu fundraiser."

"Coastal…" he said and blinked several times in thought. "And you were going to have a discussion with Sandra? About the excellent quality of her journalism?"

Sandra motioned at him, trying to make him be quiet, but he pressed on.

"Did you know about the pressure Sandra was under to both present the Townsperson contest with journalistic impartiality and try to win at the same time? The stakes were particularly high for her."

"I didn't realize there was anything out of the ordinary, no. Besides being incredibly busy." Joan smiled and nodded in Sandra's direction. "She certainly makes the folks at home love her."

"That's exactly what I wanted to bring up. Unfortunately, not everyone sees her work that way. She could go further, if she had more liberty in her decisions, don't you agree?"

Joan's gaze settled on her, and Cooper nudged her from behind. It finally clicked in her head what he was trying to accomplish, and whether or not this was the time or place, she was taking charge of the situation. Besides, she had words to say to Brad.

"Joan, the reason why I asked Lauren to host the fundraiser today for the victims of the recent apartment building was three-fold. One reason was personal—I had to convince another contestant that the town was worth fighting for. The second reason was to help the victims financially and with donations. We will hopefully provide them with the items and extra money some of them need while getting settled into new homes. And the third reason was to convince a possible source to trust me with the truth of what caused the fire. I can't say more at this time, but I have one person who admitted there was faulty wiring in the building, and another who refused to go on record to confirm there was a cover-up by the landlord, because, and I quote, "no one cares if those poor people lost everything." I had to prove that person wrong. I hope to have a message in my email by Monday, so I can bring this story to the attention of the town. We do care. And if we need to help them find justice and retribution for what they lost, then we will do it."

"Was that the source you mentioned to me earlier?" Joan asked.

"Yes, and I hope—"

Brad chuckled. "I hope this circus today hasn't chased off your source entirely. Who would take you seriously after this? A *prank war* you've engaged in for over a decade? No one will trust you with information after this."

"I have held my own finding sources for information on that building while you had me writing up trivialities about camp schedules and bogus insurance schemes. Because of you, I have to pin a promotion on outside validation, such as winning the Townsperson contest instead of being promoted—or not—according to my work. You did everything in your power to make me look bad during this contest—"

"Correct me if I'm wrong, but thirty seconds ago, you were resigning," Brad snapped.

She pointed a finger in his face. "Interrupt me one more time, and I will explain to Joan from the network how you gave instructions for my private conversation with Mr. Hall to continue being broadcast for our audience without my permission or knowledge."

"Is this true, Brad? Did you specify for this to happen?"

"There is obviously some misunderstanding here—"

"It's true," Cooper said. "The cameraman informed us. You can verify with him."

"Thank you, but I'd like to hear Brad's explanation," Joan said.

"It's part of an ongoing, behind the scenes program we have to give viewers an inside look at our work. Everyone knows when they are on the field, clips and audio can be used for the station."

"But she was having a private discussion?"

"Sandra is here to work, there is no such thing as a private discussion," Brad said.

"Well, in that case, I don't need to ask you to step aside for a private announcement I was going to make." Joan crossed her arms, as if daring him to contradict her.

CHAPTER 31

Cooper held his breath, making himself as inconspicuous as possible. If his assumptions were correct—that someone from the network that owned WCC 12 was here in person and had wanted to talk to Sandra, it could only be for a good reason.

Brad scowled, face darkening. "If it concerns me, I'd prefer to discuss in private."

"Maybe you should have thought of that before allowing my discussion to be broadcast to the entire world," Sandra said, words slipping from the side of her mouth slyly.

"Indeed," Joan agreed. "After carefully reviewing Sandra's talent for journalism the last couple of weeks, and seeing your general incompetence today, I would like to inform you that she is being offered a position in the station in Richmond, and you are being demoted and offered a position nowhere at all. I'll make a few calls, but consider this your notice. You are out."

"But I'm the producer. It's my job to organize the stories and send reporters—"

"Not anymore," Joan said, interrupting him. She took out her phone and turned her back to them, making a call.

Cooper cleared his throat and stepped next to Brad. "See you later, jackass."

Brad coughed, glanced around as though lost, then snarled at Cooper. He screwed up his face in anger and took off, weaving through the people and trees towards the street.

Sandra, though, was rooted to the spot, eyes wide. She glanced up and suddenly Cooper understood her dilemma. A promotion to go to Richmond was everything she deserved, but she wouldn't want to go. He hiked his head for her to follow him, so he could try and talk her into it, but she didn't move.

"I can't leave," she whispered. "What about you and my family?"

"I'll go with you. I've heard there are plenty of bars for me dance in at the capitol." If she wanted him to be with her, then there were only solutions as far as he was concerned.

"No joking, Coop. Not now." She walked nervously to Joan, still deep in her phone conversation, apparently telling her team they would need a new producer for Sycamore Cove's WCC 12.

Joan covered the mouthpiece and raised her eyebrows at Sandra.

"I'll take any promotion you can give me, but I need to stay here for now."

Joan cocked her head. Then her face cleared as a smile spread across it. "Of course you can stay here. How would you feel about being a producer? Listen, let's talk Monday. I'll call you when I'm in my office."

"All right." Sandra backed away, waving and grinning. "All right. I'll be there. I'll be waiting for your call."

Cooper engulfed her in a bear hug. "You did it. I was going to go all caveman and deck that jerk, but you were so amazing, all I could do was watch and admire."

"Well, I'm not done, yet." She let go and straightened her clothes. "There's still your problem. The work you've put into your business has to have some results. Tell me everything."

"There is nothing to say. I'm in the red without more clients, despite a steady growth, and now Vic has seen a lawyer about buying me out. It's over if he cuts and runs."

"But surely there must be a way. Bigger contracts for existing clients, a marketing blast to attract new ones. We can stall with Vic. Something."

He sighed, hunching his shoulders. He really didn't want to get into it, but she wouldn't let it go. "It won't help, but that reminds me a guy named Gregg is here. He might want to sign, but from the questions he asked, he's small fry. Sandra, this is life. Businesses begin and end. Life goes on."

"Where is this Gregg? Is he still hanging around?" She craned her neck at the departing crowds as if she knew who to look for.

Cooper, from his slightly higher viewpoint, checked the park, and zeroed in on an older gentleman in a straw hat and a bright Hawaiian shirt among the milling soccer moms and fishing dads. "Coffee stand. Panama hat guy. But this is just delaying the inevitable. Homeward Bound is done."

"Not on my watch, it isn't." She dragged him after her. "Don't I know him? Why does he make me think of Murphey's?"

"The karaoke guy. The one who was so chatty at the next table."

"Right," she said, breathless. She reached his side. "Hi, excuse me. Sandra Mercy Kelly with WCC 12. We've met," she said, offering him her hand to shake.

"Yes, yes. You did a lovely rendition of the Whitney Houston song."

"Thank you. I was very nervous. I have a couple of questions, if you have a moment."

Cooper coughed. "Sandra…"

"This is my job, Mr. Hall. I ask questions."

"It's no problem." Gregg tipped his paper coffee cup at her. "Ask away, Ms. Kelly. I just won a free organic iced mocha latte, so I'm happy. My name is Gregg Jones, if you need it for the paper, by the way."

"We're a news station, but this is more of a private inquiry. In fact, this is going to be painfully direct, Mr. Jones, but is there any chance you have come to support Cooper Hall in a *business* fashion today?"

"Business?"

"Did you come because you might establish a business relationship with him and his company? Are you thinking of working with him in the near future?"

"The thought crossed my mind."

"I'll be blunt, Mr. Jones. Homeward Bound is quite simply a high-quality, high-tech company with an excellent product—

"Platform," Cooper interjected.

"Platform," she continued, "and the possibility to offer large-scale..."

"Solutions."

"Solutions to companies of all sizes, but in an ideal world, it would guarantee closely tailored attention to individual clients."

Cooper nodded—apparently all the encouragement Sandra needed to plunge onwards. "With that in mind, your potential business relationship would benefit the most by you moving forward to communicate your exact needs and expectations for your..."

"Real estate group," Cooper said.

"Real estate group," she repeated. "From small to medium sized real estate groups, Homeward Bound has you covered."

"That's the first time I've heard Carlson Property Investments described as small or medium sized, but I see where you are coming from."

Cooper sputtered, choking. "Carlson Property? You're with Carlson Property? The two-point-five billion investments Carlson Property?"

"The same. I own it. My father-in-law passed away recently and my wife, before she passed on several years ago, had asked me to take over when he died. So here I am."

"Yes. Here you are." Cooper was stunned. "Why are you here? I mean, isn't your company's seat in Boston?"

"I have a sister who lives nearby. She's my only family left, so I fly down once a month or so to visit."

"There's not much that's more important than family."

"I knew there was something I liked about you," Gregg said, clapping his shoulder. "What you said that night at the bar stuck with me. You aren't afraid to lift up others, to help them reach their best. It makes you a better man because of it. I had some people look into your business, what your other customers have found, and I liked what I saw."

"You know the drag costume and the make-up, it's all—" He motioned vaguely at the park.

"It's all for fun. Except when it's to help out those around you. Then it's dead serious. In all honesty, I didn't come here to ask to sign onto your platform."

In a split second, Cooper buried his disappointment. "Well, I understand your position, and if there is anything my company can custom design to suit your needs—"

"I came to buy it. But only if you stay at the helm, of course. We can work out a new contract for the companies who already work with you."

"Buy? You want to buy..." Cooper's voice trailed off for a moment. He shook himself. "Would this require me to move the headquarters?"

"I don't see why. I'm here once a month and you seem to have a good thing going in this town. Never change a team that's winning, even if you buy them, is my philosophy."

Cooper thrust his hand out, and Gregg took it. The men smiled at each other, shaking hands.

"You'll have my offer Monday morning at the latest," Gregg said. He lifted his coffee again. "This is the best coffee I've ever had. I might have to branch out to include boardwalk cafés. Oh, and the tipping point, just so you know, was the way you support not only your competition—" he nodded at Sandra, "but also your fellow townspeople when they are down. It's how we treat others when they are at their lowest that defines our character. Don't you agree?"

"Absolutely. I'll be looking forward to your offer on Monday. Have a great afternoon. And there's a party at Murphey's tonight. Everyone is invited."

"I'm having dinner with my sister and nephews tonight, but have fun. Hopefully, a couple of these little dinosaur toys will be going with me, too." He winked at Sandra and strolled off to chat with Mackenzie, who had returned to her coffee stand.

"Did that just happen?" Cooper asked. "I have to sit a minute. I can't believe this is happening to me."

He put an arm around Sandra's waist and drew her down on a gazebo step to hold her close. "You know this means I'm dropping out of the Townsperson's race, right? I don't care what the judges say about responsibility or commitment. There's no way I'm going tomorrow and standing on that stage. I already won everything I could possibly want."

"Only if you admit I would have beaten you in the end," Sandra said. "The judges would have given me more votes. Of course, this means I'm dropping out, too. There are too many good candidates. Someone else deserves to win this time."

"That's a good point. We could try again next year."

Sandra laughed. "Then I'll beat you next year, in that case."

"So long as you end up in my bed tonight and every night from now on, you can win all the contests and prank wars you want."

The second he saw her lips part and the narrowing of her eyes as when she was about to roast him with a snarky comment, he buried his hands in her thick curls and stole her words in a kiss. She gasped in his mouth surprised, as if she hadn't expected his kiss, then she leaned into him, nipping his lower lip playfully.

He breathed her in, imprinting his mind and heart with that moment. The smattering of sun through the leaves, the freshly cut grass and hot pavement scents on the breeze, and Sandra in his arms.

"You didn't put my name on the truce," she whispered. "You know what that means?"

"It's like I just said, you can prank me all you want. So long as I get to have you in my bed every night."

"Don't worry. I'll still let you call Holy Hot Tamales when you need a break."

He laughed and shook his head. "Sandra, I promise you this—I won't need any breaks anytime soon."

"Why don't we go find out?" She stood and took his hand to lead him out of the park. He entwined his fingers with hers and followed, a smile spread across his face.

EPILOGUE

Sandra: Where r u
Cooper: home. Where r u?
Sandra: open your door

A car door creaked open and slammed shut outside his house as Cooper stood from his easy chair where he had collapsed earlier that evening. He'd put in eleven hours that day, but apparently Sandra had put in even more.

He had to hope she wasn't tired. He could always start with a foot massage and work his way up if she was low on energy. His imagination was already going into overdrive when he opened the door to find Sandra hidden behind two brown paper shopping bags. Clutched in one hand was a bottle of champagne that she jiggled.

"Take this and put it in the fridge. We are celebrating tonight," she said.

Cooper took the bottle and one of the bags. "Nice. I'll set it next to the bottle I bought to celebrate. What's this other stuff?"

"Ingredients for dinner. You have heard of cooking right? It's my sister's recipe for Mexican grilled chicken fajita salad."

"How strange. My specialty is take-away. It's delicious," he said, leading the way to the kitchen. He started shoving packages and bags of uncut vegetables into his fridge, pushing champagne and bottles of beer out of the way.

"You know the chips don't have to go in there, right?"

"Whatever. I'm not taking any chances." He brushed off his hands and turned to take her waist in his hands. He pulled her close —finally. He'd waited all day for this moment.

"Nope. First you have to tell me," she said, finger on his lips. "Did he make you an honest offer?"

"It was more than honest. It was generous. Vic will be getting more than he ever deserved, but he's already agreed to go his separate way and, as a bonus, I've already hired Gabe to help out and put in an announcement with the paper to get two more people on the team."

She tsked. "Vic gets a fair share? I'm not amused."

"Well, I was amused when I signed him up for the sex toy of the month to be delivered to his doorstep. *Fantasy Haven* has the best boxes. Very graphic. His neighbors will love it."

"So my filling his car with rubber chickens was redundant? Would you believe he leaves it unlocked?"

"Rubber chickens?" Cooper grinned. "I knew there was a reason I loved you. Can I get your naked feet in my hands now?"

She laughed as he attacked her neck with kisses, but kept her hand on his chest to keep him from getting too carried away. "Not yet, although that sounds wonderful. About that old building you're in…. My story on the faulty wiring in the apartment building drops tomorrow. I got the second source to come forward and we've verified with the electric company who was on site."

"And this has what to do with my office building?" He ran his hands up her sides and to the front of her blouse. He undid the top buttons at her neck to expose her dark skin. He leaned down to kiss the tops of her breasts.

She cupped his ass. "I've seen the inside of your building. I'd rather it not go up in flames when you are napping on that two-seater one day. So…"

He paused, sensing it was his turn to say something. "So, with my new-found riches, I need to find a new place?"

"Yes. Or," she said, yanking at his belt, "or, and this is even better, have a hard talk with the landlord about building standards and renovating. I don't want to cover any more fires in the town for a long time."

"Wait, I thought you were offered the producer position. You won't be covering any stories at all."

She stepped back, hand twisting in the top of his shirt in order to drag him to the kitchen table. "You were saying you wanted my naked feet? Why don't you grab ahold of them while I tell you about my day?" She hopped up to sit on the table, and her shoes tumbled to the linoleum.

Cooper knelt and took the first one. She groaned as his thumbs began to knead her sole. "Spill. I want all the details."

"I declined the producer position. It's not for me, and I knew Phoebe has been vying to move up. The obvious solution was for me to take her place and Phoebe to take Brad's. Voilà." She moaned as he rubbed firmly into her heel. "Yes, harder."

"You know, I would be able to access your sensitive spots even better if we were in the bed and you were naked. Relaxation as you've never had before." He kissed the sleek skin of the inside of her ankle and winked at her.

"Very tempting. But I'm also starving. I'm not sure what I want first."

He cleared his throat, standing slowly. He put his hands on either side of her legs, eye to eye with her. "My second specialty after take-away just so happens to be delivery. It's also quite delicious. We make one phone call, then go to the back and wait for dinner to show up. The best of both worlds. What do you say?"

"I'd say you are a very clever man. I had no idea." She twined her fingers in his hair.

"I didn't spend all day, every day plotting pranks, you know. This devious mind can come up with all sorts tempting proposals, and now that I can concentrate my energy, there'll be no stopping me."

"Who said I'd ever want to stop you?" She studied his face a moment, thoughtful. "You're happy, right? How things turned out? You could have stayed in the contest. It still would have been good for Homeward Bound, if you had won."

"Not an issue at this point. My bank account will be filled to the brim soon, I get to work with my best friend, and I will come home to you. Or to your home. Whatever. I'm not picky. Besides, watching Mackenzie win with her little girl bouncing across the stage to get the trophy was worth dropping out for. She needs the prize money and title more than you or me. You have your promotion, and I get to be your sex toy. It's good."

"Hey," she said, gripping his hair a fraction tighter to get his attention. "That's what I love about you, always making sure other people are taken care of, too. And speaking of sex toys, you have some promises to keep." She hiked her head towards the hall and his bedroom.

"Let's go see who calls Holy Hot Tamales for a break first, shall we?" He scooped her up in his arms and headed for the bedroom.

THE END

Thank you for reading! Did you enjoy?

Please Add Your Review! And don't miss more sexy and romantic novels like, CRAZY ON YOU. Turn the page for a sneak peek!

Leave it to me to fall asleep in the back of my car...and wake up kidnapped.

Deep voices blended into the rumble of the engine. It stuttered and shimmied before settling into a whining rest that rocked all the way to the carpeted back seat where I hid.

My eyes scrunched tight and my heart wanted to curl up and sploosh out of my chest like the last vestiges of toothpaste in the tube. Sweat trickled down the valley of my boobs and ended in the dip of my thighs.

Buried under material, each pant of breath seared my nostrils as fresh oxygen was replaced with the sour smell of the good times I'd enjoyed at dinner. Intended as donations for Goodwill, the clothes and blankets would apparently now become my funeral shroud.

Most people could escape a bad dream once they woke up. It was my luck to discover reality was the true nightmare.

A low squeal of tires pitched me forward. Cloth fibers scraped against my cheek and shoved my glasses against my forehead. My stomach swished, a wave of nausea crashing and receding against the back of my throat. Only the grace of God and a large trash bag full of clothes breaking the fall of my face kept me from moaning and drawing the thieves' attention.

I swallowed, plastic and acid bittersweet on my tongue. Whoever had said the root of all evil was money had never indulged in a bottle of Jose Cuervo.

"This car is trashed." A male spoke, tone somewhere between a two-packs-a-day habit and the wheezing of a sinus-infected bulldog. A pause. Then, "What's that smell?"

The rough crunch of paper. "Probably whatever's in this crusty old Burger King bag." This voice wasn't as deep and gravelly as the first, but still belonged to a dude.

People were in my car. Strange, judgy people at that. I'd end up an episode of Nancy Grace. Just like Mama had always warned.

My heartbeat echoed in my ears. Starbursts exploded at the sides of my vision, luring me into unconsciousness. I resisted. My glasses fogged in the confined space as I panted quietly.

"This car must belong to some hoarder or pack rat." The smoking bulldog's voice drowned out under a scrape and thump.

Whatever vestiges of alcohol were left in my system sweated out, as each frantic heartbeat replenished my blood with fresh oxygen. My fingers clutched the bag against my face. How dare these men criticize my personal habits? They were the ones stealing a car. Oakvale wasn't an urban area like New York City or D.C. but it had its fair share of crime. Joyriding and theft were common. So was murder. Kidnappings were rare but had been known to happen.

I'd never thought it would happen to me.

Not that I was above being the victim of such types of crime. I'd always kind of figured I'd be in at least one convenience-store robbery or home invasion. My house wasn't in the worst of neighborhoods, but I tended to roll out at midnight for fried pickles and iced coffee at Sheetz. I was sure neighbors and wannabe thieves had noticed. Although with the wreck my house frequently was, it could have already happened and I'd not noticed.

I released the bag. I didn't want to draw their attention, but I needed a plan to escape. The first rule of any kidnapping was not to let the kidnappers get you to a secondary location. I had to do some—

Something made a light *whoosh* as it landed on the pile on top of me. The air in my chest vanished and I swore, *I swore*, my heart stopped as well. My ears hummed as the world dissolved into a cone of white noise. But nothing was whisked away and hands didn't seize me. I shifted to ease the shirt glued to my side and something poked my boob.

My phone was in my personal pocket. Without disturbing the material covering me, I brought the screen close to my face. Almost three a.m. I'd been napping for over five hours.

I slid the silent button down.

I needed Lynnie. She'd know what to do.

I texted: HELP!

Seconds of silence. Long, long seconds.

I texted it again. Adding: KIDNAPPED to the end of the message.

More silence.

This time I sent: KIDNAPPED, NO JOKE. HELP111

I finally got a response. TO dRnK 2 CRe srRY

My jaw popped as my teeth ground. *That bitch.*

When I got out of this—if I got out of this—I was going to kill her. If by some unfortunate circumstance I didn't make it, I'd talk God into letting me haunt her white ass until she died.

The screen darkened and I hit the button to bring it back. The emergency feature in the lower corner stood out in white, blessed relief. If there was ever a time to use that, it was now.

Lord, if I make it out of this alive, I promise to consider better lifestyle choices in the future.

I tapped out 911, listening for the car to stop or movement in my direction. Nothing. Whoever was up front seemed oblivious to my presence, talking and laughing, having a grand ol' time. How that was possible, I had no idea. I thought humans had a primal sense that triggered when they weren't alone.

"911. What's your emergency?" The man's voice came through the phone bored and unconcerned.

"Help. I'm being kidnapped," I whispered.

"I'm sorry, I can't hear you. Can you repeat that?"

"Help! I've been kidnapped," I hissed, louder.

"All right, remain calm, ma'am." His voice sharpened to crisp professionalism. "Keep the line open. We're tracking your cell's location now."

I did as he said. Lights from overhead winked in and out. My eyes stared at the scraps of material hanging out of the white trash bag of donations inches from my face. Then the red tie on the trash bag. I'd never noticed how much those little strips resembled streams of blood, the bags split like overly grilled wieners. Hadn't there been a movie where someone had been choked to death with strings of sausages? These men had just stolen my beloved car and my love of hot dogs. My vision blurred as white crept up my lenses. I was beginning to fear I would survive but not have anything left to live for.

I was about to take my chances and poke my head up when the male voice yelled from the receiver. "Ma'am? Ma'am!"

"Yes," I hissed again. If it kept up, I'd sound like Great-Aunt Thelma. "Don't yell. I'm trying to survive here."

A puff of air crackled over the line. With some relief, he said, "Officers are en route. Hold on a little longer. Don't do anything to draw attention to yourself."

Well, duh.

The car hit a bump and bounced. The vehicle rocked violently, clothes and junk scattering. My elbow dug into the seat and I barely managed to keep from slamming into the edge of a wooden shelf poking through a bag. One of the idiots up front wasn't as lucky. Glass rattled and a man's yell bounced around the interior.

But that's what they got for absconding with my poor Blue.

"Why you had to get this POS, I'll never know," the young 'un whined. "There had to be another, newer car. Something with satellite radio at least."

"Those fancy-ass cars have more security than airports these days and complicated ignitions." A loud, hollow thud echoed as something slapped plastic. "Cars like this are shitty but sturdy and simple. And satellite radio isn't the be-all, end-all of quality, you know."

At least one of the guys could appreciate Japanese engineering. But if they broke my baby, I wouldn't be responsible for my actions. I'd open a can of whoop-ass and fury their kin would feel twenty years from now.

Sirens wailed faintly, but grew steadily louder with each passing second.

Thank you, Jesus.

Rescue was in reach.

What if they aren't here for you?

Man, that voice could be such a pessimistic bitch. I pressed the phone harder against my ear to deny the too-heinous-for-words thought.

"I hear sirens. Are they almost here?"

"Yes, ma'am. Hold on a few seconds longer."

Easy for him to say. He wasn't wondering if he'd live to experience Free Donut Day next month.

"Dude! The cops are behind us!"

He had to be younger by a generation at least. No way would an older man say, "dude." It made me wonder how they came to be together. Grandfather and grandson? Father and son out for a family bonding experience? I gave an inner snort. Yeah, nothing said quality time like stealin' a car together.

"Don't worry," the older man rasped, calm and even. "They can't be here for us. How would they know we stole this car? It was in an empty parking lot after the restaurant had closed. Plus, I'm not speeding and I'm using all the proper signals."

Although his vocal chords sounded like two pumice stones rubbing together, he had a soothing way about him. He wasn't addressing me directly but the odd roughness and up-and-down cadence calmed me all the same.

I needed to get a grip, not become a victim of vehicular Stockholm Syndrome.

"They don't look like they're going around."

"You worry too much." A pause. "Is this your first run?"

The little dude groaned. The edges of the trash bag against my face ruffled as the seat shifted. "It shows? I'm such a newb."

"How old are you, Ethan?" Older's voice softened.

"Twenty. Drugs weren't my first career choice, but it's a new economy, right?"

Male laughter, a light sound at odds with the roughness of his voice. "Too true. Have you heard about that mine in Logan closing?"

"I know, right." The man in the passenger seat moved, the metal grating in protest. "Stupid EPA restrictions. Can you believe—"

They thought now was a good time to discuss the state's economy? I bit the edge of plastic covering my phone to hold back a curse.

"Shit," Older said.

Flashing lights bounced above. The sirens were directly behind now.

"Man, what're we gonna do?" the younger guy whispered.

"You got your gun?"

Silence descended. I held my breath, praying someone would speak before the dynamite bordering my vision ignited.

"There's only one car. When he gets out, we'll shoot. Then vamoose down the road like nothing's happened. It should give us enough time to get to Bobby Lee's and dump this car."

The car slowed, then jerked, as my brakes struggled to stop.

Oh, God. Oh, God. Oh, God. The cop was going to get shot. Then, I'd get shot. They'd dump poor Blue in a ditch somewhere. The more my thoughts raced, the more my stomach churned. I didn't want to be another statistic. A number on a billboard counter, signaling the total people killed in traffic accidents for the year. We had enough of those already.

The back of my throat ached, burned. Swallowing made the burn worse. Too much fear, too much tequila, too much political debate. All of it was just too much.

I jerked up, screamed, and tossed the blanket off my face.

The two guys yelped, one in a wail higher than mine had been and turned to face me in the back. I threw the blanket in their general direction and scrambled out of the back door, still screaming.

I don't know how long I ran before firm fingers grabbed my shoulders. I slammed into a body. A hard *male* body. My fists swung and my feet kicked. Damn it, I wasn't dying tonight.

"Diane?" The hands shook me. "Diane!"

The voice didn't belong to one of the kidnappers.

"Calm down. You're safe," he said, his voice low and deep. So deep that even in my hysteria it caused a spasm of something down south.

I stopped screaming.

Headlights and flashing blue lights blinded me. I couldn't tell what direction I faced or where I was going. The whole world narrowed to those strong hands as they checked me over, and *that voice.* "Are you okay, Diane?"

My lips trembled with an answer, but my body shook so hard the words balled, crushed under the weight of an unwieldy tongue.

A whisper of sensation caressed my chin. Fingers moved down to my shoulders. My tongue came unstuck and my mouth opened at the audacity. I was pushed into a noticeably feminine chest before I could complain.

"Take her to the car," he of the traveling hands said.

"Yes, sir."

The woman's navy uniform blurred into the white of the vehicle as I was swept into the crook of her arm.

I blinked, regaining focus as she escorted me away from the bright lights. We were on the other side of a police cruiser in a dark part of the road. I was placed in the open back seat.

She patted my back and placed a thick blanket around my shoulders. Why, I wasn't sure. It was May and, even this early, it was hot as balls.

I shrugged, letting it drape around my elbows. I'd sweated enough tonight for a lifetime.

"Are you okay?"

I nodded and looked up. The woman was pale-skinned, dark-haired and a little taller than me. Maybe a few years older. She filled her navy uniform very stoutly. A flash of jealousy hit me. I'd always wanted to a figure like hers. It was curvy yet muscular. There was a confidence in her bearing as she stood feet apart, hands relaxed at her sides. Her eyes scanned the area while keeping me in her sights and at arms' length. My body was fine—okay, decent—but it all too often didn't move like I wanted it to. She didn't look as if she ever had such a problem.

"Thank you for coming."

"It's our job." Her smile was kind. "And Cole wasn't going to let anything keep him from helping you."

Another cop car screeched up. Followed by an ambulance. Then a fire truck. Ten minutes later, the area was filled with so many emergency vehicles it looked like the aftermath of a college kegger. With so many lights, I could see where we'd stopped. My car was over to the right, all her doors opened and officers milling in and around it. I couldn't tell where exactly I was, but I didn't think we'd gone too far outside city limits.

EMTs poked and prodded at me for a few short minutes, but as there hadn't been any damage, they moved on. They stood in the huddle of uniforms near my car. One officer separated to stride over to me. At this distance, he looked like the other officers. The closer he got, though, the more he stood out.

Dude was beyond hot.

My eyes bugged and I clutched the blanket as the fine hairs lifted all over my body. I straightened. Blinked. No one would be able to claim he had a body for radio. If anything, his voice sandbagged the package.

"Diane?" His fingers traced a gentle path across my face.

I tried to speak but didn't quite manage it. He was the man who'd rescued me?

If I didn't know better, I'd swear the love child of a wrestler and a superhero had landed in front of me. I had the urge to go Southern belle on his ass and fan myself while saying, "I do declare."

He was tall. At slightly above five-foot, most people seemed tall, but this man was up there. As in, he could have played professional basketball regardless of his skill set because he'd already be at the net. I'd need climbing gear if I wanted to look him in the eyes without cracking my back.

He didn't wear a uniform like the woman beside me, but dark jeans and a black t-shirt. And so muscular in the upper arms the material lay against it like latex. It had to be uncomfortable. There didn't seem to be any room to flex.

"Diane, are you all right? You never did answer me from earlier." He clasped my hands, bringing my attention to his face. And what a face.

His eyes were a vibrant dark brown against bronzed skin. They were so intent they almost glowed. His head did glow, so smooth the lights reflected off it. I wanted to stroke it.

Girl, you've just been kidnapped and are thinking about stroking a stranger's head. Get it together!

I shook my head. I wished I could pinch the underside of my arm to make sure I wasn't still asleep and this was the product of tequila-inspired fantasies.

"I'm fine."

I shifted on the edge of the seat. The blanket pooled around my waist, exposing my body.

His eyes flickered down then back to mine. Nuclear-level

intensity stabbed deep, penetrating, mesmerizing. As if he knew the most intimate parts of my mind and body.

He edged closer, his heat combined with that of the blanket, bringing my temperature to midday summer car proportions. Bees swarmed in my stomach. I bunched the blanket back around my shoulders, ducking my head.

"Diane, this is Trooper Peters," he said with a chin lift to the woman who'd helped me.

I smiled briefly, appreciating the brief respite from his intense maleness.

"If you're okay to talk, we need to ask you some questions." He placed his hands on his hips. "Tell us what happened."

I'd expected it. Hopefully, they wouldn't require all the embarrassing details of the night. My car didn't normally look like that, but I'd been busy—okay, *lazy*.

Peters pulled out a small notebook and pen and moved in closer.

"I'd gone with my cousin to Chili's for drinks and dinner. We decided to leave after an hour or so, but I couldn't find my keys to drive. Since I was too dr—"*cough* "tired to drive home, I figured I'd crash in the back of my car for a couple hours, then roll on home. I did, and woke up with the two guys driving my car down the road. I called you and here we are."

"You didn't recognize them?" Trooper Peters asked.

"No."

"Get a clear look at them? Anything distinctive you remember? Voice? Words?" Cole asked.

"No, but they did mention a Bobby Lee."

Cole's face tightened. "Is that name familiar to you?"

My mouth dropped open. "Dude, really? Are you not from around here? Not to perpetuate a stereotype, but that name is not an uncommon one. Not to mention, I'm not sure if it's a combination first and middle name, first and last, or just first."

"My name is Cole, as you know. Not dude." Authority rang crisp in each word. It suggested I not make that mistake again. And if the message had somehow been lost, he followed it up with, "Don't do it again."

Dude. Dude. Dude. The tone in his voice sunk his hotness level by several degrees. He might have been a cop but that didn't give him the right to order me around as if I were a dog.

"Did you hear anything else you think might be of importance?"

"I think they were Republicans."

"You didn't get a description or notice anything, but you learned their political affiliation?" It was his turn to stare. "And how is that relevant?"

I shrugged. "You asked about importance. They mentioned Bobby Lee, the new EPA restrictions hurting the coal industry, and turning to drugs out of high school because there weren't any other ways to make money." I was totally jerking his chain now. And enjoying every single minute. The fact that it was the truth was gravy.

"Drugs?" He straightened and stepped closer to share a look with Trooper Peters.

She, who had been silently observing and scribbling on the page, shot a sharp glance up. "Did you say drugs?"

"Yes. Ethan said drugs weren't his first choice, but the new economy wasn't friendly to the twenty-year set."

They shared another glance.

I turned my head from Imhotep Junior to Trooper Peters. She was definitely the nicer of the two. "Didn't you catch them? The two guys?"

It was Hottie McSnotty who answered. "No, they were able to get away."

That seemed inept of the cops, considering. Some sixth sense warned me against saying that out loud. Well, that and the burning blaze of danger rolling off him hot enough to singe my hair, and the fist opening and closing at his side. I was seriously glad it wasn't me he was angry with. I suspected someone's ass would get reamed but good come Monday.

I started pinpointing escape routes in case he decided to go full-on Hulk on the squad car.

"Did they strip poor Blue's steering column?" I hoped it would distract him and save Oakvale, as well as the rest of the county, from property damage.

"No." His lips twisted and a dark brow shot up. "Why would they?"

"How else did they get my car started?"

"The keys were in the ignition. At least I assume they're your keys. They have a little skull figurine on them."

Hmph. That explained why I hadn't been able to find them in my purse.

Stinkin' tequila.

He crossed his arms over his chest, the black shirt getting dangerously tight. The look on his face darkened and a vein stood out on the column of his neck. This dude could be a scary badass when he was of a mind to it. Oddly, I didn't get the sense he would hurt me. I was still wary, but didn't get the vibe he was physically dangerous. Maybe it was the woman calmly standing next to him.

Or I was nuts.

Either way, I wasn't afraid. His shoulders eased, the material of his shirt seeming to sigh in relief. "How much did you say you had to drink last night?"

I hadn't. "Is this important? Dude, I was just kidnapped!" Didn't that earn me some consideration? Some sympathy?

By the way that vein throbbed, apparently not. It could be because I'd accidentally—okay, intentionally—called him dude again.

"This way." He crooked his finger at me. Pointed at the straight white line on the edge of the road. "Stand."

I mentally deducted another point from his hotness scale. If this kept up, he wasn't going to star in my fantasies the next time it was personal fun time.

He pulled out a freakin' sobriety test.

"How is this fair? Shouldn't you be patting me on the shoulder or asking if I need a counselor? Not punishing me by making me walk a straight line or breathe into a machine that has probably kissed more lips than Steven Tyler?"

He ignored my ranting, studying the monitor of the machine I'd exhaled into.

His lips pinched. "You're over the limit." His serious tone contradicted the glint in his eyes.

I threw up my hands. "Seriously, dude? You're gonna arrest me for that? Did you not notice the type of evening I've had?"

Protect and serve, my ass. Where was the love?

"Diane, I've told you not to call me dude. The law's the law, and it clearly says your drunk ass isn't driving home." Another finger point. "Now, stay."

I crossed my arms and seethed.

He talked to Peters briefly.

She waved at me, then went to my car, now surrounded by the huddle from earlier. My personal bane grabbed my upper forearm in a grip all cops seemed to have. It spoke of dead men walking the Green Mile. "Come on. We'll take the rest of your statement at the department. Then, I'll take you home."

Before I knew it, he'd hustled me into the squad car I'd sat in earlier.

Specifically, the bad side of the mesh cage.

I tried, and failed, not to take it personally.

Grab your copy of CRAZY ON YOU available now. Sign up for the City Owl Press newsletter to receive notice of all book releases!

Want even more sexy and romantic fun? Try the Love in the Fast Lane series by City Owl Author, Nicole Terry, and find more from Leigh W. Stuart at www.leighwstuart.com

What will you do when love is in the fast lane?

Diane Thompson wakes up in the backseat of her car, shocked to find she's acquired a chauffeur. Realizing she's been inadvertently kidnapped, she swears off tequila—and Chili's—then dials 9-1-1.

But her rescue comes at a cost.

Her savior, too-macho-for-words Lt. Cole Anderson, refuses to let Diane out of his sight until her kidnappers are apprehended. He's already lost one woman he cared about due to his inattention; he's not letting it happen a second time.

But Diane isn't a damsel-in-distress type of girl.

When it turns out the criminals left a valuable item in her car and they want it back, involving Cole isn't part of her plan and not only because the criminals have forbidden her from involving the cops.

Men are like birds—messy, easily distracted, and only around when there's something to eat.

She's got this.

All she has to do is find and return the item in question to the drug runners threatening her life, survive a high-speed car chase, and keep her vow to never trust a man with her heart.

Please sign up for the City Owl Press newsletter for chances to win special subscriber-only contests and giveaways as well as receiving information on upcoming releases and special excerpts.

All reviews are **welcome** and **appreciated**. Please consider leaving one on your favorite social media and book buying sites.

For books in the world of romance and speculative fiction that embody Innovation, Creativity, and Affordability, check out City Owl Press at www.cityowlpress.com.

ACKNOWLEDGMENTS

Although writing can seem lonely at times, I had support and help from across the world. Therefore, I would like to especially thank:

My Wattchicks for always being there to encourage me, listen to me complain, and make me laugh. In particular, Debbie Goelz for critiquing the first couple of chapters, and helping me get the ball rolling in the right direction during revisions; and Kristin Jacques for her patience and endless supply of suggestions (and dinosaur gifs) to fix my problems. I couldn't do this without you!

Also a big shout-out to the Sprinters United group, headed by Kelly Anne Blount and populated with lovely writers from all walks of life, who believe in lifting each other up and getting words on the page. I could always count on all of you to keep me going when I was losing steam.

My husband, my partner in all things, for knowing me well enough to give me a bottle of fine, spiced rum for Valentine's Day, and to never criticize my stash of yarn in the closet. I will love you always!

Last, my editor Mary Cain, who challenged and encouraged me through the edits to make this story as shiny and wonderful as possible, and City Owl Press for believing in me.

ABOUT THE AUTHOR

LEIGH W. STUART was born and raised in Kansas City, Missouri, daughter to an English teacher. This may or may not explain her early affinity to reading books. Although she decided to be a writer by the age of six, she later talked herself out of it, studying French and German in college. She met her husband while studying abroad in Switzerland, and they now call it home with their two children. A love of reading inevitably transformed into a love of writing and she is thrilled to begin a new adventure as an author of romance novels.

Website: www.leighwstuart.com

Facebook: www.facebook.com/LeighWStuart

Twitter: www.twitter.com/LWStuart

ABOUT THE PUBLISHER

City Owl Press is a cutting edge indie publishing company, bringing the world of romance and speculative fiction to discerning readers.

www.cityowlpress.com